Thank You,
Next

BOOKS BY SOPHIE RANALD

Out with the Ex, In with the New
Sorry Not Sorry
It's Not You, It's Him
No, We Can't Be Friends
Just Saying

SOPHIE RANALD

Thank You, Next

bookouture

Published by Bookouture in 2020

An imprint of Storyfire Ltd.
Carmelite House
50 Victoria Embankment
London EC4Y 0DZ

www.bookouture.com

ISBN: 978-1-80019-042-9
eBook ISBN: 978-1-80019-041-2

For the wonderful women of STBC,
the best friends in the world. Cheese, fizz, love.

Chapter One

It was a Friday afternoon and I was sitting in a South London pub, sipping my rioja, waiting for a date with a spy.

As you do.

Of course, I couldn't be sure he was a spy. It's not like his Tinder profile said, 'My name's Smith. Brett Smith. Licensed to ghost.' But all the evidence pointed to it. Brett's profile was bland to the point of invisibility: a photo of him in a nondescript suit outside a pillared, official-looking building; another of him in a white T-shirt and camo pants against a background that looked like desert, so could have been Afghanistan or somewhere; a third showing him lying in bed, leaning back on a thin pillow, a blank wall behind him that could have been anywhere.

But Brett himself wasn't bland at all. He was downright hot, in fact, with a chiselled jaw, bright blue eyes and a cleft in his chin. I could just imagine him in a dinner jacket, ordering a dry martini with a beautiful woman in a sparkly dress on his arm. If I did the mental equivalent of squinting, I could even make that woman be me.

When I'd asked him what he did for work, he'd just said he worked for the government, but it was 'all a bit hush-hush', and he was abroad right now, so our date would have to wait until he was, as he put it, 'back in circulation'. When I asked where he was, he'd joked, 'I could tell you, but then I'd have to kill you.'

And even after that, when I'd had a text – from a different number this time; he'd explained that his phone had been stolen, but I assumed he'd been using a burner – to say he was in London now and we could make a time to meet up, it had proved surprisingly tricky to arrange. He'd suggested breakfast, but since a key part of my own job was cooking breakfast in the pub where I worked, that had been almost impossible. The same went for lunch. And so here I was, at five in the afternoon, waiting for Brett to turn up at a bar in Vauxhall that was right in the shadow of the MI6 headquarters.

If he was trying not to let on that he was an intelligence agent, I thought, he hadn't done a particularly good job of it. But what did I know?

Anyway, a date was a date and I hadn't been on one for a while, so I'd made sure I had my A game on.

My mate Dani had persuaded me to go and have my eyelashes tinted and lifted, which she'd assured me was a low-maintenance option, perfect for someone like me who could rarely be arsed with make-up, but which I thought made me look permanently surprised.

I'd bought a new, puff-sleeved black top for the occasion – well, it was off eBay, and I'd got all caught up in a bidding war with another buyer and paid well over the odds for what was only Topshop, after all, even if it was organic cotton. But it was new to me, and that counted, right?

I'd been to the salon down the road from the pub where I worked and had my nails done. I'd had an argument with the manicurist when she'd wanted to put acrylic extensions on and I'd had to explain that I'd only chop one off by accident and it would end up in someone's bean burger, so we'd settled on a sparkly gel polish instead.

Sipping my drink, I wondered what it would be like to be in a relationship with a spy. He'd be away for long periods, presumably, off doing mysterious things in dangerous places. When our friends asked about his work, he'd say something vague about it being admin, and if he ever got transferred to Moscow or Washington or wherever we'd have to pretend it was because he was exceptionally good at negotiating photocopier contracts.

Maybe his boss – who I imagined being like Judi Dench in the Bond films – would take a shine to me. Initially, she'd say, 'Of course Zoë is wonderful, so supportive and discreet,' but then she'd spot my potential and I'd train as a secret agent too, and have actual stiletto blades concealed in my stiletto heels and a tiny camera hidden in my lipstick. I'd have to flirt with men high up in foreign governments and charm information out of them, but it would never go further than that, because I was so madly in love with Brett.

Steady on, Zoë, I told myself, taking another gulp of wine. *You haven't even met the guy yet. And what would happen to Frazzle if you were off in Moscow gathering intelligence?*

This was true, of course. I was just waiting for a Tinder date. I was just an ordinary twenty-seven-year-old, chronically single, with a job and a cat and an appearance that was, given I was smallish and slimmish with lots of curly red hair, like a woman in a pre-Raphaelite painting on a good day and one of those troll dolls on a bad one.

I'd been dating, on and off, for the past six months, and Mr Right hadn't turned up. There was no reason to believe that Brett would be him, but I'd realised by now that I began every date with the same heady sense of expectation, the same wild imaginings of how my life might change if this one turned out to be The One.

And, if I was brutally honest with myself, this date had a certain feeling of being the last roll of the dice. It wasn't like I hadn't tried. I'd tweaked my online profile over and over again. I'd composed witty message after witty message. I'd put different filters on my pictures. I'd sat in bars like this one, expectant and hopeful, only to be disappointed or let down or ghosted.

And speaking of which, where exactly was Brett?

I looked at my phone, shifting uncomfortably on the bar stool, which had a rail near the bottom that my legs weren't quite long enough to reach. The two women at the table next to mine glanced at me, glanced away again, and whispered to each other.

Yes, I am waiting for a date, I wanted to snap at them. *No, he hasn't turned up yet. Anything else you'd like to know?* But I didn't say anything, because there was a text from Brett on my phone saying he was running ten minutes late – actually, what it said was, *Runign 01 mins l8 soz*, but my translation skills were just about adequate for that. Maybe spies weren't allowed to use predictive text, or he was used to sending WhatsApps in code.

We'd been due to meet at five, and it was eleven minutes past. Right on cue, I saw him through the window, hurrying down the street. There was the chiselled jaw, the smudge of designer stubble, the muscular shoulders under his grey T-shirt. I felt a little fizz of excitement.

He wasn't older than he'd said, or shorter, which I knew by online dating standards meant I'd pretty much hit the jackpot already. But there was something strange about the way he approached the bar.

He didn't walk in a straight line. He did a kind of wide parabola from one side of the pavement to the other, and back again. *Maybe it's a spy thing,* I thought, confused. *Maybe it's how you check you're not being followed.*

He reached the door, put his hand on the handle and pulled, even though the sign said push. Then he peered at it, confused, pulled again and finally pushed, so hard that he almost fell into the room. The women at the next table giggled. Clutching the door handle to steady himself, Brett looked around the bar. I raised a hand in a half-wave.

'Zoë!' his voice rang out above the hum of conversation, not the James Bond-ish voice I'd been expecting, but a normal London accent, or maybe Essex. 'There she is!'

He let go of the door and hurried towards my table, knocking into a couple of others on the way and sending a bar stool flying and a small dog darting for cover under its owner's legs.

I watched, confused at first and then horrified. *Oh no,* my mind screamed. *Oh nononono.* But I was here, he was just a couple of feet away, and there was absolutely nothing I could do to escape. I was going to have to get through a date with a man who was clearly completely steaming.

'Zoë!' He pulled me into a hug so strong and unexpected it snatched me off my stool, and my legs flailed helplessly in mid-air for a second before I slipped through his arms to the floor. His T-shirt was wet with sweat that, judging by the smell, was ninety per cent tequila. His breath smelled of fags and I could see a half-smoked one tucked behind his ear. Blurry blueish-grey tattoos covered both his arms.

'Hi,' I said, my voice coming out in a kind of squeak, because he'd squeezed all the breath out of my lungs.

'Whatcha drinking?'

I wanted to say, 'Just a glass of water,' in the hope that he might follow suit. But my half-finished glass of wine was right there on the table in front of him.

'Large merlot for the lady,' he bellowed, making his way unsteadily towards the bar. 'And mine's a double tequila shot, salt and lemon, and a Budweiser chaser.'

Except the last bit came out like 'bugwishershasher'. I watched the bartender hesitate, wondering whether to refuse to serve him, then shrug and pour the drinks. The women at the next-door table glanced at me again, concerned this time rather than amused, and whispered to each other once more.

The floor of the bar was shiny reclaimed parquet, solid as could be, which was a shame because right then I'd have given absolutely anything for it to collapse and swallow me without trace, forever.

But the floor was clearly not going to oblige. I was stuck there for the duration of this date with this man who, I was beginning to suspect, was as far as possible from being a spy. Unless he made a habit of going on stakeouts absolutely shitfaced, with the smell of tequila betraying his whereabouts for miles around.

Brett returned from the bar, his two shots clutched in one hand, his bottle of beer tucked under his arm, and my glass of wine held unsteadily in the other hand. He put it down on the table and the glass rocked, red wine slopping over its rim, then fortunately settled.

'Cheers.' Brett downed a shot, chomped a lemon slice, then poured the second shot down his neck. 'Bit pissed. It's been a long time.'

I smiled politely and took a sip of wine. 'What's been a long time?'

'Since I had a drink. Or went out with a bird. Been away, see, like I said.'

Maybe I was being unfair, I thought. Maybe it was understandable that a man who'd been abroad, doing a high-pressure job, would want to let his hair down a bit when he got back? Maybe the lairy Essex-boy act was put on to throw people off the scent? But the scent of booze and fags was for real, there was no doubt about that.

'Well, uh, cheers,' I said, taking another gulp of wine. There was no way I was going to be able to drink this date successful, but at least once I'd finished this glass I could go. 'Was it far, where you were based?'

'Not so far. Was a good long stretch though. Two years I've been away.'

He picked up his beer and took a long swallow. Shit. He was almost halfway down it. I was going to have to speed up my wine drinking so he didn't get the chance to get another round in. Or, worse still, so politeness wouldn't require me to offer him another drink.

But I needn't have worried.

'Gotta go see a man about a dog,' he said. ''Scuse me.'

He got up and made his way circuitously to the ladies' loo, then fortunately realised his mistake, turned around and stared blearily for a second before spotting the sign for the men's and heading off in more or less the right direction.

I watched him, wondering if I should just cut my losses and do a runner. But before I could get up, one of the women at the next-door table piped up.

'Excuse me?'

I looked round and managed what I hoped was a bright smile. 'Yes?'

'I hope you don't mind me asking, but it doesn't look like your… friend… is in a very good way.'

I felt a massive blush creeping up my neck and flooding my face. Not only was I on a date with a guy who was so bladdered he could barely string a sentence together, but people had noticed. Well, duh, obviously they had. Half the pub was looking in my direction with varying degrees of amusement, worry and disgust.

'He's not, is he?' I muttered. 'Oh my God, it's a Tinder date and it's just awful, isn't it?'

'You could ask for Angela,' her friend suggested helpfully.

'I could what?'

'It's a thing. If you go to the bar and ask to see Angela, they'll make sure you get out of here safely.'

'Really?' I got to my feet and was about to approach the bar, when Brett reappeared from the loo, the front of his T-shirt wet with what I hoped was water now, as well as sweat.

'That's better,' he slurred. 'Now, another round.'

He turned and strode purposefully in the direction I'd been about to go myself, but something went wrong. His brain had said, 'Go to the bar,' but his feet hadn't got the memo. One of them went one way and one went the other and his ankles got twisted around each other in a kind of French plait. For a few seconds he teetered, just like my glass of red wine had, but he didn't manage to right himself. Arms flailing, he faceplanted spectacularly, right next to the table with the little dog, which recoiled in horror.

'Just a suggestion,' said the woman next to me, who I was starting to regard as my new best friend, 'but now might be a good time to leg it.'

'If you're sure you're okay to get home,' added her friend.

'I am,' I assured her. 'I'm grand. Never been better.'

I gathered up my bag and what was left of my dignity, gave them a quick wave and headed for the door. But as I was passing Brett's prone form, I noticed something. Right there on his right ankle, between the bottom of his jeans and his grubby white sock, was a chunky plastic bit of kit on a webbing strap. I'd never seen one before, but I knew straight away what it was.

An electronic monitoring device. An ankle tag. Brett hadn't been working abroad at all – he'd been in prison.

My dating life hadn't exactly been a resounding success up until that point, but now I knew I'd hit rock bottom.

Chapter Two

Six months earlier

Today marks a turning point for you, Aquarius. Facing the future and finding the happiness you desire and deserve means letting go of the past, however painful that may appear.

I was pretty much used to waking up with a feeling of leaden sadness in my heart, and a feeling of hot, itchy softness on my head. The first was my longing for my ex-boyfriend Joe, the sense of loss and regret that had stubbornly refused to shift even though we'd split up years ago, after an intense three-month relationship at university. After many years apart, Joe had come back into my life – or I'd come back into his – and all those feelings had been painfully reignited, even though I'd realised there was no chance of him splitting up with his girlfriend, Alice.

The second was Frazzle, my fluffy ginger cat, who liked to sleep on my pillow so he could keep an eye on the birds in the tree outside.

It was Frazzle who woke me, one Monday morning in late March. There were blackbirds building a nest outside, and every cheep from the birds was met by an answering chirrup of longing from my cat.

'What are you on about, you big daftie?' I mumbled, half asleep, trying to turn over so I could maybe slip back into sleep for a precious half-hour.

But turning over was impossible, because Frazzle was lying on my hair.

'Ouch!' Fully awake now, I pushed the cat gently aside and sat up. Immediately, the birds forgotten, he jumped to the floor and stared at me, meowing plaintively for his breakfast.

'Okay, okay. Give me a second to at least wake up. Jeez, it's like having a furry dictator ruling my life.'

I slid my feet into my slippers and stood up. It was a gorgeous day – already, although it wasn't yet seven, the sunlight streaming through the window felt warm on my bare skin. The winter, which had felt like it would never end, seemed to be loosening its grip at last, being pushed reluctantly away by the promise of spring.

And something else was different too. Something inside me.

A couple of years back, I'd gone through a phase of doing yoga classes. I think I imagined that it would somehow transform me into this serene, spiritual person who cherished the gifts of the universe and spread good energy around the place and also, crucially, could touch her toes without gasping and grunting like my grandad after he'd been digging his allotment. I didn't stick with it for very long – the incense the teacher burned before classes made me sneeze uncontrollably and I was always worried I'd fart when I was doing a shoulder stand – but one thing had made an impression on me. At the beginning of every class, the teacher would ask us to do a kind of audit of our bodies: assessing ourselves from our feet up to our ankles, knees, hips and so on, identifying where we were tense or sore, learning to recognise what was going on in every bit of ourselves.

I did that now, trying to figure out what it was about me, this morning, that felt different from the morning before.

The bruises I had on my shins from my workout in the gym two days ago were still there. So was the scab on my knee where I'd cut myself shaving, and the blue plaster on my thumb where I'd missed the target while chopping onions. A tingling feeling on my top lip told me the cold sore that had been threatening to erupt was still hanging around, waiting for its moment to pounce and leave me with a gross blemish that would last for days.

All normal, all just the same as yesterday.

But what was missing was deeper inside me than any of those things. The sense of loss – grief, almost – that had haunted me since I'd split up with Joe had faded. Just like that. It was like when you have a horrible hangover and eat a huge fried breakfast, drink loads of tea and take two paracetamol, then go back to bed and wake up feeling amazing. Or when you've had a miserable cold – the kind that makes your eyes look red and piggy and your nose stream for days – and you wake up one morning and realise you're better.

Not *completely* better though. If it was a hangover I was recovering from, I'd be at the 'Okay, I'm never drinking again but at least I'm not dead' stage. If it was a cold, the skin round my nose would still be red and raw and I'd have an annoying, lingering cough. But I felt different from how I had when I'd woken up the day before, and the day before that, and... you get the idea.

All of me was still the same, except I didn't have a broken heart any more.

I sprang to my feet and almost went flying as Frazzle wound himself around my ankles. While I cleaned my teeth and washed my face, he stayed constantly half a step in front of me, trying his very best to trip me up.

'If I fall and break my neck, then who's going to give you breakfast?' I scolded him. 'You haven't thought this through, have you?'

Frazzle looked at me, his amber eyes quite clearly saying that he didn't give a shit what I thought.

Once he was fed and I was dressed, I sat back down on my bed, trying to make sense of this new feeling of lightness, freedom, optimism. What was going on? What had happened to me? Was it the advent of spring, which was meant to bring new hope but had never done anything of the kind for me before? Had my heart finally caught up with what my head had been telling me for months: that Joe and Alice were right for each other in a way that Joe and I had never truly been? And, more importantly, without my unrequited love for Joe, what was I going to think about?

Give your head a wobble, Zoë, I told myself. *You can't go around being broken-hearted because your heart isn't broken any more. That would be off-the-scale ridiculous.*

On the bedside table, my phone buzzed furiously with an incoming notification. I glanced at it, the wild hope I would have felt in the past that it might, somehow, impossibly, be a message from Joe strangely absent. It wasn't, of course. It never had been and now I found myself able to accept quite calmly that it never would be. It was just the astrology app I'd installed ages ago, which sent me a daily message. Some of them were inspirational, some all but meaningless, and some of them downright brutal.

If the app were a friend, I sometimes thought, I'd have unfriended it long ago. Not that I exactly had loads of friends to choose from, since I'd spent most of my twenties travelling – great for life experience, not so good for forging enduring bonds with other people.

You know that emptiness you feel inside? You going to fill it with something, or let it suck you in?

'Yeah, thanks for that,' I told my phone, thinking that, right in that moment, the emptiness I felt was the same kind that had made Frazzle clamour for his breakfast. But then I couldn't help thinking, *Hold on, maybe it has a point.* Maybe the Joe-shaped hole in my heart *could* be filled by someone else.

Maybe it was time for me to stop hankering after someone I couldn't have and find someone I could.

When I got to work, Robbie was already there. I couldn't even use an arduous journey as an excuse, because my daily commute consisted of stepping out of my tiny flat, locking the door behind me, walking down a flight of slightly rickety wooden stairs, pushing open a door, and voila, there I was in the Ginger Cat, the pub where I worked as a chef. But Robbie had beat me to it, as he usually did, and was already sliding two loaf tins into the oven.

It was his enthusiasm that had led me to hire him, two months before – that, and the fact that he was cheap, cheerful and touchingly grateful to be offered his first proper job in a professional kitchen. Not that the tiny cubbyhole where the two of us worked practically elbow to elbow was the most professional of workplaces. But I loved it, and so did Robbie, who worked all the hours I'd let him, with boundless energy and the ability to function on about two hours' sleep a night.

'Morning.' I flicked the switch on the coffee machine and heard it roar encouragingly to life. 'What have you got there?'

'Date and banana bread. It's gluten free, dairy free and refined-sugar free. The punters are going to love it. And so am I – was out until four and I'm hanging so badly, Zoë. Any chance of a coffee?'

'Sure. Double espresso with three sugars?'

'You're a lifesaver.'

'So what were you up to last night?'

Robbie leaned a snake-like hip against the stainless-steel worktop and ran his hand through his hair. It was dyed bright blue at the front and shaved into a careful fade at the sides, showing off his multiple piercings and ear tunnel.

'Ah, nothing much.' He ducked his head.

'Go on! You know I need to live vicariously through you, since I have no social life of my own.'

'I finished my shift here, and then I went home.'

I gave him my best hard stare. 'And then…? Don't tell me you were up watching box sets until four in the morning and getting shitfaced on your own.'

'Oh, okay. So I had a new Grindr date over.'

'What, someone you met on a dating app, over to your place? Just like that?'

'Sure. My flatmates were asleep, they didn't notice. And if they had, they'd have given zero fucks.'

'So who was he? Someone you've met before?'

'Never. And never will again. He was useless in the sack.'

Robbie peered into the oven. The kitchen was beginning to fill with the mouthwatering smell of cinnamon. Over the weeks I'd known him, I should have got used to Robbie's casual attitude to relationships, but it still had the power to surprise me. The idea of inviting some stranger from the internet over to your home, having sex with them, and then hustling them out of the door while they were still putting their socks on shocked and impressed me in equal measure.

Also, although there were only about five or so years between us, Robbie had the ability to make me feel about a hundred years old.

'I thought you Generation Z-ers were meant to be going through a sex recession,' I said.

'Yeah, well.' Robbie flicked his hair out of his eyes. 'You know the Keynesian theory of fiscal stimulus, right?'

'Course I don't. How do you know that stuff anyway?'

'Did a GCSE in economics, didn't I? I'm not just a pretty face.'

'Okay, so hit me with it.'

'Basically, I'm spending my way out of the sex recession. The way I see it, the more I shag, the more other people are shagging too. So in theory there should be more to go round. Supply and demand, right?'

'Maybe. But none of it's coming my way, that's for sure.'

Robbie widened his huge green eyes, which were framed with lashes so long and dark, Bambi would have killed for them. 'You poor woman. Why ever not?'

I sighed. The truth – which I certainly wasn't going to share with Robbie, who was not only my colleague but, in theory at least, my junior – was that I'd had sex precisely twice in the past year, both times with Sean, my ex. And the last time had been well over eight months before. If anyone was in the grip of a sex recession, it was me – but my feelings for Joe had been so all-consuming I had barely noticed.

Until now.

'That's the trouble with being single, I guess,' I said lamely.

'Nonsense! Look at me. I'm single and I get more action than the Primark sale.'

'But you're—' I stopped. Robbie was what? Gay? Twenty-two? Ridiculously pretty? Those things might be true, but they weren't the real reason why he was meeting people and I wasn't. The real reason was that Robbie put himself out there. He had a Grindr profile, he wasn't scared to meet new people, and, if they were rubbish in bed, he'd move on without a backward glance and with a good story to tell his mates.

I, on the other hand, was about as far from out there as it was possible to get. Every night after work, I went back to my flat above the pub alone and stayed there, mooning over Joe. And now, if the strange feeling I'd woken up with that morning lasted and I truly was over him, I'd spend every night alone *not* mooning over Joe. Which was admittedly an improvement, but a pretty small one.

I remembered the cutting words my astrology app had sent me. *You know that emptiness you feel inside? You going to fill it with something, or let it suck you in?*

It was a challenge, a reproof, and also a warning. I was only twenty-seven. But I wouldn't always be. What if my life was still the same in a year, or five, or ten? In the past, when I'd found myself having a surge of existential angst, I'd responded by chucking whatever job I happened to have at the time and giving notice on wherever I happened to be living, and decamping to another part of the world or the country. I'd resisted the temptation to put down roots, have serious relationships, or even make friends, preferring to see myself as an unfettered free spirit, even though deep down I knew that the price of freedom was loneliness. Over the past five years, I'd worked in Glasgow, Sheffield, Cambridge, Madrid, Warsaw and – after one particularly acute attack of 'what the fuck is my life even fucking for?' – Seattle.

But I couldn't do that any more, because now I had Frazzle. Just a few months before I'd started work at the Ginger Cat, the pub that was now named in his honour, as I'd headed home after my shift at a dodgy tapas bar in Croydon, I'd spotted what I thought was a fox: a furry ginger form trotting along the pavement, a chicken bone clutched determinedly in its jaws. But it didn't melt into the shadows and dart away like a fox would have done. It stopped, turned towards me, dropped the bone and came over, mewing urgently.

And at that moment, in the dark street, drizzle falling and litter blowing in gusts around me, I knew I'd been chosen. I did all the right things, of course. I checked the cat for a collar. Even though I brought him home with me that night, the very next day I took him to the vet to be scanned for a microchip. I posted on local Facebook groups to see if anyone was missing a cat. And only then did I allow myself to accept, relieved, that Frazzle could be my cat and I could be his human.

So, now, I had him, I had a job I loved, I had my little flat above the pub. I had a life that was beginning to feel permanent. But, apart from Frazzle, I didn't have a person who was mine, someone who I mattered to more than anyone else in the world, an other half.

The slam of the oven door, and an even more intense blast of hot, sweet-smelling air, brought me back to the present.

'These bad boys are done now,' Robbie said, 'and quite frankly, if I don't get a coffee soon, I'll be done too. The place could've burned down without you noticing. It's like you're the hungover one, not me.'

'Sorry, sorry, I'm on it.'

I made Robbie's coffee and a chai latte for myself, and raided the fridge for a portion of the previous night's veggie lasagne. Robbie's cake wouldn't be cool enough to taste for at least half an hour, I was hungry, and who doesn't love cold lasagne eaten while standing next to the fridge? Just me then?

'Robbie?'

'That's me.'

'I'm going to die friendless and alone, surrounded by cats, aren't I? At the rate I'm going.'

'Oh, I don't know about that.' He shook his head.

'No?'

'You've only got the one cat, you see. Hard to be surrounded by one of them.'

I laughed. 'I'm going to have to start dating again, aren't I?'

'What, you mean you're not? I mean, no offence, but I kind of assumed you were just being discreet about your love life, on account of being my boss and all.'

'There's nothing to be discreet about,' I said wearily.

Robbie shook his head and tutted. 'And there I was thinking you just had high standards, and that's why you weren't seeing anyone.'

'Well, I do have high standards. Doesn't everyone?'

'Not me. I mean, sometimes a shag is just a shag. And I seem to have worked my way through most of the hot guys on Grindr who live close enough for a booty call, so…' Robbie did a gesture that made him look exactly like the shrug emoji.

I felt a wave of envy for this boy, so casually, confidently in charge of his sex life. How much had I missed out on, all those years when I'd been longing and waiting for Joe to somehow magically reappear in my life? Never mind in the months since he had.

'And you don't even have to lower your standards!' he went on. 'I mean, come on. You'd be starting from scratch. You'd have your pick of the crop. I could help you write an online dating profile, and Archie who runs the beer shop next door is an ace photographer, I happen to know. You could have a new bloke every day for months without running out.'

I thought, *I don't want a new bloke every day for months. I just want one. One special one.*

But I said, 'You might be on to something. Let me give it some thought. But in the meantime, we've got the bean burgers to make for lunch, and those carrots that were on special are looking a bit sad, so we should turn them into soup. And I'm not sure those avocados are ripe yet, so we might have to do hummus instead of avo smash on the snack menu.'

'On it,' Robbie said, doing a brief juggling performance with three of the bendy carrots, keeping the limp vegetables together in the air as easily as he managed his multiple men.

Chapter Three

You've been thinking. Made up your mind yet? Remember, fortune favours the brave and love will only find those who look for it.

For the next few hours, I successfully managed to avoid thinking about my love life – or rather my lack of one. I made a batch of sourdough bread and left the loaves to prove. I seared a mountain of mutton for a curry and ground a load of brick-red spice paste to flavour it. I made breakfasts, brunches and lunches to order.

And when three o'clock came and it was time for my break, I was determined not to start thinking then, either, if I could possibly help it.

'I'm heading to the gym,' I told Robbie.

'Cool,' he said. 'I'm off to get my eyebrows threaded.'

And so we left the pub together, but then went our separate ways, Robbie to Alina's chichi salon on the high street (which I kept meaning to visit myself to get the untamed jungle of my bikini line sorted, but then kept not bothering because, really, what was the point?), and me to the Dark Arch, the gym under the railway tracks.

I'd never been much of a gym bunny before. Well, to be honest, I'd never been one at all. The idea of joining a Zumba class set my teeth on edge, spin bikes left my bits so bruised I couldn't sit down for a week and, like I said, my enthusiasm for yoga had petered out after about three classes. So when I'd been working with Sean, my ex, at our food cart at the local market and a guy asked if I'd mind him leaving a few flyers on our stand for the new fitness studio he was opening, I'd agreed, with no intention of ever going there myself.

But then I'd picked one up, just out of curiosity. And, just out of curiosity, I'd dropped in later that day to take a look. At first I wasn't sure I'd come to the right place. The signage was spray-painted like graffiti on the metal roll-up shutters that covered the front of the railway arch. The entrance was a small door to the side, with a threshold across it that could have been put there intentionally to trip unwary feet. Inside, it was dark and cavernous, and would have been echoey if it hadn't been for the black rubber matting that covered every inch of the floor.

There were no piles of fluffy towels, no smiling receptionists, no lush plants in pots. There was nothing at all that suggested leisure or luxury: just racks of shining chrome bars and black rubber-coated weights, mysterious pieces of machinery that looked like they might attack you if you got too close, and bars and pulleys fixed to the walls like something out of a sex dungeon – or at any rate, like I imagined a sex dungeon might look. Right now, my chances of ever going to one seemed about as good as my chances of taking a trip on Virgin Galactic – and I wasn't sure which of the two I'd find more terrifying. The only colour in the place came from a stack of brightly painted iron balls that I later found out were called kettlebells.

I was about to step right back out again and never return when I saw a woman in one of the shadowy corners, lit by a string of fluorescent red lights. She had one of the silver bars over her shoulders, laden with weights, and she was doing squats. She was about my age, and slim like me, and the plates looked huge on her shoulders. I could see her face contort with effort as she moved the bar, but she managed it, and when she'd replaced it on its rack there was a smile of pure, triumphant happiness on her face.

And I thought, *I want to be able to do that.*

Almost a year later, I still couldn't. Not that heavy, anyway. But I was getting there, and I was hooked. I loved the smell of the place: rubber and sweat and disinfectant. I loved the sounds of iron meeting iron, people gasping with effort, heavy weights thunking on the rubber floor. I loved the new muscles that had appeared with surprising speed on my arms and thighs, and the calluses that had appeared on my hands alongside the ones left by my chef's knives.

Most of all, I loved how, when I came here, there was no space in my head for anything at all except the awareness of what my body was doing, the effort every move took, the longing for it to be over, the elation when it was.

Now, walking through the door felt like stepping into my happy place – which I guess it was. Mike, the owner, was on the phone, but waved a greeting. The woman I'd noticed on my first day there was in her usual spot by the far wall, doing some warm-up stretches. I walked over to join her, dropping my bag next to hers.

'Hey, Zoë.'

'Hey, Dani. How's it going?'

Dani stood up, took a gulp from her water bottle and twisted the bobble more securely around her ponytail. When I'd started at the gym, her beauty had been one of the many things about it that had intimidated me. Her mahogany-coloured hair was always straightened and glossy, even when she was literally wringing sweat out of it. Her arms and legs were long, smooth and perfectly tanned. She always wore make-up, and even the toughest workout didn't seem to shift it. She looked like she'd stepped straight out of one of those Instagram posts with a #fitspo hashtag.

'Ugh, same old, same old,' she said. 'Started work at seven this morning, and as soon as I sat down a patient was screaming down the phone at me because he'd forgotten his appointment and we'd charged him for it and somehow that was all my fault. I was tempted to tell him to adjust his own bloody braces if that suited him better, but I didn't, obviously.'

I made sympathetic noises and dropped down onto the mat to start my own stretches, and we were still chatting away about nothing much as we started our workout together. I noticed Mike glancing over to us, a benevolent smile on his battered ex-boxer's face.

It was he who, a few months back, after he'd given me what passed for a formal induction into the gym – where everything was, how everything worked, how to secure the weights on the bars, that sort of thing (the more advanced stuff, he said, he'd show me as I went along) – had said, 'In the meantime, if you need a workout buddy, chat to Dani.'

In those first few weeks, at times when Mike wasn't around, Dani had shown me some of the ropes – literally, because it turned out

I was going to have to learn how to skip for the first time since I was about seven. She'd been friendly and patient but also kind of remote. We'd chatted a bit while we worked out together; I told her I was a cook, working freelance for a catering company and manning a food cart with my short-lived then-boyfriend, Sean, at weekends, but that I dreamed of having a kitchen of my own one day, maybe in a pub, a place I could make my own. She told me she was a receptionist at a nearby dental surgery, and when I asked if she enjoyed it, she shrugged and said it paid the rent. Then she'd flashed a brief, dazzling smile and said, 'Plus I get my teeth whitened for nothing. Good for business, right?'

When Sean and I split up, I'd told Dani and she'd said she was single too, and weren't blokes more hassle than they were worth. When I started working at the Ginger Cat, she'd congratulated me and told me I'd be brilliant, and she must drop in for a pint sometime, although she never had. When she moved into a new flat, she'd shown me pictures and asked for my advice on paint colours, and we'd started following each other on Instagram.

So, for a while, we were kind-of friends.

Then, one day a few weeks back, things had changed. That day's workout had been particularly brutal, and although Dani had raced through it way faster and more easily than me, by the end we were both flat out on our backs on the mat, just as knackered as each other, gasping for breath and soaked in our own sweat like we were being marinated for a cannibal barbecue. I glanced over to her, ready for our usual high-five, but she didn't stick her hand out.

She pressed both palms over her face, and I realised she was crying.

'Hey.' I sat up, reaching over to touch her shoulder. 'What's up?'

She tried unsuccessfully to laugh. 'Don't tell Mike. He'll think the workout was too hard for me.'

'And it so wasn't – you totally smashed it. But there's something the matter, isn't there?'

She shook her head, her hands still covering her face. I could see her shoulders shaking with sobs. I jumped up, my legs somehow finding strength I wouldn't have believed they had, and grabbed a wad of paper towel from the enormous roll mounted on the wall.

'Do you want to talk?' I asked, squatting down next to her.

'No. Yes. But it's just a stupid thing.'

'It's not, if it makes you feel like this. You can tell me, if you like.'

She peeled herself up off the floor and leaned her face forward between her long, slender thighs.

'It's my birthday,' she said, her voice muffled by the curtain of her hair.

'Oh no! Why didn't you say? Happy birthday! Are you doing anything nice?'

'Not really. Might go out with some mates. But that's not the point.'

She lifted her head. For the first time ever, I saw her make-up smudged, her nose and eyes red.

'What is it?' I asked.

'My mum didn't ring me. Not a card, not anything. I should be used to it by now, we're not close, but it still hurts so much.'

And she made a strange keening sound, and I hugged her, not caring that we were both drenched in sweat and totally minging.

'She never wanted me to move to London,' Dani explained between sobs. 'She wanted me to stay in Liverpool and marry the boy I'd been seeing since high school, because he was so nice and suitable and about to qualify as a dentist. But I couldn't do it. I just thought about my life being the same for ever and ever and I wasn't in love with him any more, so I ended it and came to London. And it's like she's never forgiven me. I can't even go home for Christmas and stuff because there's always rows, so I make up excuses about having to work, and I just feel so alone.'

I'd listened, passed her tissues and waited for her to finish crying. I didn't tell her then, because I didn't want to make it all about me, but I totally got what she was saying. I sometimes felt like I'd missed out on the window of opportunity when everyone else had seemed to build up a close network of people they could hang out with, go on holiday with, make memories with. All documented with accompanying Instagram stories and hashtags.

The next day, I turned up at the gym with a cake I'd baked, Mike and all the regulars sang 'Happy Birthday' to her, a group of us went out for a few beers, and that had been that. Dani and I were mates. And still, months later, I caught Mike looking at us with a slightly smug expression on his face, and I knew it wasn't just because he saw us challenging each other, motivating each other, but because he knew he'd been instrumental in giving us what we'd both been missing: a friend.

'Shall we do chin-ups next?' Dani asked now. Chin-ups were her favourites, and watching her pull herself up on the bar again and again, her strong arms straining until she got her whole head over it, was total life goals.

'Sure. I'm just going to get some water.'

I crossed the gym towards the water cooler, glancing around me. It was quiet, as was usual for the middle of the afternoon –

there were only a couple of hench guys doing bench presses by the weights racks, a woman chatting to Mike by the doorway and a guy finishing off a run on the treadmill.

The machine slowed as I watched, and he stepped off, towelling his face. He was tall and lanky, and something about his easy grace reminded me of Joe. I waited for the familiar twist of pain, but it didn't come – I could just discreetly and appreciatively check out this sweaty but handsome stranger, who was also approaching the water cooler, his aluminium drinks bottle swinging from one hand.

We reached it at the same time.

'After you,' he said.

'No, it's fine – no rush. You go first. You look like you need it.'

He wiped his face again, making his damp hair stand on end, and grinned ruefully. 'That obvious, is it?'

I smiled back. 'Yeah, it kind of is.'

'Well, I'd better go ahead then, before I collapse from dehydration.'

'We wouldn't want that to happen.'

He leaned over and pressed the tap, and I enjoyed the view of his broad shoulders under his wet Lycra vest. We'd only exchanged a few words, but there'd been something in the way he'd looked at me that was – maybe? – flirtatious. But what did I know? I hadn't flirted with anyone since forever. My memories of flirting were dim, ephemeral things, lost in the mists of time.

He turned back to me and smiled again, showing straight white teeth Dani's boss would have been proud of – or possibly not, if they were like that naturally rather than representing her next Caribbean holiday.

'All yours,' he said.

'Thanks.' I bent over to fill my own water bottle.

'Do you mind if I ask you something?'

I felt my heart give a little jump that had nothing to do with the thousand metres I'd just completed on the rowing machine. Was he about to ask me out? Me? Right here, in the gym, on the very day on which I'd decided that it was time to do something about my single state? I remembered the last words the Stargazer app had pinged into my phone: *Fortune favours the brave.*

If he did, I resolved, I was damn well going to say yes.

'Ask away,' I said, turning and sipping water as alluringly as I could.

'Um… my name's Stephen, by the way. I'm here most afternoons, same as you.'

I nodded. I'd seen him there, just never had the benefit of a close-up before.

'I'm Zoë.'

'Hi, Zoë. Uh… God, this is awkward.'

I smiled, touched by his shyness. 'Take your time.'

I looked over to the pull-up bar, where Dani was finishing off her second set, and his gaze followed mine. Dani dropped down off the bar and rubbed her trembling arms.

Now, Stephen's words came out in a rush. 'Your friend – the girl you train with?'

'Dani.' My warm glow of anticipation melted away, like I'd just chucked the contents of my water bottle over my head.

'Dani.' His tone was all kind of reverent. He might as well have been saying 'the blessed Virgin Mary'. 'Does she have a boyfriend at all?'

*

'Ooof,' Robbie said, when I relayed the story to him over our shepherd's pie prep later that afternoon. 'That must have smarted a bit.'

'Tell me about it. And when I told Dani afterwards, she just laughed and said he was on a hiding to nothing, because he's not her type, and if he asked her out she'd knock him back in a kind way, and I was welcome to him. But that's not the point, is it?'

'Zoë.' Robbie put down his wooden spoon and folded his arms across his chest. 'May I have your attention for just one second?'

'What?' I kept my eyes fixed on the pan of chopped onions I was stirring, so he couldn't see that I might be about to cry.

'Ahem.' He picked up the spoon again and tapped it on the worktop.

Reluctantly, I turned and looked at him.

'That's better. Now, listen up. You are bloody gorgeous. I've never seen this Dani and I'm sure she's smoking too, but just because your man in the gym fancied her and not you, doesn't mean you get to be down on yourself. I won't have it. Okay?'

'Okay.' I sniffed and blinked my eyes rapidly a few times. 'But…'

'But what? She's tall and dark, you're petite with red hair. Different strokes for different folks, am I right? I bet there are plenty of blokes out there who'd look at her and go, "Eeeuuuw," and look at you and go, "Phwoar."'

'I guess. But the thing is, if you're dating, you're basically putting yourself out there for people to go eeeuuuw or phwoar at, over and over again. And I just don't know if I'm up for that.'

Robbie twirled the spoon in his fingers like a cheerleader's baton, sending minced lamb spattering against the wall.

'Ooops.' He grabbed a cloth. 'What you need is a resilience strategy.'

'How do you mean?'

'I mean…' He looked at the spoon again, then replaced it in the pan. 'You need to be able to deal with knock-backs. Because, I'm not going to lie, you'll get them. But dating's meant to be fun, not hard work. You need to treat it like a game.'

'More like the flipping Hunger Games.'

He tutted. 'Don't be so negative! If the idea of on-tap no-strings nookie isn't enough to motivate you, then we're going to have to find something that will.'

'Meeting my Mr Right, so I'll never have to date anyone else ever again?'

'Won't work. That way, you'd settle for Mr Good Enough, and then realise he's not actually good enough, and before you know it you'll be back to square one. You need to challenge yourself to date lots of people so you can figure out what right looks like.'

'But I don't want—'

'Zoë!'

'Sorry. What do you mean, though? Like, work my way through the alphabet, from Alfred to Zachary, and hope I get lucky round about Christopher?'

'That could work. Although if you got as far as Q you might get stuck.'

'Yeah, there aren't that many Quentins about, are there?'

'Exactly. You need something where there's an even distribution.'

'Like what?'

Robbie stirred the sauce for a moment. I could see his mind working furiously.

'The zodiac!' he said. 'Oh my God, that's inspired. No wonder you hired me, I'm a strategic genius.'

I couldn't help laughing. 'What, you think I should date a guy from every star sign until I find one I click with?'

'You've got it.'

'But…' I paused, thinking of the Stargazer app on my phone. I'd installed it a year or so back. It had seemed like a bit of fun, at first, even though it claimed to base its predictions on big data derived from international space agencies and a load of other science stuff that had completely lost me. Still, sometimes the messages that pinged onto my phone seemed almost uncannily accurate.

'But what?'

'Is that stuff actually real? I mean, how can it be?'

'Don't knock it until you've tried it. Astrology has been regarded as a scholarly tradition throughout history. It's the wisdom of the ancients.'

'And Mystic Meg in the *Sun*.'

'Okay, and Mystic Meg. But that's not the point. The point is to make dating fun.'

I switched off the gas burner under the potatoes.

'I suppose anything that'll make this whole finding-a-man malarkey feel like fun has to be worth a go,' I said.

'So you'll do it?'

Abruptly, my enthusiasm deserted me. 'I'm not sure.'

'Go on, I dare you.'

'Robbie, I—'

'Double dare you!'

'Robbie!'

'Triple dare with a cherry on top and sprinkles!'

'I'll think about it.'

It was after eleven thirty that night when Frazzle and I arrived home. As I unlocked the door of my flat after climbing the stairs, my legs so tired and heavy it felt almost like I might not make it to the top, I heard the click of Frazzle's cat flap and he wiggled his way in through the window, hopped up onto my bed and settled down for a good wash.

'Where have you been then?' I asked him. 'Busy day?'

He glanced at me, blinked, then carried on scrubbing his face with his paw like he was going in for a mega exfoliating session.

As usual after a long day, I felt knackered but also too wired to settle down to sleep. There was nothing I wanted to watch on TV. I would have loved a hot bath but the flat had only a tiny shower cubicle that provided hot water in a way I guess you'd describe as quirky, if you were its mum and wanted to make it feel better about itself. I'd eaten dinner earlier in the pub kitchen, so there was no point in making myself a piece of toast.

Instead I found myself pacing up and down, waiting for the nervous energy that had carried me through the day to dissipate enough to allow me to rest. Not that pacing in my flat got you very far – twelve steps, fifteen if they were small, took me from the front door to the bed, and eight from the bed to the bathroom door. The place was tiny, poky even. I wasn't naturally a tidy person, but I'd quickly realised that I'd need to clean up my act or risk drowning under a rising tide of my own stuff, so the room was neat, the bed made, most of my clothes folded tidily away in the chest of drawers.

I sat down on the bed next to Frazzle and took out my phone, flicking reflexively through to my astrology app.

It's okay to admit that you're a bird who'd be happier in a cage than flying free, it told me.

What? Surely no bird was happier caged?

Today offers challenges in work and creativity, it went on. *But let's be honest, it's love you're struggling with right now, Aquarius.*

'You don't say,' I told it. Frazzle looked curiously at me.

What would it be like, I wondered, having a man with me in this tiny space? Having someone's warm body next to mine in the small double bed, someone cleaning his teeth while I had my morning shower? Although I knew the answer to that – it would mean my morning shower would be more of a morning trickle, the water pressure being what it was.

What would it be like to share routines and private jokes with someone who didn't have four legs and stripy orange fur? What would it be like to hear someone say he loved me?

I flicked back to the app. Although I'd had it on my phone for months, I'd never fully investigated its functionality. The one-line daily readings it gave had been enough for me, up until now. I'd glanced at the push notification when it flashed up on my phone each day, laughed or tutted or wondered briefly what the hell that even meant, and moved on.

But now it was like the pesky thing was getting inside my head, and I wanted to get inside its head, too. But I was a grown-up. I knew, rationally, that my personality and my life's path hadn't been determined twenty-seven years ago when I'd entered the world, or nine months before that, when my mum and dad had— Yuck, I wasn't going to think about that.

If I was going to accept Robbie's challenge, though, I'd need to understand a bit more about how this whole astrology thing worked, and what the app could do to help me in my mission.

I clicked on the tab that said 'Love'.

You're fiercely independent, I read, *and you think you can manage just fine on your own. And that's true, up to a point. But no woman is an island, and sometimes you feel your soul crying out for its twin, its other half, your soulmate. But how do you find that person – and how on earth (or in the stars) are you supposed to know when you have?*

Bloody good point, I thought.

Under that little chunk of text was a link that said 'Find your love match in the stars'. I clicked it.

Cerebral and intellectual, you can come across as emotionally detached. But still waters run deep, and that's never truer than in your case, water carrier. You have reservoirs of love and passion waiting to be tapped.

Okay, this was getting technical now. And me, cerebral? Come on. I was the woman who spent her days up to her elbows in mac and cheese and the last time I read a book was just before I dropped out of uni. And emotionally detached? That certainly hadn't been the case earlier, when the sexy gym guy had seen my face fall as I realised it wasn't me he fancied but Dani. Maybe that was those reservoirs the app was on about. I'd certainly cried enough to fill one – or maybe empty one that was already there inside me.

'Okay, so air signs,' I said to Frazzle, who'd finished his wash and curled up next to me, his head on my knee. 'What do you reckon those are?'

I tapped another link.

Gemini, Libra and Aquarius are governed by the Air element, the app informed me. *These most spiritual members of the zodiac are often blessed with highly attuned intuition, the ability to read others and even, in some cases, the skills to reach realms of the psyche beyond our own.*

This sounded kind of familiar. I remembered going to see a tarot-card reader when I was sixteen, and she'd told me I was highly spiritual, too. She'd also told me I'd have four children before my thirtieth birthday, which would be giving it some considering I was already twenty-seven. Maybe there were triplets in my future.

'That litter tray of yours isn't going to clean itself, is it?' I said to Frazzle. Putting my phone aside, I got up off the bed and went through my night-time routine, scooping out Frazzle's poo and topping up his water bowl, washing my face and brushing my teeth, slathering on some of the night cream I'd bought because it was organic and on special offer, but which smelled faintly of boiled cabbage.

I put on my pyjamas and got into bed, and Frazz immediately wormed under the duvet to lie by my feet. But I wasn't ready for sleep just yet, so I turned back to the app.

If air signs were right for me, what did wrong look like?

There was another link on the app that said 'Seeking a challenge?' I wasn't; it was after midnight, I was in bed with my cat and I had to be up at six. But I clicked it anyway.

Love moves in mysterious ways, the app told me. *And sometimes, in the stars as in life, opposites attract. These matches might seem unlikely on the surface, but they could send astrological sparks flying.*

Pedantic, routine-loving Virgo might seem the worst possible partner for head-in-the-clouds Aquarius. But their stability and steadfastness could give you the security you crave.

At my feet, I felt Frazzle curl up into a tighter ball, and I heard him let out a loud snore. Clearly, he'd had quite enough excitement for one day.

But I'd made up my mind. I was going to get myself set up on a dating app, and I was going to find a Virgo. And if he was completely wrong for me, that wouldn't be a problem. After all, I didn't want to peak too soon.

Chapter Four

Today is a good day for decision-making. With the sun in Taurus, it's time to take the bull by the horns. You might not be feeling confident, but that's no excuse to set aside your dreams.

I actually beat Robbie to the kitchen the next day, and I'd made a batch of granola and got eight sourdough loaves shaped and proving before he arrived for work. Even though I'd been busy, I'd been glancing at my watch every couple of minutes, muttering, 'Where the hell is that boy?' – not because he was late, but because I was itching to talk to him.

'Morning, morning,' he carolled, breezing through the door at twenty past seven. 'I was all tucked up in my bed – alone, I hasten to add – by ten last night. I feel bloody marvellous. Is this how married people feel, like, every morning?'

'Doubt it,' I said. 'I reckon they toss and turn for ages wondering about the mortgage, or the baby wakes them up at four a.m., or maybe they don't get to sleep until late because they're out having fun or in having sex.'

'Imagine,' Robbie said. 'Just for a moment. Imagine only having sex with one person again, ever. For the *whole* rest of your life.'

I imagined it. I couldn't imagine the actual person, of course, but I was right behind the idea. I didn't get a chance to say so to Robbie, though, because he carried on, in full flood.

'Doesn't bear thinking about it, does it? I mean, I know you could argue that once you've seen one penis you've seen them all, but I'm just not willing to accept that theory until I have in fact seen them all. Courgette and tahini muffins this morning, right, boss? Since it's Thursday?'

'That's the one,' I said. 'And we got that load of chicken wings from the farm shop, so those are going to need putting in a marinade, if you don't mind? Maybe two – one hot, one not so hot?'

Although my job made it impossible for me to be as strictly vegan as I'd like – only a crap chef wouldn't taste their food, and the Ginger Cat's clientele wasn't quite ready for a totally plant-based menu – it was still a massive relief that Robbie was on hand to help prep ingredients that had once had a face.

While he busied himself feeding courgette after courgette into the grating blade of the food processor, I made coffee for us both.

'So I've been thinking,' I said, handing him a mug, 'about this dating malarkey.'

'You're going to do it!' he breathed. 'Finally! After all this time! The only woman in the world not to have Tinder on her phone has come over to the dark side!'

'Not yet,' I admitted. 'But I'm going to. I've decided. And I've got a plan. Have you ever heard of an app called Stargazer?'

'Is the pope Catholic? I've got it on my phone, I check it all the time. Oh, the burns it gives! Just this morning, right, it told me age might just be a number, but that doesn't stop you getting older every day. So no more early nights for me. I'm back to living life to the full.'

The problem with trying to have serious chats with Robbie, I'd discovered, was the challenge of keeping him on any kind of conversational track. If I wasn't fast enough, he'd be telling me the story of how his grandpa once put his nan's hair removal cream on their poodle by mistake. Again.

'Yes, well,' I said. 'Me too. This morning Stargazer told me if I wanted love to find me, I wasn't making it easier by hiding away.'

'Ouch. You know, my mate Damian – he's a physicist – reckons it's all bullshit, but if the moon controls the tides, how come the position of the stars when we're born can't have some influence on our lives? I mean, it's science, right? Literal science. I told Damian…'

I half-listened, waiting for Robbie to run out of stuff to say. At last, his story concluded (with Damian admitting that there might be something in Robbie's theories, although probably because he knew that was the only way to get some peace and quiet), and I was able to carry on.

'So I was thinking,' I said. 'What if I accept your dare, but start with the signs that are meant to be least compatible with me. That way I can manage both of our expectations, and also test out how accurate the app is.'

Robbie put his head on one side, half looking at me and half watching the muffin batter he was carefully spooning into compostable paper cases.

'Which sign would that be, then?'

'Virgo.'

'So, like, if your Virgo dude turns out to be totally fugly or have bad breath or hate Ariana Grande or whatever, then you bin him off and you won't be disappointed?'

'That's right. I mean, imagine if I had a first date with a Gemini, my ideal match, and he was awful? What would happen to my blind faith in the power of the stars to reveal our destiny?'

'But what if Mr Virgo is hot as fuck, and you click right away?'

'Well, that doesn't necessarily prove anything, does it? I mean, the app says that there are always exceptions and sometimes the stars align in surprising ways. But I'd have a hot boyfriend, so I wouldn't care, would I?'

'Sounds like a win–win situation,' Robbie agreed. 'So now what we need to do is get you a killer profile set up. No duck face. No filters. And no pics of your cat.'

'What? But Frazzle's gorgeous.'

'Not bad for a cat, I suppose. But still. Photos of pets are a no-no.'

'Why?'

'They scream crazy cat lady, Zoë. Come on. No bloke wants to think if he dates you he's going to have to play second fiddle to a bloody cat.'

'But I am a crazy cat lady,' I said. I didn't add that any guy I dated would have to accept that Frazzle was my first priority, and if they didn't like that they'd be out on their ear.

'Tell me about it.' Robbie rolled his eyes. 'Okay, one pic with the cat. But only one. And he'd better not be making that face he does.'

'What face?'

'The one that's like, "I see you. I know you forgot to send your mum a card for Mothering Sunday and told her it must have got lost in the post. I know you washed your hair with Fairy Liquid once for a whole week because you were too skint to buy shampoo. I can tell you eat Pot Noodle sandwiches when you're hungover." You know what I mean. That face.'

'But all cats look like that.'

'God. How do you ever manage to have sex with him watching you?'

I wasn't going to tell Robbie that since Frazzle had come into my life I'd had sex precisely zero times, so I kept schtum.

'Right, it's almost eight thirty,' I said instead. 'We'd better get our skates on.'

'Not so fast, young lady,' Robbie countered. 'We're going to get that Tinder profile of yours set up right now, before you chicken out.'

'But I should prep the mango for the smoothies.'

'Did it last night; it's in the fridge.'

'How about the celeriac soup for lunch?'

'The veg is already done, and it'll take half an hour to cook. Come on, Zoë, if you don't crack on I'll take your phone off you and do it myself. "Flame-haired temptress seeks Jared Leto lookalike for nights of passion. Must be hung like a moose." And I'll set the password so you can't change it.'

When I'd taken Robbie on as my sous-chef, I'd been very clear that I believed in a collaborative working environment, and there'd be no hierarchical management structure in my kitchen. But now, the urge to pull rank on him was stronger than it had ever been.

I resisted it, though. 'Okay, okay, I'll do it.'

I tapped my phone, creating a new account in record time before I could change my mind, using Frazzle's name as a password even though I knew it wasn't particularly secure. If some random wanted to hack into my online dating, they were most welcome – a Russian bot would probably do less damage than my colleague, who was hanging over my shoulder offering advice.

'Your profile needs to stand out, Zoë. Be funny but not try-hard. And don't say you like nights out and nights in.'

'I can't remember what a night out even is any more. How about this?'

I passed him my phone and he read aloud from the screen. '"Me: Aquarian, vegan, feminist. I care about the planet and creating a more equal society. Looking for a like-minded Virgo." You can't say that.'

'Can't say what?'

'That stuff about being a feminazi social justice warrior.'

'Why not? I'm allowed to want to date someone who cares about the same stuff I do, right? And don't say feminazi – it's highly offensive on all sorts of levels.'

'Sorry. But seriously, you'll scare ninety-nine per cent of blokes off before you've even started. And given you're already ruling out the ninety-one per cent of them who are the wrong star sign, you can't afford to do that, can you?'

'But it's only temporary. I'm going to work my way through the whole zodiac until I find the right person.'

'Even so. Come on, I know what I'm doing here. Trust me.'

'Okay... Do your thing.'

Five minutes later, *Zoë, 27, London*'s profile was live. It described her as a fiery redhead with abs of steel and killer knife skills, and quite frankly she sounded absolutely terrifying. Robbie and I had been through my photos and selected three: one of me cuddling

Frazzle (in which he, too, looked kind of terrifying, even I had to admit, making Robbie tell me darkly not to say he hadn't warned me); one of me in the gym (in which some trick of the light did actually manage to make me look like my abs were half decent); and one of me taken when I was working in Paris, with the Eiffel Tower in the background. (I'd objected to that on the grounds that my hair was all frizzy and I had a spot right next to my nose, but Robbie insisted it made me look well travelled and sophisticated, and I had to relent because he'd let me have the abs one.)

'Good to go,' he said. 'Look, someone's swiped right on you already. Strong work.'

'Oh my God, my first match! Give me my phone, let me look.'

'Hold on. Tom, 28, loves Star Wars and pepperoni pizza. Sounds promising. I'm liking him back.'

He held my phone up high over his head so I couldn't reach it, and I cursed being only five foot three inches tall, for about the millionth time in my life.

'Robbie! Give me my phone!'

We had a brief tussle, which I eventually won, mostly because the oven beeped and Robbie whipped round to take out the muffins before they burned. Before I could check out Tom's profile in more detail, though, a red dot flashed up next to the messages tab at the top of my screen.

'Shit. He's messaged me. What do I do?'

Robbie laughed. 'You read it, obviously. Come on, it's not brain surgery.'

My finger was literally trembling as I hovered over the tab, then tapped it.

There were no words in the message, just a picture. It was kind of blurry and the lighting wasn't the best, but I could still more or less make out what it was.

It looked like a penis, only smaller.

Chapter Five

Others will be drawn to you today, Aquarius. Make the most of your attractions while you can.

That might have been my first dick pic – the breaking of my dick-pic virginity, so to speak – but it wasn't the last. Over the next few days, wang after wang popped up in my inbox. If I'd been concerned that my period of celibacy had gone on for so long I'd forgotten what a cock looked like, Tinder would have put me right in no time at all. At the rate this was going, it wouldn't be long before the number of penises that had landed in my inbox would exceed the number that had landed in me, which was a somewhat depressing thought.

'What's wrong with these people?' I complained to Robbie. 'Seriously, what do they actually think they'll achieve by doing this? Do they do it to blokes, too?'

'Hardly ever,' Robbie said wistfully. 'And I wouldn't mind too much if they did. I like having a good look at a nice hard-on. But it's just rude, isn't it? Block the fuckers.'

'It's about control, right?' Dani said later in the gym, once we'd recovered our breath enough after our workout to talk at all. 'It's like, I want to show you my junk and I don't care about what you want.'

I rolled over on the mat, leaving the sweaty imprint of my body behind. 'What do they think is going to happen? Like, does any woman ever receive a dick pic and immediately be like, "Oh yes, bring that right here and let me see if it's that good in the flesh"?'

'Maybe they do,' Dani mused. 'I mean, maybe if you were on Tinder for booty calls, it would work. Like a try-before-you-buy kind of thing.'

'Maybe they think you'll be flattered. Maybe they're trying to show you that reading about how you love Quentin Tarantino movies and halloumi fries has given them the raging horn.'

'God, the idea of halloumi fries is giving me the raging horn right now,' Dani said. 'I'm always starving after a workout. I could totally inhale an entire portion of those bad boys to myself and move on to potato wedges and it wouldn't touch the sides.'

'Oh my God, potato wedges.' I levered myself to my feet, waited a second to make sure my legs would actually hold me up, and took a gulp from my water bottle. 'We've got them on the menu in the pub tonight – it's burger night. The punters will be lucky if there are any left once I get my hands on them.'

'It's protein you need after a heavy workout, you know, ladies,' said a voice behind us. I turned around and Dani sat up. 'You've heard about the thermic effect, right? The calories burned in protein metabolism are twenty to thirty per cent higher than when metabolising carbs and fats. Plus proteins trigger the release of satiety-inducing hormones in the brain's hypothalamus, while inhibiting the release of ghrelin, the hunger hormone.'

Normally, I'd have rolled my eyes at the tedious inevitability of having fitness mansplained to me by some random dude in the gym. But I couldn't roll my eyes now, mostly because they were in danger of popping out of my head. Not because the man who'd spoken was hot – although objectively he was: six foot two of pure, rippling muscle, with an elaborate sleeve tattoo wrapping around one bulging bicep, tousled dark brown hair and Hollywood-perfect teeth – but because of who he was.

Fabian Flatley. The same Fabian Flatley who'd made a bid to purchase the Ginger Cat last year, wanting to close it down and turn it into luxury apartments. In the end there'd been a massive scandal over his tech start-up squirrelling away funds in the Cayman Islands to avoid taxes, as well as dodgy quality and extortionate service charges in the apartment blocks he'd already built (never mind his habit of talking loudly on his mobile in the gym, which as far as I was concerned should have carried a custodial sentence), and he'd disappeared to San Francisco, where I'd assumed he still was.

But he wasn't. He was here, and he was bad news.

'That's really interesting,' Dani was saying. 'So if you eat, like, an egg, that's got the same number of calories as a piece of toast, you basically get fewer calories from the egg?'

'Correct,' Fabian said, squatting down next to her and taking out his phone. 'There was a great article about it recently in *Fitness* magazine. Why don't you give me your number and I'll WhatsApp you a link?'

'That would be great! I'd be really interested to read that,' Dani said, reciting her number, although I knew she was as likely to read an article about calories as *The Complete Works of William Shakespeare*.

I hesitated. I could hang around, wait for Fabian to go away and carry on sweating all over the weights bench, which he never wiped down after he'd used it, and warn Dani to give him a wide berth. Probably it was what I should have done.

But he didn't look like he was going to make himself scarce any time soon; he'd stretched his legs out on the mat next to Dani and was settling in for a good old chat about whey-powder shakes (yawn). Also, his presence was making me feel really weird – almost like there was some kind of force field coming off him that was interfering with the signals in my brain, or I was allergic to his super-strong piney deodorant. And anyway, I needed to get back to work.

'I'll see you tomorrow, okay?' I said to Dani, who gave me a half-wave before turning back to Fabian, as mesmerised as a mouse watching a snake that was about to swallow it whole. I'd have to warn her about him – although, from the way she was looking at him, I wasn't sure she would listen to me.

I hurried back to the pub, showered and changed in my upstairs flat, and was back in the kitchen with plenty of time to get ready for evening service. But I didn't start shaping the burgers and frying the onions. Instead I pushed open the door to the pub and went to look for Alice.

It was a strange thing. Last year, after I'd unexpectedly encountered Joe after so many years and he – with a good-hearted obliviousness to other people's darker feelings that was typical of him – had offered me their spare room when I told him I had nowhere to live, I'd seen Alice as a rival. I'd persuaded her to give me the job at the Ginger Cat not just because I saw the potential the pub had, but because it was another way to get closer to Joe. But over the months we'd worked together, I'd got to know Alice as a person. She loved the pub and the community it served. Together, we'd fought off the threat from Fabian Flatley and worked our butts off to make the Ginger Cat the thriving business it was now. And during the course of all that, I'd realised Joe and Alice were rock solid and I would never be able to come between them – not that I wanted to, any more – and come to regard her as a friend.

And so, now, I was going to mention that I'd seen Fabian again. Just, you know, in case.

At first I couldn't see her, then she straightened up from behind the bar, where I guessed she must have been checking the stock in the wine fridges. Her hair was scraped back in a ponytail, there was a smear of dust on her cheek and a pencil behind her ear, and she looked stressed and knackered. For a second I wondered whether this was a good time to bring up Fabian Flatley's reappearance, but then I was pretty sure there never would be a good time.

'Hey, Alice. How's it going?'

'God, it's been the day from hell. The beer order hasn't turned up and the Wi-Fi's been down and one of the kids in the mums and tots group puked all over the carpet this morning. And I've got a meeting with the bank tomorrow to discuss our mortgage and I haven't had a second to get the figures in order. And, worst of all, bloody Drew's let me down.'

Okay, so maybe now wasn't the best time. Alice's brother had worked in the pub for a few months, and still played an active role in organising the packed calendar of social events. Everyone loved him, but everyone – including or maybe especially Alice – knew that he was about as reliable as a plastic chip pan.

'What's Drew done?'

'You know the fantasy role-playing game night he was meant to be organising? Nerd central, but we've had quite a lot of interest.'

'The Dungeons & Dragons game? It's been in my diary for ages. I'm taking the night off, remember, so I can join in. I've wanted to play D&D for ages, ever since I saw it on *Stranger Things*. The nerd is strong in me. Eight weeks on Tuesday, right?'

'That was the plan. Only now Drew's gone and had a poem he wrote long-listed for some award, and the ceremony is guess when?'

'Eight weeks on Tuesday?'

'Correct. I mean, obviously I'm thrilled for him, but he was going to be the Dungeon Master and apparently you really need to know what you're doing and understand the rules and stuff, and I don't, and even if I had time to learn them, which I don't either, it's got to be the same person every time, apparently, so you can get to know the players' characters and everything. So he can't do it – not ever.'

'Can't we put off the first game?'

'We could, I guess, but we've been promoting it on our social media and we've already got people signed up and they're really keen and you know how I hate letting customers down. And we planned the social events calendar so carefully so there was a good mix of stuff and nothing clashed. Zoë, I don't suppose you could…?'

I felt a familiar twist of guilt. Alice was my boss and my friend, but she hadn't always been. Before, she'd been the woman whose boyfriend I was in love with. The Zoë who'd behaved that way seemed almost like a stranger now, but I could still clearly remember the doubt and confusion in Alice's face when she'd seen – and how could she not have; I hadn't exactly been subtle about it – that I still had feelings for Joe.

But still, however much I wanted to help Alice, I was pretty sure that running a Dungeons & Dragons game when I'd never even played it was beyond my limited skill set. I thought of the multifaceted, sparkly dice in the box that Drew had bought, the innumerable variables of character attributes and monster lethalness and treasure value I'd have to get my head around – all while I was trying to have a life and actually date people.

'Leave it with me,' I said. 'I can't do it myself, but I'll try and find someone who can.'

*

Every day for the next couple of weeks, my first thought on waking in the morning was, 'Shit, I need to try and get a Dungeon Master sorted for Alice.' But it didn't happen. Partly, this was because I had no idea where to even start looking for one. I mean, there's not a Dungeon Masters' college, is there? And it's not like you could ask the JobCentre to advertise for one, like I did when I was recruiting Robbie. I posted on my Instagram asking about it and got nothing beyond a few random likes – far fewer than when I posted pictures of Frazzle. Clearly, accumulating a following made up of cat lovers and foodies had been a major tactical error and I should have gone after the hardcore nerds who used hashtags like #pathfinder and #instarpg.

So every day, I moved the notification in my calendar a day forward, and every day nothing happened.

It didn't help that work was crazy busy – it was half-term and the pub was packed with groups of mums (and sometimes dads) bringing their kids in for breakfast in the mornings before heading off to the park, the lunchtime regulars, and bigger throngs than usual in the evenings, because the weather was fine enough for us to set up a barbecue in the tiny beer garden. Robbie, wearing a stripy butcher's apron and tall white chef's hat, clearly thought he was the dog's bollocks and wouldn't let me have any say in his mysterious marinades, sauces and skewers, so I was stuck in the kitchen keeping the regular menu ticking over. I began to think that maybe it was time to employ another sous-chef, before I remembered that there was barely room for two of us in the Ginger Cat's cramped galley kitchen.

And it didn't help, either, that my phone kept pinging with notifications from Tinder. I tried to be methodical about it, checking in every morning, swiping left on lots of people and right on a few, responding to the messages that came in (unless they had pictures of penises in them, which many did – by the time I'd been doing this a couple of months, I reckoned, I'd have quite the collection, enough to open a gallery or maybe publish a glossy coffee-table book) and sending a few new messages of my own.

But the process took ages. I mean, like, ages. Looking at guys' profiles and trying to think of interested-sounding questions to ask them, weeding out the ones who appeared normal but within a couple of messages revealed themselves to be pervs. ('Do you do that thing where you cross your legs and dangle your shoe off your toes?' asked one. I mean, come on. I'm as broad-minded as the next person, but I was pretty sure I wasn't in the market for a foot fetishist.) Then trying not to keep checking over and over again and not feel hurt when ones who seemed normal and nice descended into total radio silence when I suggested actually meeting up. Not to mention that, under my self-imposed rules, I had to rule out all the ones whose star sign wasn't right.

So I was relieved when schools went back, a week of solid rain was forecast, Robbie was able to return to his usual post in the kitchen and the daily rhythm of the pub, from opening time to Maurice and his friends, the local retiree regulars, arriving at eleven for their daily dominoes game, to lunch and on through the afternoon and evening, was able to resume. And, one evening, I stuck my head around the door to check that Robbie had everything under control, because I had the evening off and I was going out.

His eyes widened when he saw me. 'You've got a date! Oh my God, Zoë, you've actually got a date! Your first one!'

'What makes you think that? I could just be meeting a mate for a pizza.'

'Yeah, right. Dressed like that? I don't think so.'

'Dressed like what? Is it too much?'

'Course not. You look stunning. Just, date-stunning, not meeting-a-mate-for-pizza stunning.'

I paused, tempted to ask if he was sure, and whether my green midi dress, denim jacket and gingham Converse were too girly, too frumpy, too try-hard or too something else, and whether my hair looked okay or had managed to explode into frizz in the time it had taken me to walk down the stairs.

But as I was trying to find a way to do that without sounding pathetically needy, Robbie demanded, 'So who is he? Go on, spill.'

'Just a guy off Tinder.'

'Just a guy off Tinder! Come on, Zoë. That's not good enough and you know it. Details, please.'

'Okay, okay. His name's Dominic. He's thirty-one and he works for a construction company – I don't know what doing, he could be the MD or a scaffolder or anything in between. Plays football on weekends, has a dog called Rufus, is a Virgo and is decent-looking.'

'Ooooh, I shagged a Rufus once; he was lovely. And a Dominic, now I come to think of it. Let me see his piccy.'

Reluctantly, I handed him my phone with Dominic's profile on the screen. I'd looked at his photos often enough to know what Robbie was seeing as he swiped through them: Dominic drinking beer out of a plastic pint glass at a festival, Dominic pressing his face up to his chocolate Labrador's, Dominic holding his phone up to his bathroom mirror to take a shirtless selfie. Okay, that last one suggested that he might have a bit of a high opinion of himself, but I'd told myself I needed to be open-minded. And besides, anyone with pecs like that was entitled to want to show them off just a bit.

'Hmmm. Bit hairy, isn't he?'

'I don't mind hairy. Better than a man who waxes his chest, right?'

Robbie's face fell. 'I wax my chest.'

Oops. 'It's just personal taste,' I soothed. 'But I'd better get going or I'll be late. Full report tomorrow, I promise. Sure you'll be okay here?'

Robbie nodded, wished me luck and turned back to the stove, and I hurried out to the station. The evening was cool and fresh after yet another rain shower, and I glanced anxiously up at the sky, wondering if I should have brought an umbrella. But it was a clear, washed-looking blue, with just a few clouds receding to the horizon. A good omen, I told myself.

Half an hour later, I was perched on a bar stool in a packed central London pub, nervously sipping a glass of white wine and trying not to jump out of my skin every time the door opened, which was often.

Seven o'clock came, then five past. I glanced at my phone. My Stargazer app had told me that Virgos were meticulously punctual – clearly Dominic hadn't got that memo. To pass the time, I flicked the app open and turned again to the entry that was meant to tell me what to expect from my date.

As steady as the earth element that governs this sign, your Virgo fella is hard-working, meticulous, patient and kind. He's a perfectionist and good with his hands – so maybe a scaffolder, then, not the MD of a construction company. And good with his hands? I could get behind that, depending on where said hands were at the time. *The downside? Picky Virgo can be critical and stubborn, prone to overthinking.* Well, he was fifteen minutes late already. *I'll give him some bloody criticism when he turns up and let him overthink that,* I thought.

When it comes to intimacy, your virile Virgo is a slow-burner. He waits for love before rushing into a physical relationship, and as a lover he's caring, romantic and skilful. And did we mention good with his hands?

That was all very well, but it didn't mean a row of beans if Mr Meticulous wasn't going to show up. I checked WhatsApp, my text messages and the Tinder app, but – apart from a couple of new 'Hey girl' messages, which I always ignored, and a new dick pic to add to my growing collection – there was nothing. I double-checked the messages we'd exchanged; I was definitely in the right place. And it wasn't like the pub was called the King's Head or something, and there might be another half a mile away with the same name. The Horse and Feathers was about as uncommon as pub names got, possibly even better than the Ginger Cat. It was a pub-name googlewhack.

My wine glass was empty and I was starting to feel that toe-curling awkwardness you get sitting alone in a bar, like everyone there knows you're single and your date's stood you up.

Maybe, I thought, Dominic was sitting somewhere at a table just a few feet away, waiting for me. Maybe, even though the photos on my profile were all less than eighteen months old, he'd somehow failed to recognise me. Maybe – I died a bit inside at the thought – he'd actually turned up, seen me, and turned right around again and left. I scanned the room again, but there was no stocky dark man sitting alone looking out of place and anxious. No stocky dark man sitting alone at all, in fact.

Enough, I decided, was enough. It was seven twenty-five. I was done here. I was going to get the train home and see if Robbie could use any help, and if he couldn't I was going to go up to my flat and get into bed with Frazzle like the sad loser I was.

No – I wasn't, I told myself. I was going to pull up my big-girl pants and go to Din Tai Fung, a restaurant right round the corner, and order their famous soup dumplings and eat them by myself, with my head held high, like the strong, independent woman I was. Or the strong independent woman I wished I was. There wouldn't even be a wait for a table, since there was only one of me. And I was a chef – it was basically research, as opposed to having a meal alone like a saddo.

I stood up and put my phone in my bag, after giving it a final scan for messages but drawing a blank. With an attempt at nonchalance, I strolled towards the door. *I had an hour to kill between a work meeting and cocktails with some of my glamorous, fascinating friends,* I told myself. *I enjoy a glass of wine alone in bars all the time. It doesn't faze me in the slightest. I'm independent Aquarius, among the crowd but not of it.*

If I'd had a bit longer to work on my technique, I might just have convinced myself that all that was true. But I didn't – and I'd failed to convince someone else.

'Excuse me,' a voice said, just before I reached the door.

'What?' I snapped, as unlike a nonchalant, independent haver of fascinating friends as it was possible to get.

Spinning around so fast I practically put my back out, I found myself face to face with a man who definitely wasn't Dominic. He was tall and lanky; my should-have-been-date had been sturdy and shortish. He was fair; Dominic's photos had shown a man so dark-haired and olive-skinned he looked almost Mediterranean.

'I'm sorry,' he said. 'I don't mean to intrude. It's just, I was meant to be meeting a Tinder date here, and she hasn't shown up. I may have this totally wrong, but I was watching you and I kind of wondered if that was what was going on with you too.'

For a second, I thought about drawing myself up to my full height, giving him a haughty stare and telling him not to be absurd, who would have the gall to stand me up? But five foot three isn't much full height to speak of, and my dignity was so tattered by that point that I simply didn't have enough of it to cloak myself in.

'Actually,' I said, 'it is. You've got me bang to rights.'

He smiled ruefully. 'I'm sorry. It sucks, right? However many times it happens. But – and I know this is kind of left field – maybe we could have a drink together? A kind of un-date?'

I looked at him. His eyes behind his thick glasses looked kind. He was smiling in a cautious, self-effacing sort of way, and the smile showed clean, even teeth. His denim shirt looked freshly ironed, and he smelled of some kind of mildly floral, slightly earthy cologne.

I'd have scored him a high seven and a half, maybe even eight if I was feeling generous. But I had different standards to uphold.

'Just one thing,' I said. 'Do you mind me asking what your star sign is?'

'My what? I'm sorry, I don't really follow all of that.'

'That doesn't matter. Just tell me when your birthday is.'

'Ninth of September – 1992, if that matters. And my name's Justin.'

'Zoë,' I replied, frantically trying to remember whether that date fell within the sign of Virgo, and realising that it did. 'And you're on. What can I get you?'

Chapter Six

Following your dreams doesn't always mean getting what you desire. But you're not going to give up that easily – are you?

'Oh my God!' Dani lowered her barbell, its ends loaded with metal plates, back onto the squat rack. 'Fuck me, that hurt. But that's so romantic! I can't believe it! That's a meet-cute straight out of a movie. It's almost as good as if he'd rescued your cat from a tree or you'd met each other's eyes in a Tube station going in different directions and he'd run down the up escalator to find you and get your number. You'll be able to tell your grandchildren! I'll use it in my speech at your wedding!'

'Steady on! It was only the one date.'

'So what happened next?'

I moved some of her weights off the bar and positioned myself underneath it. I hadn't needed her to tell me – this was going to hurt. But it would be worth it; already, I could feel my hangover receding a bit, and I was pretty sure I was sweating pure sauvignon blanc. After this, I promised myself, I'd head for the local café that did vegan breakfasts and have a massive stack of pancakes with blueberries and coconut yoghurt, and then I'd feel as good as new.

I hoped so, anyway, because after that I needed to go to work, and there was no prospect of the long nap I so badly needed.

'So, after that,' I stepped carefully back from the rack, the weight on my shoulders, lowered myself into a squat, then straightened up again, my thighs already burning, 'I bought us a drink – white wine for me, red for him – and he managed to find us a table, which was pretty impressive because the place was totally rammed by then and the one I'd been sitting at got nabbed as soon as I stood up.'

I did a couple more squats, by the end of which I was too out of breath to talk.

'Go on, you've got this,' Dani said. 'Two more, then you can carry on with the story, right?'

'Right.' I finished my set, replaced the weight and stood there for a moment, breathing hard, my eyes stinging with perspiration.

'So you bought a drink and you sat down,' Dani prompted, wide-eyed. 'And then?'

'Then we chatted a bit, like you do. It was weird because I kept wanting to ask him all the questions I'd planned to ask Dominic.'

'What happened to him, anyway? Did he get in touch with a grovelling apology?'

'Nope. Nothing. And he's blocked me. I've got absolutely no idea what that was all about.'

'Bastard,' she said. 'He probably got a booty call – some girl he's shagged before and knew was a certainty – and he couldn't be bothered to think of an excuse. He should be ashamed of himself.'

'Maybe, but I bet he isn't. Anyway, so I had to keep reminding myself not to say something like, "How is a luffing crane different from a normal crane anyway?" to Justin, like I'd been planning to say to Dominic. So I asked him what he did for work and he told me he was an accountant, so of course I couldn't think of anything even slightly interesting to ask him about that.'

'"What is double entry anyway, I've always wondered?"' Dani suggested, and we both giggled childishly.

'"Do you have an asset or a liability?"' I suggested.

'"Are you single and ready to commingle?"'

I stepped under the bar and did another set of squats, racking my brain and then racking the weight.

'Sorry,' I said, when I'd finished. 'That's it. No more accountancy puns. I've got nothing else.'

'Just as well,' she admitted. 'I'm all out too. It's not exactly a field that has many opportunities for lolz, is it?'

I shook my head.

'Anyway, never mind about that,' she went on. 'Back to Justin. So you had your drink and you talked about what he gets up to between the spreadsheets.'

I groaned. 'Badoom-tish.'

'Thank you, I'm here all week.'

'Anyway, yeah, so he actually did talk about being an accountant. Like, a lot. He talked about how it requires integrity, precision, attention to detail and stuff like that. And he talked about how it's given him this great grounding in managing his own personal finances, and how he was able to put down a deposit on his first flat when he was twenty-three, because he'd always saved between ten and fifteen per cent of his income – net, not gross, whatever that means – since he got his first summer job when he was sixteen, and invested it across a spread of short- and long-term instruments, carefully selected to manage risk and maximise growth whilst offering a steady rate of return.'

I paused for breath, and Dani said, 'Oh. Right.'

'And he said he'd started paying into a pension as soon as he got his first job, so that he'd be able to enjoy a comfortable lifestyle in retirement, thanks to his prudent financial planning.'

'Right,' Dani said again. 'So by this point you must have been practically whipping your knickers off and waving them round your head?'

'Exactly. Nothing turns me on like a good chat about fiscal responsibility.'

'So I guess he isn't The One, then? No story to tell your grand-children?'

I shook my head. 'Sorry about that. I did try, honestly. I thought maybe I could drink him interesting, so we had, like, three more glasses of wine and I swear to God, he just kept getting more and more boring. I'm sure he'll be an amazing husband and father one day, but…'

'Not for you?'

'Not for me. And there was another thing.'

'Don't tell me it gets worse?'

'I'm afraid it does. So when I bought the first round, I left my card behind the bar to start a tab, like you do. I mean, everyone does it at work. It saves the staff having to put through a payment every time. And when eventually I just couldn't try to fancy him any more, and I said I was going to call it a night because I was knackered and I had an early shift the next day – not true, obviously – he was like, "Why don't I get our drinks next time and you pick up the tab tonight?"'

'What? The tight fucker! No wonder he's looking forward to a comfortable retirement if he never buys his own bloody drinks!'

'I know, right. And my card was behind the bar and I couldn't exactly force him to get his wallet out of his extremely deep pocket with his extremely short arm, could I?'

She shook her head.

'So there we go. A date with the dullest man in the world ended up costing me the best part of eighty quid.'

We stripped our weights off the bar and moved over to the mat. I got down into a plank and Dani put a weight on my back. As I always did, I started off thinking this was really quite easy, and wondering if I would try a heavier one next time. And as always, after about thirty seconds, I felt my arms and legs start to tremble and my mind begin to tell me insistently that this was a really terrible idea and I should stop right now.

Dani's voice distracted me from the growing urge to give up. 'I'm so sorry you went through that. Honestly, what a wanker. That really sucks. What kind of dick expects a girl to pay on the first date? I bet he hadn't even been stood up, I bet he was just on the scrounge to be bought a few drinks and wang on about interest rates. Loser. Time's up, you can stop.'

I dropped to my knees and we swapped over.

'No, but the thing is,' I said, 'I actually don't mind at all. I didn't want to meet Mr Right on my first go. Well, I did, obviously, but

Robbie says I won't know who Mr Right is until I've been out with loads of Mr Wrongs, so that's what I'm doing.'

'But isn't that – surely I'm done now?'

'Ten more seconds. Isn't it what?'

'It all sounds a bit… I don't know. If it was me, I'd want a bit more romance. Like, your eyes meet across a crowded room and suddenly your heart skips a beat and you know that he's The One.'

I sighed. 'That's what happened with me and Joe, and look where it got me. Back at university we were in the same queue for beers at a festival, we got talking and bam – I thought we'd be together forever. Then three months later I got an attack of commitment-phobia and ended it, and I spent six years regretting it. This time, I'm all about the scientific approach.'

I didn't mention that the science I was basing my approach on was what lots of people would regard as next-level woo. I did too, quite a lot of the time – except when my phone buzzed with one of the app's spookily accurate messages. And besides, I'd accepted Robbie's dare and taken on this challenge – project, whatever it was – so I might as well see it through.

My turn in the plank was over and I lay on the mat for a bit, waiting for my arms to stop feeling like they were about to fall off. Then I rolled over and sat up. To my surprise, Dani wasn't standing next to me, waiting for me to start her timer. She was in her plank already, the metal plate on her back. I could see drips of sweat from her nose landing on the mat.

And there next to her, looking intently at his watch as he counted down a minute for her, was Fabian Flatley.

I had no idea how long he'd been there, listening to us.

*

Challenge or no challenge, project or no project, it was hard not to let my first date make me doubt my decision to leap into the murky waters of online dating, which, if they were infested with men like no-show Dominic and dull Justin, no doubt contained far worse, too. And it made me doubt myself, too. If I wasn't good enough for Dominic to even turn up and meet for a drink, what hope did I have of finding an actual, proper relationship? And what right did I have to decide that Justin – who was, after all, perfectly normal and pleasant and some would consider quite the catch – wasn't good enough for me?

Was I going to have to lower my standards? Were there men out there who'd have to lower theirs to consider me good enough?

It wasn't devastating, exactly, but the whole experience had been enough of a let-down that I approached my phone in the mornings to check Tinder with far less enthusiasm than previously, and far more trepidation.

'How do you do it?' I asked Robbie, as we made sandwiches one lunchtime.

'I just slice the bread, butter it, spread on the filling, top with another bit of bread and cut it in half,' he said. 'Voila.'

'Not this, you doughnut! The dating thing. Like, without it totally destroying your self-confidence?'

'Oh, Zoë,' he said, with a sigh that seemed to come all the way from the AirWear soles of his Doc Marten boots. 'You poor love. It's tough at first, isn't it? You're going to have to develop a thicker skin, stat.'

'But how do you do that? I mean, surely getting knocked back hurts every time? Or do you get used to it?'

He paused, biting his lower lip reflectively, and spread mustard onto a slice of ham. 'You don't have to get used to it. It might always smart a bit. But why not tell yourself there's a reason for it? If someone's a dick, or flaky and doesn't turn up, or ghosts you after you've shagged or whatever, then actually you've dodged a bullet. Because if someone does that after one date, how badly could they break your heart after a year? And how much of your life would you have spaffed away if you ended up marrying them or something, and only realised they were a dick after that?'

'I suppose that's true. But it's kind of disheartening, putting all this time and effort into it on the off-chance that the right person could be out there, when your chances of finding them must be pretty microscopic really.'

'It's not about finding The One, though, is it? Not at first, anyway. You've got to play the long game. Kiss a few frogs, go for drinks in a few places you wouldn't normally, build up some experience of what the world is like, learn a bit more about yourself. That kind of thing. Oh, and have masses and masses of sex, obviously.'

He yawned hugely, stretching his arms high up over his head so the sleeves of his T-shirt slipped down over his lean biceps.

'Isn't it weird? The whole hook-up thing?' I asked.

'Weird? It's like being a kid in a candy store. Actually, it's not. It's like being the candy in a candy store.'

'How do you mean?'

'Zoë, I'm twenty-two. I won't be forever. But for now, I can log on to Grindr and twenty minutes later be walking into a guy's house for a fuck. I can take my pick, as well. I'm in high demand and I intend to make the most of it.'

Often, I'd noticed that Robbie made me feel absolutely ancient, but now, he was making me feel like a mere child, still wet behind the ears.

'You mean a guy you've never met before?'

'Usually. Sometimes it's a second bite of the cherry. But you know, so many men, so little time. I may as well work my way through them while I can.'

'So what, you go online, someone sends you a message, and you go round to his and…'

'Have sex. That's right. Sometimes they're quite sweet and want to romance me with a glass of wine and a chat. But usually it's walk in the door, shoes off and upstairs we go. If it wasn't for my housemates I wouldn't have to leave my bedroom, but I can't really have people turning up at all hours of the morning, so I go out mostly.'

'What if you don't fancy the guy?'

'We exchange pics first, of course. I like to know what I'm getting. No old blokes, no hairy blokes, no blokes with tiny cocks. I make my standards clear.'

'And if he doesn't look like his picture?'

'Then I turn right around and walk back out again. Or sometimes I can't be arsed with that and I just go through it anyway. It's just sex.'

Just sex. I thought about that for a moment while I sliced a cucumber. I couldn't imagine doing what Robbie was describing: walking out of my flat at three in the morning, getting on a night bus or into an Uber, turning up at a stranger's house, going upstairs and having sex. I'd be terrified.

But it didn't seem to bother Robbie in the slightest. Part of me wanted to warn him to be careful, to give him a massive hug and tell him he was worth more than that. But it was his life and none of my business. And, also, that wasn't what he was telling me to do, I reminded myself. All I had to do was exchange a few messages with people, delete a few dick pics, then go and meet someone for a glass of wine and see if it worked out well enough for a second date.

'You're right, I guess,' I said. 'Back on the horse. Or rather, back on the fish. It's Pisces' turn next.'

'Ooooh,' Robbie sighed. 'I dated a Pisces boy a few months back. He was proper gorgeous. Just so needy. If I didn't reply to a text in about five seconds he'd start freaking out and asking me why I was ignoring him. Far too high-maintenance for me, so unfortunately I had to tell him to sling his hook. See what I did there?'

I laughed. 'Did you draw a line under it?'

'I did. He got a bit chippy with me, I can tell you.'

'But the experience must've been worth it, since the sex was off the scale.'

'I'm still a bit gutted about it, if I'm honest.'

We hooted with laughter at our lame puns.

'Robbie?' I said. 'Since you know everything, apparently, can you tell me how to find a Dungeon Master?'

'What? Christ, Zoë, I don't want to kink shame or anything, but I had no idea that's what you were into.'

'No! Not that kind of dungeon. Or that kind of master, either. Here, take these sandwiches through to the bar and I'll explain.'

Robbie picked up the platter of artfully arranged food, pushed the kitchen door open with a snake-like hip and disappeared into the bar. While I waited for him to return, I checked Tinder and updated my profile to say I was looking for a Pisces man to date.

Plenty more fish in the sea, I told myself, feeling another giggle rising in my throat. Just as well I was easily pleased – I was going to have to be, if I was to find anything in common with a bloke who, my Stargazer app told me, would be introspective, scatterbrained, forgetful and sulky. Hard work, in other words, I thought despondently.

'So what's this, then?' Robbie burst back into the kitchen. 'There's a massive crowd out there today. Alice reckons we'll need more sangers and we're out of ham.'

'Let's do beetroot hummus and avocado. I feel bad about the avos coming from Peru and they're certainly not organic, but what can you do? How many years on and we still haven't reached peak avocado – people can't get enough of them.'

'Never mind about avocado air miles,' Robbie said, pulling a tub of purple hummus out of the fridge. 'Talk me through the dungeon thing. Whips and chains, or just a bit of light restraint?'

'None. Of. The. Above. Honestly, if you'd been paying attention for five seconds, you'd know that Alice is organising a Dungeons & Dragons group in the pub. Or rather Drew was, but now Drew can't, so I am. At least, I've been delegated to find someone who can, and I don't know where to start.'

'Google?'

'Tried that. And there isn't a version of Tinder that matches Dungeon Masters to groups of players that don't even actually exist yet, unsurprisingly.'

'Reddit?'

'I never go on there; it's too scary.'

'I know, right? Full of weirdos and incels.'

Since I was quite the involuntary celibate myself, I didn't feel qualified to comment on that.

'We've got six people signed up for the game already,' I said, 'and I'm sure others will join nearer the time. But if we don't have someone in charge who actually knows what they're doing, it'll be a massive flop, Alice will be disappointed and we'll have to find something else to go on the social calendar for Tuesday nights.'

'And we've already got the monthly open-mic poetry slam, the board-games evenings, the bingo nights on Thursdays…'

'The stitch and bitch sessions, the pay-what-you-like lunches for pensioners…'

'Live music once a month…'

'The mums and tots groups…'

'Maurice and his mates teaching people dominoes, although that's not really a formal thing…'

'But we've got to keep coming up with new stuff, to keep the place buzzing.'

'Although quite how bringing a bunch of nerds in once a week to fight pretend monsters counts as buzzing, I'm not entirely sure,' Robbie said.

'Don't knock D&D – it's massively zeitgeisty right now,' I argued. 'Alice said so, anyway. And Drew Barrymore's a fan. Anything she does basically comes with a badge of cool, right?'

Robbie looked unconvinced, but he said, 'One of my mates from school plays, I think. Well, when I say mate, more someone

I know. Anyway, I'm pretty sure I've seen pictures of dice and shit on his Insta feed. I'll ask and see if he has any ideas.'

For Robbie to make such a concession was pretty good going, and as much help as I was going to get from him, so I thanked him and we both turned back to the sandwich platters. Then my phone buzzed, then buzzed again – a double notification. I reached for it and flicked the screen to life.

Is it feeling kind of like groundhog day there, Aquarius? asked the astrology app.

And Tinder had a message for me, too. Well, an image. An image of a penis that looked almost uncannily like a potato. A dodgy, misshapen one that would have been on a one-way street to the compost, had it turned up in my kitchen.

'You're not wrong,' I told Stargazer grimly.

Chapter Seven

Is that romance making your heart beat faster, Aquarius, or did you just run up the stairs?

Over the next couple of weeks, I spent many, many hours on Project Pisces. Just narrowing down my pool (gettit?) of potential dates to those who had actually been born between February 19th and March 20th was my first challenge. It felt kind of rude and abrupt to ask someone their zodiac sign as soon as I'd matched with them – but then, if I was going to do this thing systematically and scientifically, as I'd promised myself I would, I couldn't go wasting my time and theirs exchanging chit-chat with blokes who were born under the sign of Sagittarius, when I was only going to get around to dating them in several months' time – could I?

So I kept my approach pretty simple. I got a match, maybe a bland 'How's it going?' message (or maybe a dick pic, but I was getting so used to those that they barely registered – the 'delete, block, ignore' sequence was so ingrained now, I was sure I could do it in my sleep), and I replied cheerfully with a 'Hope you don't mind me asking, but what's your star sign?'

Helpfully, some guys already had theirs listed on their profile, and that made it easier, although I didn't swipe right on every Pisces man – of course not. There were just as many of them, it seemed, who had pictures of themselves with some poor drugged tiger in Thailand, or with their ex-girlfriend's face half cut off at the edge, or wearing a baseball cap backwards, and I had standards to uphold.

The responses I got to my question varied. A high number thought it was hilarious to reply informing me that they'd been born under the sign of the ram, bull or goat, and therefore – you guessed it – they were horny. Delete, block, ignore. Some asked, 'My what?' in which case I'd ask the question again, and helpfully tell them that if they told me when their birthday was, I could work it out myself. And, of course, a high proportion simply ignored my question and never messaged me again.

Lying on my bed with Frazzle purring on my feet, I asked myself over and over again whether all this was worth it, and whether I shouldn't find some other way to spend hours and hours of my leisure time, like training for a marathon or painting the ceiling of the Sistine Chapel or something. But I'd set myself this challenge, embarked on this project, and now I felt strangely compelled to carry on with it.

By the end of April, I was regularly exchanging messages with Mitchell, who met my criteria but was working away in Glasgow for a couple of weeks; Rich, who was a nurse working in accident and emergency and whose shifts seemed to have been planned to coincide with my time off; and Paul. Pisces Paul – it had a nice ring to it. His pictures showed a nice-looking guy with glasses and a beard, he lived in South London too, and soon he suggested that we should meet up one evening in a local park for a glass of wine, as the weather was so nice.

At first, when he'd suggested it, I'd fleetingly thought, *In a park? What's wrong with a pub, like normal people go to on dates?* But I'd dismissed the thought – the early May weather was glorious, the cherry trees laden with blossom and the sky a clear blue day after day – not that I got to enjoy very much of it, because I spent all my days inside a pub. So I decided that Paul was on to something. An al fresco date would be fun. It would be different. And crucially, it would be cheap – my wages didn't amount to much and Paul, who'd told me he was studying for a PhD in medieval literature, was probably even skinter.

When the day of our date came, I finished the prep for the Sunday roast at the Ginger Cat and the main rush of service, and escaped upstairs to my flat at three o'clock to get ready, leaving Robbie in charge. I showered and washed my hair, then stood in front of the mirror trying to gauge its mood. My hair, I often thought, was like a particularly troublesome child. I was like the little girl in the nursery rhyme, except instead of one curl I had about a million of them, and it wasn't me who was very good when I was good, and horrid when I was bad, it was my stupid hair.

If I spent a fortune on sulphate-free shampoo, argan oil conditioner, mousses and serums, it often behaved itself, falling obligingly into ringlets that looked more copper than ginger. But if I compromised on products, if the weather was wet, if I'd been simmering stock in the kitchen, or sometimes just because it felt like it, it rebelled and transformed into something you'd scrub a burned pan with. If I resorted to straighteners, it threw an almighty strop and turned into a mass of broken strands and split ends.

Compared to my hair, Frazzle was totally undemanding.

Today, I carefully soaked the excess water off it with an old T-shirt, ran three different smoothing potions through it, and ever so gently allowed my hairdryer's diffuser to breathe on it for a few minutes. There was a moment when I thought it would take exception to that and poof out into a frizzy mess, but I stopped just in time, added more serum and ran my fingers through it gently, then sighed with relief as it dropped into soft curls.

I pulled on a yellow cotton skirt I'd found in a charity shop, my trusty canvas trainers and a white T-shirt, hastily applied some make-up and headed out, stopping at the corner shop for a bottle of Californian rosé and a bag of cashew nuts. I was starving, and Paul hadn't mentioned anything about food. Maybe, if it went well, we could grab a takeaway pizza later or go for a curry, but I wasn't going to ruin the date before it even started by unleashing my hanger on poor, unsuspecting Paul.

As I hurried towards the park, I checked my phone. There was no message from Paul cancelling; just a screen grab of a map with a pin dropped in the centre of the park – where he wanted us to meet, I guessed, which was thoughtful. The Stargazer app reminded me again of the romantic nature, thoughtfulness and sensitivity of Piscean men – he certainly seemed to be living up to that so far.

The park, on this beautiful day, was full. There were kids playing on the swings, groups sitting at the wooden tables outside the café with coffee and (I noticed enviously) cake, a group of teenagers playing volleyball, and couples strolling hand in hand along the pathways. For a second, I allowed my mind to imagine that, soon, Paul and I might be among them, but then I pushed the idea aside.

It was only my second date; there was no way I'd meet Mr Right – or even Mr Right for Now – so soon. And besides, if the app was to be believed, Pisces wasn't even a good match for me. This wasn't supposed to be love at first sight.

I made my way towards where the pin on the map had directed me, which I realised was the bandstand, perched high on the hill. The wine bottle was running with condensation by the time I reached the top, and I could feel sweat trickling down my back. I willed my hair not to frizz in the heat, and congratulated myself on my good sense in wearing trainers.

But, when I neared the bandstand, my steps slowed. There must be some mistake. There was something weird going on. There were two men waiting there together, both in dinner jackets and bow ties. Sometimes couples posed there for wedding photographs, but this wasn't that – there was no bride in a white dress. A gay wedding? But one of them was seated at a table right in the middle of the bandstand, which had been set with a sparkling white cloth, and the other was standing next to him, rigid, as if at attention, a napkin draped over one arm.

I stopped and took out my phone, looking around me as I did. There was no sign of any single man perched on a bench or a picnic blanket, or even just looking around awkwardly like I was. Apart from the groups scattered around – many, I could see, staring at the bandstand and speculating among themselves about what might be going on there – there was no one apart from the two men and me.

My phone vibrated in my hand.

Is that you, Zoë? Your date awaits!

*

'Oh my God, cringe!' Dani said.

We were at the café next door to the gym, both drinking enormous iced coffees with squirty non-dairy cream on top and eating carrot cake, still in our workout gear.

'I know! Cringe, cringe, cringe, to the max. I was cringing so hard I almost swallowed my own head.'

'Who was the other guy?'

'Paul's flatmate. He'd got him there to be our waiter. I think his name was Imran. Lovely guy and everything, but...'

'Cringe.'

'Yep. So, so cringe. Everyone was looking at us. People were taking photos and everything.'

'You mean you actually stayed for the date?'

'How could I not? What could I have done, said, "Sorry mate, your romantic gesture is making me die inside and I'm going to fuck off home to my cat?"'

'Must've been tempting.'

'Oh God, it so, so was. But at the same time...'

'Awww?'

'Exactly. He'd done this mad romantic thing, he was willing to make a total tit of himself in front of loads of people, I couldn't be like, "Not working for me, soz, bye."'

'Yeah, I can kind of see how that would be.'

'So what could I do? I walked over and he got up and – no word of a lie – he kissed my hand. Like I was the queen or something. I nearly died.'

Dani had a mouthful of coffee and I saw her cheeks bulge as she struggled not to choke on it. 'He what?' she spluttered at last.

'You heard right. And then Imran pulled my chair out for me to sit down and poured us both champagne, and Paul gave me an enormous fuck-off bunch of roses, and I didn't know where to put them so I sat there clutching them like a wedding bouquet or something, until Imran took them off me and stuck them in the ice bucket the fizz was in.'

'And you still had your bottle of cheap wine and your packet of nuts?'

'I did. Oh my God, it was awful. I didn't know where to put those either. I ended up kind of hiding the nuts in my handbag and putting the wine on the ground by my feet and not mentioning it because here he was with this bottle of Moët that had cost, like, twenty quid.'

'Oh, Zoë. Is it wrong that I'm really glad it happened to you? It's, like, once-in-a-lifetime mortifying. What happened next?'

'So then Imran opened this massive cooler box – what with that and the table and the two chairs and the flowers the two of them must've looked like they were going on an expedition to summit Everest when they walked up that hill – and got out a plate of oysters.'

'Oysters? Oh no.'

'Oh yes. And I don't have in my profile that I don't eat meat because, you know, everyone takes the piss out of vegans for saying all the time that they're vegan. I thought if we ended up going out for food I could just order what I wanted and not say anything.'

'But you couldn't.'

'I couldn't. I feel terrible, Dani, but I ate them. I felt too bad not to. I mean, I try to avoid meat but I have to taste it sometimes for work and I told myself this was kind of like that. He had put so much effort in. But it was gross, like swallowing snot, and I read afterwards that the poor things are actually alive when you eat them and I tried to make myself sick but I couldn't. Anyway, I'm getting ahead of myself, because after he'd opened the oysters, Imran… Oh my God, I can't actually bring myself to tell you.'

'Go on!' Dani leaned in, grinning delightedly.

I covered my face with my hands and muttered, 'He only took out a bloody violin and serenaded us.'

'Waaah!'

'Waaah. He's obviously really good at playing the violin, and he got really into it. He was doing that thing of closing his eyes and kind of throwing his head around. And by this stage, people weren't just taking photos, there was this whole little crowd around the bandstand videoing us. I'm sure I was literally everyone's Insta story yesterday. I haven't logged in because if I saw it I'd legit die.'

'Oh fuck.' Dani wiped away tears with her napkin. 'So what happened next?'

'It was so awkward. I couldn't even have a proper conversation with Paul, because all there really was to say was how much trouble he'd gone to and how mad it all was, and anyway, even though he was doing the violin thing, obviously Imran would've been able to overhear anything we said. I tried to ask Paul about medieval literature, but he kept getting interrupted when Imran stopped playing to top up our glasses or put more food out or whatever.'

'There was more food?'

'There were olives and asparagus and strawberries dipped in chocolate, so that was okay in theory. But actually I didn't feel like eating anything after the oysters. Why does anyone think those things are an aphrodisiac?'

'I've never had oysters,' Dani said. 'But I'll take your word for it. And stick to cake for now, obviously.'

'Obviously.' I forked up a huge bit of my cake, which I'd checked had been made with dairy-free cream cheese frosting to help alleviate my guilt about the oyster. It was delicious – melting and sweet and studded with walnuts and, crucially, not a bivalve mollusc. And I was eating it without an audience.

'Anyway, so go on,' Dani urged. 'I need to hear what happened next.'

'It was a bit better once the food was finished,' I admitted. 'I was a bit pissed by then, and Imran had moved away to the other side of the bandstand so it didn't feel like he was hanging over us earwigging. But to be honest, I was so over the whole thing by then and it was just so toe-curlingly awful I just wanted to go home and never think or speak of it again.'

'Why didn't you? Why didn't you invent a text from a mate or an emergency at work or something?'

'Dani, I couldn't! It was like I was paralysed. It was the most awkward thing ever. Paul was so proud of himself and he kept going on about how he wants to treat a woman like a princess, and did I like the food and would I like more champagne, or would I prefer white wine, and I just couldn't leave. And anyway by that stage it was starting to get dark and I thought that would probably give me an excuse to go.'

'And did it?'

I nodded. 'Eventually. But not before he'd got Imran to take a photo of us with the sunset behind us, and said he wanted something special to remember our date by, and he'd send it to me and we could both make it the background on our phones.'

'Wait, what?'

'Yup. That was the weird thing. Like, up until then, I'd thought it was really all quite sweet, even though it was the most over-the-top and mortifying thing ever, but after the first hour or so he started talking like we were going to be together, like it was a given.'

'How? What did he say?'

'He said he wasn't going to kiss me, because he wanted the first kiss to be special, and something we'd always remember, and we should wait until the perfect moment. And he started talking about how he'd always thought solitaire diamonds were the best for engagement rings.'

'Oh, no!'

'Oh, yes. And seriously, that was the moment when I finally got the guts to get up and say it had been a lovely afternoon, but I had to get back because I had an early start for work the next day. And he said, "Every moment with you is special, and longing to see you again will be special too."'

'And you must've been like, "Glad you'll enjoy that, because you'll be doing it for a long time."'

'I was. But I couldn't actually say that to him. I got home and I texted him and thanked him for the date, but said I wasn't sure we were right for each other.'

'Good for you. What did he say?'

I sighed. 'He called me an ungrateful bitch and said I'd never meet anyone as good as him and if I stayed single it would serve me right, and he wouldn't be surprised because I'm an ugly cow.'

'Oh. Oh shit. What a bastard.'

'Yup. So you know the drill.'

'Delete.'

'Block.'

'Ignore.'

'Move on.'

Chapter Eight

Unrealistic expectations can lead to disappointment, and promises made too hastily are easily broken. Your head may be in the clouds, Aquarius, but keep your feet on the ground.

After that, I found my thoughts returning quite frequently to my date with Paul. When I was doing some mindless task in the kitchen like chopping onions or rubbing butter into flour for scones; when I was in the shower, Frazzle watching me with an expression that quite clearly said, 'What on earth are you doing in there, human? It's wet, you know'; when I was lying in bed at night, staring at my phone and scrolling left over and over again.

Clearly, he thought he was a nice bloke. A true romantic. A guy who was prepared to go to an enormous amount of thought and trouble for one first date with someone he'd only been messaging for a few days. A man who, he claimed, wanted to treat a woman like a princess.

And yet, when I told him quite gently that he wasn't right for me, he'd turned into someone else entirely, sending that nasty, abusive message that had actually made me feel a bit sick for a second, like he'd punched me in the stomach.

What the hell was that about? I found myself asking the question over and over as I stared at my phone, or my knife, or Frazzle's judgy ginger face. And, in the end, I found myself seeking advice from someone who I reckoned knew a hell of a lot more about men and relationships than I did, given she'd managed to sustain a pretty functional and healthy one for more than two years.

'Alice,' I said, one afternoon when the pub was quiet and we'd finished going through the budget for the next week's food order, 'can I ask you something?'

'Sure.' She pushed back her chair, twisted her silky blonde hair into a knot at the back of her head and secured it with a pencil, her expression neutral and curious, then suddenly doubtful. 'Is it about the D&D game?'

'No,' I said, feeling a twinge of guilt and anxiety because, with the inaugural game drawing nearer and nearer, I was no closer to achieving what she'd asked me to do. 'It's about a date I went on. It got kind of weird.'

And I spilled out the whole story.

Unlike Dani, Alice didn't piss herself laughing. But, unlike when I'd told Dani about my date with Paul, I didn't play it for laughs. I tried to explain how deeply uncomfortable I'd felt, how embarrassed, how much the focus of attention I hadn't expected and didn't want.

'And then,' I said, 'after he'd been so romantic and lovely the whole way through, when I said I didn't want to see him again, he got all shitty with me. Like, really shitty.'

In spite of myself, I felt a lump forming in my throat. I mean, it's not like I cared what Paul thought of me really, but I'd tried to be nice and he'd called me an ugly cow. It wasn't the words that hurt, because I knew deep down that they weren't true, so much as the fact he'd needed to say them.

I tried to explain that to Alice, but I don't think I did a great job of it.

'There's something you're missing, though, Zoë,' Alice said, pulling the pencil out of her hair again and chewing the end of it a bit.

'What's that?' I asked, thinking for the millionth time how amazing it would be to have hair that fell into a smooth, glossy curtain like that every time.

'There were red flags all over the place, right from the beginning.'

'Really? I thought it was so sweet and romantic – although totally mortifying, of course – and that's why I couldn't just walk away.'

'Yep. That's what he was counting on. And that's manipulative, quite frankly. You can't go love-bombing someone like that, not on a first date. It's meant to be about getting to know each other first. I mean, Joe's a big one for the grand romantic gesture but not unless he's sure it's appropriate, right?'

'Right,' I said hastily. 'Okay. I get that. He was counting on me being too wrong-footed and too embarrassed and too flattered – which I guess I was, in a way – to tell him he had to be having a laugh and I wasn't going to play along.'

'Exactly! And all that stuff about being treated like a princess – *really*?'

'Why? What's wrong with that? Isn't it just one of those things people say?'

'It is and it isn't. Think about it for a second. What do princesses do? Do they have opinions, or do they sit around looking pretty?'

The only princess that sprang to mind wasn't actually one, but the Duchess of Cambridge was married to a prince, so she'd have to do. She probably did lots of stuff, I thought. Looking after her kids and being involved with charities and maybe a bit of gardening or photography or whatever. But Alice was right – she spent an awful lot of time, in the public eye at least, sitting around looking pretty.

'I see what you mean,' I said slowly.

'Right. And when you were caught off guard, he showed his true colours. That there is a guy who basically doesn't like women.'

'Okay,' I said. 'I mean, the things he said to me afterwards, those were pretty nasty and misogynistic. But surely he wouldn't want to go to all that trouble on a date if he didn't want to have a relationship?'

'I expect he does. But only with someone who's totally compliant and admiring and passive. Look what happened as soon as you stepped out of line. How do you reckon that would play out if you disagreed about him staying out late with his mates while you were left with the kids, or about politics, or about what colour to paint your front room, or whatever?'

'It's like what the app says about Pisces,' I said. 'Oversensitive, needy and inflexible.'

Alice managed not to roll her eyes, but I could tell it was a struggle. 'Maybe it's a Pisces thing, maybe it's just a character trait. But the point is, do you want to be treated like a princess or like a person?'

I opened my mouth to tell her that what she'd said made perfect sense, and thank her, but the door of the Ginger Cat swung open and Maurice, Ray, Sadiq and Terry strolled in, ready to start today's dominoes game, and Alice sprang to her feet, sliding through the hatch and behind the bar in one graceful movement.

'Morning, gents. Your usual?'

The pub suddenly got crazy busy after that, the way it sometimes did, with waves of people coming through the door for no discernible reason – other than the fact that the Ginger Cat was the best pub in South London, obviously – and I had no time to think more deeply about what Alice had said. I barely had time to slip to the gym in the middle of the afternoon, and I rushed through my workout.

Dani wasn't there, and when I asked Mike if he had heard from her he said she'd been in earlier. He said it in a way that seemed kind of evasive, like he wasn't telling me the full story, but I didn't have time to think about that much, either, only to send her a quick text saying I hoped she was okay, and we'd see each other soon.

The evening got even busier, and it was eleven thirty before I made it back up to my flat. Frazzle launched immediately into a vocal campaign for second dinner and a series of detailed complaints about humans who stayed out until all hours and neglected their cats, before flopping down on my bed and asking for his tummy to be rubbed.

I lay down next to him and took out my phone, tapping and scrolling with one hand while fussing Frazz with the other.

Least compatible signs with Aquarius, I read. *Virgo and Pisces* – well, I'd tried those and as far as I was concerned the app had been bang on the money so far. Third on the list was Scorpio.

Your Scorpio lover operates at a higher level of intensity than most men. His emotions run deep and he feels them keenly – but he will avoid showing what he perceives as weakness at all costs. To avoid getting hurt, he may close his heart and repel emotional intimacy – because he knows that when he falls he'll fall hard. Prickly and intense, the sting in the scorpion's tail will be felt if he is angered or wounded.

Jesus, he sounded like an awful lot of hard work. Couldn't I just skip him and move on to someone who was a bit less of a pain in the arse?

Then I reminded myself that I'd set myself a challenge, and it would be pathetic to give up. I read on.

The upside? Ruled by Mars and Pluto, Scorpio is the most primally passionate sign in the zodiac. Your Scorpio man brings all his emotional intensity into the bedroom – or the kitchen table, the shower, the bondage dungeon; when it comes to matters of intimacy, it's no holds barred for your sexy Scorpio. As a lover, he is inventive, skilful, enthusiastic and often surprisingly tender. It's in relationships where he is physically satisfied that Scorpio will reveal the loyal, compassionate and devoted side of his personality.

Oh, right then, I thought. *Why didn't you mention that in the first place?* If there was one thing that was lacking in my life, it was a good bit of inventive, passionate sex.

'Come on then, Scorpio,' I said, tweaking my profile. By the time I'd finished, my eyes were drooping with tiredness and my phone was slipping out of my hand, but I forced myself to get up, scoop out Frazzle's litter tray, wash my face and brush my teeth before falling back into bed.

Just as I was sinking blissfully into sleep, my phone flashed with a message from the dating app. Half awake, I fumbled it to life in the dark.

Oh God. A dick pic.

But this time, I smiled and looked at it properly. And, for the very first time, I didn't ignore, block or delete.

*

'Holy shit, Zoë, what have you been doing with yourself?' Robbie demanded when I stumbled into the kitchen the next morning, my eyes half closed still. 'You look like you've been on a massive bender. You look like me after a heavy night. Actually, you don't – you look worse.'

'Cheers for that,' I said. 'I can always count on you for an ego boost. I didn't get a whole lot of sleep.'

Robbie looked at me appraisingly. 'Well, you're going to have to tell me all about it. But first, you're going to have to go back upstairs and put your T-shirt on the right side out. And I'll get some coffee on.'

I left the kitchen and walked back upstairs to the flat. Actually, it didn't feel like walking – more like floating. As if my feet were somehow on a cushion of air, like when you're wearing expensive brand-new trainers. For the first time in my life, I got what the phrase 'on cloud nine' meant – although it was entirely possible that I'd skipped that and gone directly to cloud ten.

As I walked, I checked my phone, but there were no new messages from Seth, not since we'd signed off three hours before.

'Now,' my sous-chef thrust a triple espresso into my hand, 'what's all this about? Share it with the group.'

'Nothing,' I muttered, trying to keep the silly grin off my face and prevent a massive blush making its way up my neck. 'I was just chatting to someone online, and I lost track of time.'

'Chatting, you say? And what form exactly did this *chat* of yours take?'

'It got… kind of flirty.'

'Flirty, or filthy?'

'Oh God. Both, I guess.'

'Good girl! Up all night sexting a stranger, that's what I like to see! Who is he?'

'He's a Scorpio,' I said. 'The app reckons they're all passionate and stuff, so when he sent me a dick pic I didn't delete it. I decided to kind of go with it.'

Robbie gave me that hard stare again, which reminded me of the way Frazzle looked when he wanted his breakfast. 'I take it this was no ordinary dick pic, then? Or rather, a pic of no ordinary dick.'

'I didn't say that! It was just… You know.'

'I certainly do not know. And I won't, unless you give me details.'

'Robbie. Let me remind you that this is a place of work and I am technically your boss.'

'Okay, fine. Sheesh, you're no fun.'

'That's enough of that. We've got the tofu to press for the vegan stir-fry, so let's get cracking.'

We did, but as we worked I kept catching Robbie casting side-long, speculative glances at me, and I knew he must be thinking, *I never knew she had it in her.*

And he wasn't alone – I hadn't known, either, until the messages I'd been exchanging with Seth had... well, escalated (and judging by the pictures he'd sent me, they weren't the only thing that had). It was bizarre. For the first time in ages – possibly the first time ever – I'd felt purely, viscerally physical, a bit like how I did when I was in the gym, but also so very differently.

I felt consumed by desire, but also felt desirable – like there was some kind of digital thread of lust connecting me to this man I'd never met. We didn't even appear to have that much in common, and we hadn't talked about anything meaningful – well, I suppose sex is meaningful, isn't it? And we'd talked about that, a lot. I'd promised myself that if I felt uncomfortable at any point, I'd stop and block him – but I hadn't felt uncomfortable. Not one bit.

From his pictures, he wasn't even anything special – nice enough to look at, with cropped dark hair that was covered by a hat in quite a lot of his photos, and eyes that were a kind of tawny light brown, but not the kind of handsome that stops you in your tracks. He was older than I'd have ideally wanted, too, right at the upper limit of the age range I'd specified.

But none of that mattered. I was like a woman possessed. In spite of my tiredness, I felt giddy with excitement all that morning, racing through my tasks in the kitchen, running up the stairs to change into my gym kit at three in the afternoon, almost unaware of how tough my workout was, or that Dani wasn't in the gym at her usual time – again.

Oh, and checking my phone. I did that a lot. Every time it chirruped with an alert, I grabbed it like I was worried it might run away. When it was only a calendar reminder or a push notification from Stargazer, or a message from someone I'd been speaking to on and off on Tinder and assumed had gone off the boil, I felt a lurch of disappointment, but that did little to dull my giddy excitement.

I understood, now, what Robbie had meant when he talked about going to a stranger's home for sex. Not caring if it was dangerous, or reckless, or stupid – just feeling a total, all-consuming longing to tear off my clothes and sleep with someone. A particular someone.

And Seth felt the same, I was sure. When we signed off the previous night, he'd said that, next time, it would be in real life. I didn't care if we had a drink first, or even if he liked cats.

Robbie, to his credit, managed to put up with my distractedness all day. It was only when we were cleaning up after the evening service had finished that he said, 'Now. Listen up.'

'What?' I jerked out of my reverie.

'I know you're my boss and everything. But you need to get your shit together, Zoë. Today you left the deep-fat fryer unattended and you could have burned the place down. You almost used the tongs I'd been turning chicken with to serve up the tofu. You would've sent a dessert out with beetroot ketchup on it instead of raspberry coulis if I hadn't stopped you.'

'I know. I'm sorry. I've been all over the place. It's lack of sleep. I'll be fine tomorrow.'

He gave me a hard stare. 'You will not be fine until you get that man out of your system. When are you seeing him?'

'Weeelll… he did mention meeting up on Thursday. But that's your night off, and—'

'Night off, schmight off. I'll swap with you. You go off on your date, and afterwards maybe you'll be able to get through a service without bringing shame on this pub.'

I didn't need telling twice. I thanked him, apologised again, and got straight on my phone to see if there was a local salon that could fit me in the next day to have every surplus hair on my body waxed off in preparation for my date with Seth. Bollocks to my feminist principles.

Chapter Nine

Passion is your governor today, Aquarius. Be guided by your heart, but remember that those who play with fire risk getting scorched.

I lifted my martini glass, carefully so as not to spill any of the clear, icy liquid that filled it, and took a sip. My lipstick left a red smear on its rim, and I wondered what I was supposed to do about that – ignore it? Try to lick it off? Wipe it with a napkin? I'd never been much of a make-up wearer, but tonight I'd gone full femme fatale. My eyelashes were curled and mascaraed to within an inch of their lives. My freckles were blotted out with foundation. My eyebrows – normally almost invisible – had been pencilled in with countless tiny strokes and gelled into place.

I was wearing dark skinny jeans, a silky black top I'd had for years and never worn because it had scratchy beading on the neckline, and a pair of kitten-heeled mules I'd bought in a charity shop ages ago for a party, then discovered that they slipped off my feet with every step.

I didn't feel even slightly like me. I felt like someone daring, alluring and sexy. At least, I would, once I'd got half this cocktail down me.

Seth had suggested a swanky cocktail bar in North London for our date. It was near to where he lived, he'd said, and I knew that what he meant was, convenient for going back to for a shag afterwards. The thought made my stomach turn a somersault, and I saw my hand trembling slightly as I lifted my glass for another sip of what was basically cold, neat gin.

Zoë the femme fatale would feel entirely comfortable perched on a bar stool sipping a dry martini while she waited for her date. I just wished she'd hurry up and take over from the regular Zoë, who was twitching with nerves and whose arse was slowly going numb from the bar stool's slippery marble top.

'Hello, Zoë. There you are. Did you find it okay? Sorry I'm late – I got held up at the office.'

I wasn't sure what I'd been expecting Seth to do – greet me with a sleazy, 'Hey, baby,' and stare down my cleavage or something – but this totally normal, casual greeting surprised me and put me a bit more at ease.

'That's okay. I haven't been waiting long.'

He slipped onto the stool next to mine and looked at me for a moment, smiling. His teeth were slightly crooked, with a bit of a gap between the front ones. He was wearing jeans and a white shirt, the top button undone, and I could see that his brown leather belt had recently been let out a notch.

Liam Hemsworth he was not. He was just an ordinary, decent-looking guy in his mid-thirties, average height, average build, average everything – everything except his eyes. They were the most amazing colour. Light brown? Hazel? Whatever you called it, they were almost golden, and a fine black line surrounded each iris, as perfect as if it had been applied with liquid eyeliner (at least, by someone who could apply liquid eyeliner perfectly, so not me). And when he looked at me with that curious, smiling stare, I felt something happening inside me – a loosening, melting feeling that made me even more worried that I might slide off the bar stool. It was like he'd sprayed himself with some mysterious pheromone-boosting cologne, or clicked on one of those emails that always go into your junk folder saying they've got the secret that will make you irresistible to women.

Or maybe I was so desperate for a shag I'd imagine anyone as the next Casanova, so long as they weren't actively repulsive. But that wasn't the case, I told myself – I hadn't felt this way about Paul or Justin. I wasn't accosting random men in the street and begging them to come back to mine and bump uglies.

Whatever it was Seth had, he had it in spades, and I was in no fit state to analyse it.

He ordered an Old Fashioned for himself and another martini for me; the first one seemed to have mysteriously disappeared. We drank our drinks and we talked about perfectly ordinary things: his job doing something complicated involving buying online advertising space, my job in the pub, places where we'd travelled and books we'd read. He asked me stuff about myself like he was really, genuinely interested. Everything I said seemed to make him laugh, and when he did, those amazing eyes sparkled like shards of amber glass in the sun.

But afterwards, I could hardly remember a thing we said, because it seemed like every word was about something else. When he lifted his drink, I found myself staring at his hand, looking at his blunt fingers wrapped around the glass and wondering how it would feel when he touched me. When he took a sip, I wanted to run my finger over his bottom lip. When he rubbed his shorn head, I wished it was my hand doing it, and I could almost feel the suede-like smoothness on my palm.

What the hell is wrong with you, Zoë? I asked myself, but my brain wasn't able to engage even in that simple question. It was like I didn't even have a brain any more, only a body that wanted to get as close as possible to this irresistibly sexy man.

As if Seth sensed my feelings, he nudged his chair closer to mine, so that our denim-clad knees were just an inch or so apart, and when I uncrossed my legs to cross them back the other way, my thigh touched his. Our eyes met again, he smiled and I felt his hand on my leg, resting there, heat spreading through my jeans and my skin and my whole body.

And when he finished his drink and said, 'Shall we go?' I could only nod, watching mutely as he paid the bill and letting him guide me to the door, a warm, strong arm around my shoulder. He was taller than me but only just, thanks to my unfamiliar heels. If he kissed me, he'd only have to lean down a tiny bit.

It was still light outside, so bright after the gloom of the bar I felt almost disorientated – although that might have been the gin. Pavement tables were crowded with people eating, drinking and smoking, enjoying what would be almost the longest day of the year. The air was cool against my skin, and I realised my whole body felt hot, as if I'd been lying in the sun.

'So,' Seth said. 'Back to mine?'

'Sure.' I tried to sound casual, like I did this sort of thing all the time, but part of me was terrified. What was I doing? No one knew where I was. This man could be an axe murderer.

'I'm not an axe murderer,' he said.

'Like you'd admit to it if you were. Imagine. "Come back to mine – oh, by the way, I'm an axe murderer."'

He laughed. 'Not the strongest of pick-up lines. Which is why I stopped using it years ago.'

It was my turn to laugh. 'So what line do you use now? When you're not meeting people online, that is?'

'I don't. I just rely on personal magnetism.'

That was it, I realised. This average-looking dude – above average, maybe, but not someone whose picture you'd put on your bedroom wall and daydream over when you were fifteen – had magnetism. Charisma. Some elusive quality which, whatever you called it, made me go weak at the knees and made me self-conscious of my lips in a way that had nothing to do with lipstick, and of my breasts in a way that had nothing to do with the lacy bra I was wearing, which was digging into my ribs and itching like a bastard.

'It's just down here,' Seth said as we turned off the main road onto a side street lined with tall stucco-fronted houses, most of them painted white but the occasional one pastel pink or green. The one he stopped in front of was pale yellow.

He unlocked the front door and gestured to me, and I climbed a narrow staircase, up and up to the third floor. My heart was hammering by the time we got to the top, and not just from the many steps. He followed me onto the landing and seconds later we were in his flat.

It was a gorgeous room – high-ceilinged, with the evening sunlight streaming in through tall sash windows. But it didn't stream for long, because Seth crossed the room, lowered the blinds and switched on a lamp, bathing the room in a soft glow like honey and transforming it instantly from an ordinary lounge into a love nest.

'Drink?' he suggested, and I accepted gratefully. 'The bathroom's just through there.'

A few minutes later, I was sitting next to him on a squashy cream sofa, sipping another martini that was just as expertly made as the one I'd had in the bar. This, I realised, was a practised seduction scene: the lamplight, the gin, Seth's arm along the back of the sofa almost but not quite touching my shoulder.

'So,' he said, 'here we are.'

'Here we are,' I agreed, carefully putting my glass down on the polished wooden coffee table and turning to face him.

'You're very beautiful, you know,' he told me, and then he kissed me.

I wasn't the most experienced person in the world, when it came to sex, but from that moment on I knew I was in the hands of an expert. Seth's kiss was perfect: not too hard, not too tentative, not too much tongue and no teeth whatsoever. I kissed him back, my lipstick forgotten, my hands reaching up around his shoulders, feeling the breadth of his back and the softness of his cotton shirt.

Expertly, one-handed, he undid the few tiny buttons of my top, and I felt the fabric sliding off my shoulder and his lips move from my mouth to my neck, then down to my chest. I unbuttoned his shirt too, not so expertly, needing two hands, and felt the heat of his skin, smelling shower gel or cologne or deodorant and something more primal that was pure man.

I slipped my feet out of my shoes and felt the plushness of the rug between my toes, then lost myself again in his kiss, feeling the softness of his lips, the scratch of his stubble, the silkiness of his chest hair under my fingers. His hands brushed against my breasts and I felt my nipples almost painfully hard against the lace of my bra. I opened my eyes and saw him looking at me, and we both laughed, breaking off the kiss.

'Come on.' He helped me to my feet, which was just as well because I was sure I wouldn't have been able to stand otherwise. He unbuttoned my jeans and slid them down my legs, then gently lowered me back onto the sofa and pulled them over my feet, kneeling on the carpet in front of me.

My bare thighs looked slender and pale against the cream velvet; my skin was very white against my black lace underwear. I could see myself through his eyes and, for the first time in what felt like forever, I felt potently sexy, desirable, desired. He unhooked my bra and bent his head to kiss my breasts, and I closed my eyes again, losing myself in the sensation as his lips found my nipples and his hand moved lower to ease my pants down over my hips. I felt like my whole body was melting, becoming boneless, liquid with pleasure.

He was kissing my thighs now, his hands easing my legs apart so he could see me, open me for his tongue. I heard myself gasp with pleasure, then almost cry out as his mouth found the perfect spot.

It had been so long – too long – since I'd last been given an orgasm, but in the next hour I more than made up for lost time. Seth brought me to the brink over and over again, then let me slip over it once, twice and a final time before he even took off his jeans. By then I was limp with longing, and when he slid his cock into me I legit thought I'd arrived in heaven.

I know, right? A bit of a fuss about what was, after all, just a shag (well, three shags, strictly speaking – Seth didn't exactly stint on the orgasms for himself either). But as shags go, that night was right up there. It was a Michelin-starred dinner of shags, a shag Oscar winner, the kind of shag that would earn Olympic gold. It really, really was that good.

It was almost midnight when we finally admitted defeat, too satiated and sore to attempt round four. We'd moved to Seth's bedroom by then, and I was lying in his arms, both of us sweaty and panting and entirely satisfied.

Reluctantly, I eased myself out of his arms.

'I should really go,' I said.

'Sure? You could stay.' He smiled at me, one arm behind his head instead of a pillow, because we'd knocked them all to the floor.

I shook my head. 'I have to get home to my cat. And I've got work at seven in the morning.'

He stood up and pulled on his jeans. 'I'll order you an Uber and see you out.'

He waited until the cab came, one warm, strong arm around my shoulders, and when we said goodbye he gave me one last, lingering kiss that felt like – and surely must be – a promise.

My elation lasted all the way home. I slept like I'd necked a handful of Xanax but woke up in the morning feeling alert and rested. I actually found myself singing in the shower, and I skipped downstairs to the kitchen and was already two coffees down by the time Robbie arrived for work. He didn't ask me how my date had gone – he didn't need to, I suppose, because my face must have said it all.

As I worked, I imagined what it might be like to have sex like that all the time. If I was Seth's girlfriend, would I wake up every morning feeling like this? Would people look at me in the street and guess that I was a woman who had multiple orgasms every night, because how else would I get that glow on my skin, that spring in my step, that secretive smile?

Would our friends say knowingly, 'Of course, he's a Scorpio, isn't he?'

Or would it get old after a bit? Would I find myself turning away from him in bed and saying I was tired, or had a headache, or thought my period was about to start? I had no idea. I wasn't even sure that I wanted to be his girlfriend. Nowhere near sure. But I did know that when he messaged me and suggested meeting up again, I wouldn't be able to say no.

But he didn't message me. As the day passed, I felt my elation draining away. When I checked my phone after my workout and there was still nothing, I felt suddenly weary in a way I hadn't even when I'd been caning it on the rowing machine. It wasn't surprising after barely any sleep, I told myself, and somehow I struggled through my evening shift, thinking that he was clearly a night owl and would message me later, even if I was asleep when he did.

But there were no messages from Seth that night, even though I waited up until two, restlessly hoping. And the next morning when I woke up, there were none either. And when I went onto Tinder to find him, I couldn't. His profile wasn't there. The messages – and the pictures – we'd exchanged weren't there. I switched my phone on and off again, but nothing changed. I deleted the app and reinstalled it, but that didn't work either.

I stared at my phone in bafflement for a while, and then I realised with a thud what had happened. He'd blocked me.

I wasn't exactly a battle-hardened veteran of online dating, but I knew this stuff happened. I knew that there were people who were just there for sex – if I hadn't, Robbie would have set me straight. I knew that online dating was fickle and cruel. But knowing all that stuff didn't stop it hurting like a punch to the ribs when it happened to me. I remembered that night with Seth – how completely I'd let myself open to him, how I'd abandoned any thoughts of playing hard to get the second he'd walked into the bar, how I'd urged him to carry on and on and not stop ever. I cringed remembering how blithely I'd assumed that he would contact me again – why wouldn't he, since it had been just as good for him as it had for me?

I didn't feel a glow of remembered pleasure any more. I just felt disappointed and stupid. I felt like I'd been duped into something I wouldn't have agreed to otherwise, even though I knew that wasn't true at all. I picked it over and over in my mind, trying to figure out what had made him behave that way. I couldn't talk to Dani about it, or even Robbie. Even though I was pretty sure it wasn't my fault, I still felt strangely ashamed, like I'd been made a fool of somehow. I knew that Dani's sympathy and understanding would make me feel a million times worse, and Robbie's kindly but sharp advice to move on was advice I'd already given myself. But I remembered what Robbie had told me about his own online hook-ups – how sometimes, even most times, the whole point of it was that you could have sex with a new person every night if you wanted to.

I thought of Seth – just your average bloke, not that good-looking or wealthy or even interesting – suddenly finding himself with unlimited girls like me, there for the asking. I couldn't blame him for it, not really. He was a Scorpio, after all. Every time I opened the Stargazer app, I expected to see a message saying, *Don't say I didn't warn you*, but the app clearly thought I could figure that out for myself.

And then – I'm not proud to admit it, but it was like my fingers were possessed – I couldn't stop myself from stalking him. It wasn't easy, because I didn't know his last name. But how many Seths could there be in London, working in advertising sales? As it turned out, there were loads. I spent ages looking for companies that sold online advertising and were based near Old Street, where he'd mentioned he worked, and trawled their websites clicking the 'Our Team' button over and over again, until I found him. Seth Davidson.

I looked at his LinkedIn profile, but I couldn't see much on there because I didn't have an account of my own, and I wasn't going to create one in case he somehow knew I'd looked. Plus, that seemed a bit too stalkerish, even for me. I found his Twitter feed, but that was full of technical work stuff and retweets of motivational sayings – although funnily enough, 'Fuck 'em and forget 'em' wasn't one of them. I found him on Facebook but his profile was locked down tight.

Next I found him on Instagram. There was nothing there to torture myself with: no pictures of him with a girlfriend or a wife.

Just innocuous photos of him at a rugby match with friends, throwing a tennis ball for a dog, opening a bottle of expensive red wine.

And then there was a photo of a chocolate cake, crowded with candles, Seth's face blurry in the background as their flames danced with the force of his breath. The post said: 'Spoiled rotten by my mum on my thirty-fifth birthday.'

Hold on. His thirty-fifth birthday? The image had been posted two months before. His birthday shouldn't have been until late October or early November.

He wasn't a Scorpio at all.

Chapter Ten

Wise decisions made now will bear fruit in the future. The subtle energies in play today may not appear to be placing your dreams within your grasp, but be sure the universe holds the key to your desires.

Somehow, I muddled through the next morning, feeling sick with disappointment. I tried to tell myself that I was stupid to get so worked up over what had been nothing more than a one-night hook-up. But I couldn't help it. I felt wounded, angry with myself and with Seth, and ashamed that I'd let myself expect it to become something more. I'd have to go back to the drawing board, I determined, try to take comfort from the fact that I'd had the best sex of my life and move on to the next star sign.

Robbie had the morning off, so at least I didn't have to deal with his well-meaning curiosity. I worked alone, as I had for the months before he'd joined, glad to have the kitchen to myself, able to play music loudly through my headphones and not have to talk to anyone or pretend I was okay when I wasn't.

But there was no fooling my kitchen. Like the cranky old campervan I'd bought a few years back when I was travelling around Europe, it seemed to sense my moods and play up if my mind was in a state of anything other than zen calm. The oven, which normally had to be set at least ten degrees higher than its temperature dial claimed to be, put on a power surge and almost burned the breakfast muffins. The food mixer blew a fuse when I was halfway through blending a vat of spring vegetable soup, so I had to pretend it was supposed to be chunky, and hastily amend the description on the chalkboard in the bar. My knives, which weren't due to be sharpened for another two weeks, all seemed to have gone dull overnight, and the blade of one of them slipped on a sweet potato and cut my thumb.

So, all in all, I was massively relieved when the lunchtime rush was over and it was time to take my break and go to the gym. There, at least, I could lose myself, burn off some of my misery, sweat out the creeping sense of shame I felt and reset my mind ready for the evening.

I cleared everything away, wiped the surfaces, told the kitchen to have a good long think about what it had done and decide it was better than this, quickly changed into my workout kit and headed out through the bar.

It was quiet, almost empty, as was usual in the afternoons. The dominoes players had left, the mums had taken their toddlers home for their naps, the estate agents who always came for lunch were back in their office across the road. Only Fat Don remained in his usual place on a stool by the bar, slowly making his way down his

fourth pint of the day, which would extend to five or six more by
closing time.

But he wasn't our only customer. Alone at a table next to the shelf
of board games was someone I'd never seen before, a man about
my age, with a dark beard and glasses. He was drinking coffee and
reading. Nothing new there – mostly, people who came into the
pub in the mornings and afternoons had laptops with them and
spent their time intently focused on those, but sometimes people
read books or magazines or whatever.

But this guy was reading something different. My hand was
already on the door when I noticed, and I paused. He was engrossed
in one of the books that had come with the Dungeons & Dragons
set – the thick, heavy one. The Dungeon Master's manual. The box
was open on the table in front of him and dice were scattered around.

I thought for a second. I needed to get to the gym; I only had a
couple of hours before I was due back in the kitchen to get cracking on the evening meal. But I'd promised Alice to try and find
someone to be the Ginger Cat's Dungeon Master, and this bloke,
with his fancy watch and his leather sandals and his T-shirt that
had an algebra equation printed on it, certainly looked the part.
He was right out of nerd central casting.

I turned and walked over to his table.

'Hi,' I said, wondering if I should add, 'Live long and prosper,'
or something.

He started like I'd poked him with something. 'Uh… hi.'

'My name's Zoë,' I carried on. 'I'm the chef here.'

I extended my hand, and he hesitated a second, like touching
me was the last thing he wanted to do, then shook it briefly.

'I'm Adam.'

I saw his eyes flicker back to the page he'd been reading, before turning back towards me.

'I'm sorry to bother you,' I said, because it was as clear as anything that I had, 'but I couldn't help noticing you were looking at our D&D set.'

'It was right there on the shelf,' he said defensively.

'I know, it's cool – people browse through the games all the time,' I soothed. 'But I was wondering – do you play at all?'

'Only online.'

Again, there was that flicker of his eyes, that slight tightening of his face into a reluctant half-smile, which quite clearly said, 'I wish this woman would leave me alone.'

'Only we're starting a group, here at the Ginger Cat,' I burbled on. 'We're looking for someone to be our DM. Well, I'm meant to be looking, but I've got nowhere so far.'

Admittedly, that was because I hadn't tried particularly hard. But I wasn't going to admit that to him.

'There are forums,' he said. 'Boards on Reddit where you could ask. Or you could try the Orcs Nest – you know, the shop in the West End?'

'But you're here,' I persisted, with my best attempt at a winning smile. 'And you know how to play.'

'I might not be here long,' he said. 'I'm waiting to view a flat round the corner. I haven't made up my mind. Mostly I've been looking in Hackney, where I live now.'

'Oh, you should totally move here! The area's so fun, there's loads going on and the Ginger Cat is a real community hub.'

'Why's it called the Ginger Cat?' Adam asked.

Finally – a question. Perhaps I was getting somewhere with this grumpy, frankly quite rude stranger.

'It's actually named after my cat,' I said proudly. 'He's called Frazzle. He lives with me in the flat upstairs, but he hangs out in the pub sometimes, when it's quiet.'

Right on cue, Frazzle came padding in through the door that led to the tiny beer garden outside. His tail was held high, and the breeze was ruffling his long fur. I was biased, obviously, but he did look utterly gorgeous. He strolled over to us and miaowed a greeting.

'Hello,' Adam said, with far more enthusiasm than he'd displayed when I approached him. 'You're a handsome boy.'

He bent down, and Frazz pushed his face into Adam's hand for a fuss. Seconds later, he'd jumped up onto his lap, and I heard thunderous purring.

'He likes you. He never normally does that until he gets to know people better.'

'I like cats,' Adam said unnecessarily. 'He's cool.'

'He's great,' I agreed, and I found myself pouring out the story of how I'd come to adopt Frazzle – or rather, how he'd come to adopt me.

'I used to have a cat,' Adam said. 'Well, I kind of had a share in one. He belonged to our neighbours, but they had a baby and needed to move to a bigger house. So he's gone with them. His name's Freezer.'

'It sounds a bit like Frazzle, doesn't it? Is he white? He must be, with that name.'

Adam nodded. 'White with one blue eye and one green one.'

'Adorable. But Frazz says ginger cats with yellow eyes are better.'

Frazzle rolled over on Adam's lap so he was upside down, inviting him to rub his fluffy belly.

'Okay,' Adam said. 'If I move here, if the flat I'm seeing isn't a total dump, I'll consider being your Dungeon Master. Just for a few games, to see how it goes.'

I sent up a silent prayer of gratitude for my cat's unique charisma and charm.

'Amazing! I'd be so grateful, I really would. Let me give you my number, text me and let me know how the viewing goes. And if there's anything I can do to help set up the game, I will, obviously, although I don't actually have a clue how to play or anything.'

Adam tapped my number into his phone. 'We'll see. I'd rather stay in Hackney, but if this place is decent and I take it, I'll let you know.'

I sensed that that was as much of a commitment as I was going to get, so I thanked him again, wished him luck with his flat viewing and headed out to the gym, leaving Adam chatting away to Frazzle, far more animatedly than he had to me. As the door of the pub swung shut behind me, I could hear him asking my cat, 'Who's got the most magnificent whiskers in all Lewisham? Who's got the fluffiest ears in the world?' which of course Frazz already knew the answer to.

Dani was in the gym already when I got there, but she put down her kettlebell and hurried over when she saw me.

'Hey, Zoë! I thought you weren't going to turn up. Sorry I missed you the past couple of days, work have been dicking around with my shift pattern and I've been doing afternoons, so I've been coming here in the mornings.'

'That's okay. I was late today anyway; I got held up at work.'

I gave her a brief overview of how I had used my cat to – hopefully – persuade someone to move to the area and volunteer to lead our Dungeons & Dragons group, and Dani laughed. I considered filling her in on the Seth situation, too, but something stopped me. I wasn't ready to laugh about it or chalk it up to experience yet, and besides, there was a part of me that was still hoping – although the hope was faint and I secretly hated myself for it – that he'd get in touch again after all.

'So,' Dani said, picking up her kettlebell again and starting to swing it in a way that would have terrified me a year ago, 'it's weird here in the mornings. Different crowd.'

'Oh yeah? Who did you see?'

'Some of Mike's personal training clients – my God, but they're hardcore – and a woman who is apparently a professional dancer and is so bendy you won't believe.'

This was interesting enough intel, but I sensed that there was more Dani wanted to reveal, so I shut up and waited for her to carry on.

'And you know that guy we saw here a while back? The totally shredded one with the American accent?'

Fabian Flatley. But I didn't want to say his name – it felt, stupidly, like it would be summoning Lord Voldemort.

'Yeah, I remember him.'

'He's called Fabian. We worked out together a couple of times. He says he's going to show me how to do clean and jerks.'

As far as things Fabian Flatley might get up to went, coaching a compound barbell lift didn't sound too sinister.

'Cool,' I said.

'He's really interesting,' Dani went on, 'as well as being hot, obviously. He works with loads of tech start-ups. One of them's that thing with scooters that you can access through an app and use when you need them. It's fantastic for the environment and getting people active.'

Especially the kids that hack into the software and then chuck the scooters in the river, which is obviously awesome for the environment, I thought, but I didn't say that. Dani was looking so fired up and happy, and I didn't want to warn her off Fabian – until I had to, at any rate.

'And he's got shares in a bar in Bethnal Green,' she went on. 'It's called Last Resort, and it sounds really cool. They make their own bitters for the cocktails and cure their own olives and everything. Fabian's asked me to go there. With him. Like a date.'

A date? With Fabian Flatley? My reaction to the idea was physical – visceral, almost. I could literally feel the hairs standing up on my arms and the back of my neck, as if the industrial-strength fans Mike had installed in the gym had suddenly been turned on full and pointed at me. *But why?* I asked myself.

Fabian had tried, and failed, to buy the Ginger Cat from its previous owner and turn it into luxury apartments. He'd tried – also unsuccessfully – to float his property business on the stock exchange. He'd siphoned money from his businesses into offshore tax havens. Certainly, all of these things were a bit dodgy, a bit unscrupulous. But they were no worse than things other ambitious young entrepreneurs might do when trying to claw their way to the top. My own interactions with Fabian had been limited to seeing him sometimes in the gym, and being annoyed when he had loud conversations on his phone or didn't wipe his sweat off the equipment – but there were plenty of other people who did that stuff too.

Still, Dani's news made me want to bundle her up and whisk her off to a convent where she'd never be able to date anyone ever again, if that was what it took to stop her dating Fabian. There was something about him that just gave me the creeps. Actually, there were lots of things. The stretch marks on his arms and shoulders that suggested he'd bulked up really quickly. The row of gleaming-white veneers that showed when he smiled, like he had unchewed chewing gum instead of teeth. The way he looked at you with dark eyes that were narrow, unblinking and had no light in them at all, like a snake's.

People born under the sign of Aquarius, my Stargazer app had told me, had highly developed levels of intuition. I wasn't sure whether that was true, but Fabian Flatley certainly sent my intuition into overdrive, and not in a good way.

But then, Dani was a grown-up woman. She was perfectly capable of making her own decisions about who to go out with – and, after all, it was just a drink. For now, at least.

'That's exciting,' I said. 'It'll be fun to go somewhere fabulous. But Dani – be careful, okay?'

'Careful of what?'

'It's just… I think Fabian might be a bit dodgy. The apartment blocks he owns…'

'But I'm not looking for a flat, am I?' She smiled.

'Well, no. But his tax affairs…'

'And I'm not his accountant, so that's not my problem, is it? He's just a guy. It's just a date. Besides, I spoke to Mum last night and she was like, "I take it you're still not seeing anyone, Danielle?" and I had to fess up that I wasn't. Next time, I'll be able to tell her I had a date with a hot entrepreneur.'

'But, Dani…' I hesitated. There was nothing concrete I could warn her about, nothing much more than the feeling Fabian gave me of deep-down wrongness. But clearly he didn't give Dani that feeling, or she wouldn't have agreed to go out with him. 'Just don't rush into anything.'

'Ha! I'll be rushing into that bar for sure. It's ages since I've been anywhere that cool.'

'Me too, if I'm honest.'

I sighed, realising how true that was. When I'd thought about dating, I'd imagined that it would involve – you know – actual dates. As opposed to sitting alone in my bedroom looking at my phone for hours and hours, trying to find people I wanted to date who wanted to date me back. And so far, I'd managed a few drinks in a dull pub with an even duller man, a picnic in the park that still made me die inside a bit when I remembered it, and a hook-up that had got me ghosted faster than you could say, 'Thank you, next.'

I could hardly blame Dani for jumping at the chance when she was asked out by someone without having to go through all that rigmarole. And Fabian was, on the face of it, quite the catch. He was handsome, if you could overlook the fake teeth and dead eyes. He must be intelligent, to have all those business ideas. And if the sleek black Lexus he parked on double yellow lines outside the gym was anything to go by, he was wealthy too.

Not that I was jealous – I wouldn't have dated Fabian if Tinder lived up to its name and burned to the ground along with every man in it. I just wanted Dani to not have her confidence knocked the way Seth had knocked mine, not be disappointed like Justin had disappointed me, not have a load of abuse hurled at her like Paul had hurled at me. I just wanted her to not get hurt, and I suspected Fabian was the hurting type.

Chapter Eleven

With Venus rising, love is in the stars – and you could find it where you least expect to…

'I mean, I'm sure he's just busy,' Dani said. 'He must be, right? With all those businesses to run and stuff.'

I delved into the bowl of Doritos and took one with loads of chilli seasoning on it. We were in the living room of Dani's shared flat, with the place to ourselves as her flatmates were all out – one having tea with his mum, one away for the weekend camping with her boyfriend, and one at an all-day work conference with drinks afterwards in the evening. Nothing wildly exciting, admittedly, but it made Dani's and my lack of dates or social lives feel all the more tragic by comparison. So when she'd suggested earlier, after our workout, that I drop round to hers in the evening for Netflix and a takeaway, I'd jumped at the chance.

Even if it meant listening to her agonise about Fabian on repeat.

'You mustn't let him treat you like a doormat, Dani. Seriously. How long does it take to send a text?'

'I know, I know. But we've only been on one date. It's not like we're serious or anything. Yet.'

He might not be, but you are, I thought. I splashed some more of the pinot grigio I'd brought into our glasses.

'I could call him, I suppose,' Dani said, as if the idea had only just occurred to her for the first time, quite out of the blue.

'No, you couldn't.'

'Why not? It's the twenty-first century.'

'Because you have already.'

Dani met my eyes with a look of wide-eyed innocence, then dropped her gaze and giggled. 'Okay. I have.'

'How many times?'

'Just the once. Well, once that I left a message.'

'And how many times when you didn't?'

She checked her phone, even though I knew she didn't need to. 'Twice.'

'And how many times with your number withheld, to see if he'd pick up if he didn't know it was you?'

'Bloody hell, Zoë. This is like being on *Burden of Truth.*'

'So? How many times?'

'Five,' she admitted.

'And did he pick up?'

'Nope.'

'So you see. That's good really. It means he probably is actually busy, and he isn't just avoiding you.'

Although it could equally mean that he was one of those people who no one ever rings without arranging a time first, and so a bunch of calls, three from Dani's number and five from an unknown one, were all blatantly the same person. But of course I didn't say that.

'Do you really think so?'

'It's possible. But don't call him again, okay? Otherwise I'm going to have to take your phone off you and hide it, and then when he does ring you won't be able to answer.'

'Promise.' Reluctantly, Dani put her phone down. Then she picked it up again. 'Shall we order food? And find a movie to watch?'

'And open another bottle?'

'Done. Pizza or curry?'

'Pizza. I cook spicy food all the time at work, and I've been craving pizza ever since I heard Papa John's are doing one with fake cheese and jackfruit pepperoni,' I said.

'And I love their ham and pineapple.'

'Pineapple? On pizza? Who are you and what have you done with my mate?'

'I know, I know. It's my guilty secret,' she replied.

'So when you see Fabian again, and you're in bed with him after a totally mind-blowing shag, and he suggests you get a takeaway, you'd order ham and pineapple?'

'No! God, no. Not in front of him. I'd have something proper posh, like with anchovies and olives and those caper things, and then I'd be thirsty for about the next week from all the salt. But I bet he doesn't eat pizza. Remember what he was saying at the gym that time? I think he's one of those guys who lives on a diet of one hundred per cent grass-fed beef.'

It wouldn't surprise me if that was the case, I thought.

'Can we get some of those potato popper things as well?' I suggested.

'And a tub of Ben and Jerry's. They do dairy-free ones now.'

'And shall we watch *The Haunting of Hill House*?'

'Hell, yeah.'

So Dani and I spent the rest of the evening huddled on the sofa under her duvet even though it was a hot night, scaring the living daylights out of ourselves, stuffing our faces with junk food and drinking far too much cheap white wine, and it was totally brilliant and reminded me how fabulous it was to have a friend after telling myself for so long that I was this independent free spirit who didn't need other people. She didn't mention Fabian again and quite honestly, for those few hours, I wouldn't have cared if I never went on a date again.

Around midnight, her flatmates came home and went to bed, and I heaved myself up off the sofa, yawning so hugely I thought I might dislocate my jaw, and said I'd better do the same.

'I've got the day off tomorrow,' I said. 'My first Saturday off in ages. I can't wait. I'm going to lie in bed with Frazz until lunchtime and then maybe get the Tube to Kensington or somewhere and browse posh charity shops for clothes.'

Dani stood up, too. 'I'm going to… dunno really. Bake cupcakes with my flatmate, maybe. Watch more telly. Do some ironing. Weekends suck when you're single.'

I said I'd been single for so long I could barely remember what they were like when you weren't, or even, after years working in a job with the world's most antisocial hours, what a proper weekend was like. But Dani wasn't listening; the mention of being single had made her reach for her phone, which she'd managed to ignore ever since ordering the pizza.

'Zoë!' Her whole face was lit up as brightly as her phone's screen. 'He texted! He actually did! Two hours ago, and I missed it!'

'Don't text him back now!' I practically dived across the sofa to stop her. 'It's too late. Plus, he took his time replying, didn't he? Wait until the morning. He'll think you've been off doing something fabulous. What does he say?'

'He's asked me out! To the launch of a bar his mate's opening in Soho!'

Which was all very well, I thought, but not exactly a date. And I couldn't help wondering whether the guest list for the launch was looking a bit thin, and Dani, who was total eye candy by anyone's standards, was just the kind of person Fabian's mate needed to make up the numbers.

'He says I should bring a friend,' she went on, confirming my suspicions. 'You'll come, won't you, Zoë? It's at half five tomorrow, there's going to be a private drinks thing and canapés and stuff and then the doors open to the general public at seven. Here's the website – it looks amazing.'

She passed me her phone and I scrolled through a minimalist page that suggested the web designer had been briefed to make it look hyper exclusive, as opposed to including any actual information beyond some artfully photographed cocktail glasses and a neon sign on a bare brick wall that said, 'Alcorithm'.

But there was no way I was going to let Dani see that I wasn't convinced this was the best thing ever.

'Of course I'll come. It'll be brilliant. But what the hell am I going to wear?'

I ran through my wardrobe in my head, thinking of my jeans, T-shirts and Converse, and regretting my resolution to buy no new clothes for a year in a one-woman bid to save the planet.

'Whatever you find at your posh charity shops,' Dani said. 'Or, failing that, go to TK Maxx. You'll look amazing whatever you wear, anyway. This is it, isn't it? He must really like me!'

*

In my flat the next afternoon, I found myself wondering if Dani had developed a sudden case of adult-onset blindness. I looked as far from fabulous as it was possible to get. My hair had staged a protest and was standing out from my head in a shock of frizz. My legs were milk-bottle white and I had no fake tan to put on them, not that that would have helped, because I knew from experience that they responded to that by turning a violent shade of yellow, like your wee does after you've drunk a Berocca.

The dress I'd bought, a lilac satin slip with black lace edging, made me look like the heroine of a Victorian novel who was about to die of consumption and was – I could now see in the full-length mirror – totally the wrong length, hitting my legs at the widest part and making them look the shape of milk bottles, as well as the colour.

'Shit, Frazz, why did I agree to this?'

My cat opened one eye and turned over, saying quite clearly that if I changed my mind about going out, that was absolutely fine with him.

But there was no way I could let Dani down. I slapped on some foundation that was meant to make my skin glowy and pearly, but was slightly the wrong shade and made me look like I needed a good wash. I tried to tame my hair with serum, but it refused to co-operate so I attacked it mercilessly with straighteners, knowing I'd pay the price in split ends.

I might as well give up, I decided. It didn't particularly matter what I looked like – this was going to be Dani's night. And I had no intention of pulling one of Fabian Flatley's friends, no matter what the Stargazer app said about the location of Venus in my rising sign. I'd settle for being her corpse-like, frizzy-haired wingwoman, and make my excuses and leave as soon as I could see things were going okay with her and Fabian.

I looked longingly at my trusty Converse, lying next to the bed ready for me to slip my feet into them as I did practically every morning. 'Come on,' they seemed to be saying, 'wear us! We could do with an exciting outing! We've barely left the postcode in months! And we're so comfortable!'

But there was letting myself be outshone by Dani, and there was letting the side down entirely. Besides, I'd painted my toenails for the first time in ever so long, and I wasn't going to let that annoying, tedious effort go to waste. I rummaged underneath my bed, which was where my shoes lived because the flat had no wardrobe, and pulled out my one and only pair of high heels. I'd last worn them when I was a bridesmaid at my friend Nadia's wedding four years ago, before she'd moved to New Zealand with her husband. Four years is a long time, but the blisters were as fresh in my memory as if it was yesterday.

Too bad, I told my feet, *deal with it. Strappy silver stilettos it is today.* I forced on the shoes, put my phone, keys and lip balm in my little silver backpack (which I promised myself was actually quite retro cool and didn't make me look like I was hopelessly unprepared to climb Ben Nevis), kissed Frazzle goodbye and headed out, resisting the temptation to stick my head round the door of the pub kitchen and face Robbie's excoriating criticism of my outfit.

Dani was waiting for me outside the station, as we'd agreed. Any smidgeon of doubt I might have had that she wouldn't outshine me as comprehensively as Mars outshines Pluto vanished as soon as I saw her. She was wearing a nude lace bodysuit that looked almost like she was wearing nothing at all, high-waisted satin combat trousers that showed off her tiny waist and incredible bum, and black heeled gladiator sandals that made my shoes look like something your nana would slip on to take the dog out. Her hair was as smooth and glossy as dark chocolate, flowing down her back like it had melted there. Her make-up was flawless and, apart from her extravagant lash extensions and coral lipstick, almost invisible.

'Wow,' I said, hugging her. 'Knock-out.'

'You too,' she said kindly. 'Love the dress! So cool! Unlike me, I'm sweating like a horse I'm so nervous.'

'Don't be. You look amazing, and we'll walk really slowly so we don't get too hot.'

As if, in those shoes, I had a choice.

We got on the train and sat in silence next to each other. Dani kept checking her phone, tapping from WhatsApp to her map, anxiously making sure she knew the way and even more anxiously looking for a message from Fabian. But I could tell from the expression on her face that there was none.

At last, we emerged from the roasting heat of the Tube at Charing Cross in the heart of London. Outside, it wasn't much cooler – on this midsummer day, the sun was beating down on us like a blowtorch caramelising crème brûlée, and I could feel the heat of the pavement coming up through the thin soles of my sandals. Dani flapped her hands frantically in front of her face, and I assured her that her foundation hadn't melted, her mascara hadn't smudged and she didn't have lipstick on her teeth.

'Okay then,' she said, and in spite of it being so hot, I was convinced I could hear her teeth chattering, 'let's go. It's just off Trafalgar Square – we don't have too far to walk.'

And she strode off, confident and agile in her high heels, while I teetered behind her on mine.

'It's just here, isn't it?' I asked hopefully.

'Round the corner, I think, and down a side street.'

But we couldn't find the side street, so we walked around some more, Dani's eyes fixed to her phone as she got more and more stressed. Finally she muttered, 'Shit! It's supposed to be right here!' before stopping outside an anonymous black-painted door with 'AR' on it in tiny orange letters, which we'd walked past about four times.

'Do you think this is it?'

'Must be. There's literally nowhere else it could be, unless we've entered some kind of wrinkle in the fabric of the Matrix.'

I pushed open the door. Beyond it, we could hear the buzz of conversation, the hum of some kind of trance music and the clink of glasses. The air smelled of paint, the way new buildings do. At a little mirrored table by the door was sitting a beautiful blonde woman in a black dress, who looked us up and down with something close to contempt.

'Can I help you?' she asked, her tone so dismissive she might as well have said, 'Can I be arsed to help such sorry specimens as you?'

'We're on the guest list for the launch,' Dani said. 'Danielle Fletcher and Zoë Meredith.'

'Right.' The woman picked up an iPad from the table and flicked its screen a few times. Her nails were long coffin shapes, painted lime green.

Then she looked at us and shook her head.

'We're definitely invited,' Dani said, attempting an ingratiating smile. 'Fabian said so. Fabian Flatley?'

Again, the woman shook her head. 'No Fletcher, no Meredith.'

'How about just our first names?' I suggested. 'Zoë and Danielle?'

'Not on the list. Excuse me.'

The door behind us had opened again and two girls in floaty white broderie frocks gave their names and were waved through.

'Why don't you call Fabian?' I said.

Dani nodded, looking almost green under her make-up. With the blonde woman watching us expressionlessly, Dani pressed buttons on her phone, held it to her ear and waited. And waited.

'He's not answering.'

The blonde woman looked pointedly at the door.

'Come on,' I said, bundling Dani outside. 'We can't just stand there with her watching us. Too mortifying.'

'But he said.' Dani sounded like she might be about to cry. 'He promised me our names would be on the list.'

'But they're not,' I said gently.

'We could come back later, when it's open to the public.'

Privately, I thought this was a terrible idea, but agreeing to it at least gave me an hour or so to persuade Dani of that.

'Okay. Let's go somewhere else and get a drink, and you can try calling Fabian again. I'm sure there's just been some kind of fuck-up, but he might be busy and not answering his phone.'

She nodded, dabbing her eyes with a tissue. 'Where shall we go?'

'I used to work round here – there are loads of places. There's a decent pub just the other side of Trafalgar Square. Let's head over there.'

The Griffin only just warranted the description 'decent', but it was close and it would be quiet, so I could sit down and assess the damage my shoes had done to my feet. There was a bit of my ankle that felt ominously cold when a breeze brushed it, and I suspected I'd already lost a chunk of skin.

'I just don't understand,' Dani said. 'He said to come. He even asked for both our surnames so he could add us to the list. You don't think he did it on purpose, do you?'

'I'm sure he didn't. I'm sure you'll be able to get hold of him on the phone and he'll explain and we can go back and it'll all be… What the hell's that noise?'

We'd headed back off the side street onto one of the busier roads, but even so, even though it was right in the centre of town, it shouldn't have been as noisy as it was. Behind us, I could hear shouting, chanting, drums and even something I was pretty sure was a vuvuzela.

'Is it the Hare Krishnas?' Dani said. 'They come down Oxford Street most days, don't they?'

'They don't make as much noise as that.'

We stopped and turned around, and, as we watched, a huge crowd poured into the street. There were so many people they filled it right from one side to the other; it must have been closed to traffic somewhere because there were no cars or buses and no space for any. There was just a wall of people, moving slowly but inexorably towards us, a wave in which we'd have no choice but to be swept up.

As they drew closer, I could make out banners and placards saying 'Rebel for life', 'Act now' and 'Tell the truth'.

'Shit,' I said to Dani. 'It's the Extinction Rebellion demo.'

'What, that march against climate change thing?'

I nodded. 'I'd forgotten it was today.'

Forgotten almost deliberately, because I'd seriously considered going but sacked it off in favour of being Dani's wingwoman and felt guilty about my lack of commitment to a cause I cared about. But now, like it or not, we were going to have to join the march, because there was literally no way around it.

'Come on.' I grabbed Dani's arm and we headed up the street, the chanting crowd growing closer and closer behind us.

'You can't eat money! You can't drink oil!'

'There is no Planet B! Declare climate emergency!'

Soon, the lead marchers caught up with us, and Dani and I, in our going-out clothes and high heels, were enveloped into the jeans-and-T-shirt-clad throng, carried along like overdressed twigs in a fast-flowing river. Someone thrust a placard saying 'We can't eat money' into my hand, and someone else gave Dani the corner of a 'March now or swim later' banner to hold. She gripped it awkwardly in the hand that wasn't holding her little sparkly clutch bag, her eyes wide and alarmed.

I was struggling to keep up in my high heels, but I had no choice; the press of bodies all around me made it impossible to slow down. We passed another side street, but there was no way of escaping the throng.

I heard my voice joining the chant: 'I don't know but I been told, fossil fuels are getting old.' Dani caught my eye, horrified, then started singing too. In our going-out clothes, surrounded by a sea of people, we couldn't have looked more out of place if we'd tried. It was like one of those dreams where you're on your way to a job interview and you realise you've forgotten to put any clothes on, and for some reason you decide to style it out and go ahead anyway.

And now, just like in those dreams, I was unable to escape. I was falling behind Dani, though; as she strode unwillingly along, I found myself dropping back, slipping through the crowd towards the side of the road, my aching feet literally unable to go any faster.

The marchers turned a corner and I lost sight of Dani for a moment, and then my heel got caught in a crack and I stumbled, tried to right myself, made it worse and ended up in a heap on the cobblestones, surrounded by my silver bag and my placard. Oblivious, the marchers carried on past me, now chanting, 'What do we want? Climate action! When do we want it? Yesterday!' and one of them actually stepped on my dress and gave me a brief, impatient scowl like it was my fault.

My knees were bleeding, the hem of my dress was ripped and, pathetically, I'd started to cry. I rummaged in my bag for a tissue but found only my phone, my bank card and a lipstick, which of course made me cry even more. The day, which had started out not exactly promisingly, had gone completely and utterly wrong. I had no hope of finding Dani now, and there was no way I could go into a bar anyway, with my knees all bloody and my dress torn. If Dani had any sense she'd escape from the protest as soon as she could and make her way to the station and home, and I was going to do the same, and text her as soon as I was out of this madness and enough time had passed for there to be no chance she'd suggest giving the party another shot.

I struggled to my feet, cursing my stupid shoes and my stupid lack of balance and stupid Fabian Flatley and his stupid guest list, and waited for the tail-end of the march to pass me. A couple of people looked at me curiously but didn't stop, for which I was quite grateful. And then someone did: a guy wearing a Campaign for Nuclear Disarmament T-shirt and camo trousers, with long brown hair and an array of piercings in his ears.

'Are you okay?' he asked, propping his placard against the wall next to mine. He smiled, and I realised he was seriously hot, with the kind of chiselled features that would be more at home on a movie star than a climate-change protester. 'These events get emotional, don't they? I was nearly crying, too, during the speeches in Parliament Square. I didn't see you there. I'd have noticed, even in that crowd.'

I wasn't sure whether that was a dig at my inappropriate attire or a compliment.

I sniffed and wiped my eyes with the back of my hand. 'That's because I wasn't there. I wasn't meant to be here at all.'

'How so?'

'I was on my way to a party with my friend and we just kind of accidentally got caught up in it, and then I fell over because I'm wearing ridiculous shoes.'

He looked me up and down appraisingly. 'Yes, you're not exactly dressed for it, are you? I mean, you look lovely and everything, but…'

His lips twitched as he tried to suppress a smile, and I found myself giggling too. There was something about the way his teeth flashed in his tanned face and his eyes crinkled up at the corners that made me feel suddenly much, much better, like something good might come out of this disaster of a day after all. And I remembered the message from the app, saying that I might find love where I least expected.

'I haven't exactly got my protest-march A game on,' I admitted.

'I guess the party's loss was the protest march's gain.'

'Not really. I mean, I wasn't going to make much difference to global warming sitting on the pavement having a cry.'

'Crying for climate change. That's a new one on me.'

'I guess it's never going to catch on.'

We both laughed again. He had a great laugh, totally infectious.

'Show's over, now, anyway. Fancy a drink?' he asked.

I felt a little leap of excitement. Could this be about to turn into an actual date? A date with a man I realised I properly fancied? Then I looked down at my scraped knees and torn dress, and realised that my make-up must be all smudged from crying.

'I can't, really. Not like this.'

I gestured to my grazed knees and he winced sympathetically. 'I'd suggest going back to my place to get you cleaned up, but that's in Bedford at the moment, and I'm not sure a two-hour train journey is worth it for a bit of Savlon.'

'Probably not. Mine's closer, so I should get home and sort myself out.'

'Sure. Well, I guess I'll see you around, if social justice is your thing.' He half turned away, then turned back again, like he didn't really want to leave.

I felt like I ought to wave goodbye and say I'd see him around too, even though I knew I wouldn't. But there was a voice in my head practically jumping up and down waving its arms and saying, 'No! Don't! What if he's The One that Got Away and you're about to let him do just that?'

He was still standing there, looking down at me, and I was looking back. It was like there was a thread running between us that we were both about to break, despite not wanting to, because we didn't know how not to. He held out his arms and I moved into them for a hug, and he held me close for a moment. I could feel his breath ruffling my hair and the heat of his body through his T-shirt, and I didn't want him to let go.

'Hey, what star sign are you?' I asked, my voice muffled by his chest.

'You normally ask random guys that question when you don't even know their name?'

'Hardly ever. I guess it must be something about you. I'm Zoë, by the way, and Aquarius.'

'The sign of spirituality, intuition, creativity, idealism and vision. I'm Gemini. Outgoing, intelligent, optimistic, passionate and dynamic. Name's Jude. Oh, and Geminis are also highly impulsive, and highly compatible with Aquarius. Just saying.'

'In that case,' I said, 'why don't you come back to mine?'

Chapter Twelve

*It may feel as if your dreams are slipping through your fingers
today. But maybe you've just been dreaming of the wrong things?*

'Right, our lamb's ready for the oven.' Robbie gave one of the
garlic-and-rosemary-studded legs a fond pat. 'How's that nut roast
looking?'

I poked at the mass of pulverised nuts, herbs, onion and
breadcrumbs in the roasting dish. To be honest, it looked like a
dog's dinner.

'It'll be grand once it's cooked and covered in gravy,' I said. 'I'm
all over the place this morning. And you're not looking too sharp
yourself. You almost put the crumble topping on the broccoli. You
thought I didn't notice, didn't you?'

'But I have an excuse.'

'You do? What's that?'

'Oh, Zoë.' Theatrically, Robbie wrapped his arms around his
thin shoulders. 'I'm smitten. Properly smitten, with a bloke who
came round mine last night. He's called Rex. Isn't that just the
most amazing name ever? He's older than me, right up against

the upper limit, a whole thirty-two. But when has age ever been a barrier to true love?'

I could have pointed out several situations in which it would be just that, but I didn't want to dim his enthusiasm – and besides, I found I was dying to hear more. Not least to deflect Robbie's thoughts away from the fact that I was, indeed, all over the place.

'Steady on. You can't be in love when you've only seen him once.'

'But I can! You just know, don't you, when you just click with somebody.'

Did I know, now? I wasn't sure I knew anything; my heart and my mind felt like they'd been put through a mixer on high speed.

'Go on then. Tell me all about sex with Rex.'

Robbie giggled. 'I know, right? How could someone called that be anything other than hot AF in the sack? But there's so much more to it. It was like we really connected. He…'

He carried on, and I listened, peeling potatoes and trying not to allow my gaze to stray upwards, beyond the extractor fan to the ceiling, wishing it was made of glass so I could see through it, into my flat.

When I'd left it that morning, Jude had been in the shower.

We'd walked to the station together – or rather, he'd walked and I'd hobbled, declining his kind offer of a piggyback because, well, I wanted to salvage what scraps of dignity I could – and boarded a train together. After I'd texted Dani to check she was okay, we'd shared the rest of the water from his water bottle and the rest of a pack of nuts and raisins he'd found in his backpack, and we'd talked.

He told me he was a vegan, just like me. His parents were divorced, just like mine. He'd even grown up in a nondescript small town about forty miles from the nondescript small town where I grew up. He'd travelled around Europe after dropping out of uni, just like me.

It was the weirdest thing, like meeting my own shadow. We got back to the flat, stopping on the way at Craft Fever to buy some beers (he liked cucumber saison, obviously, because it was my favourite), and after I'd cleaned up my knees we decided we were both starving, so I made us beans on toast, explaining that all the proper cooking I did was in the pub downstairs, and my kitchen wasn't equipped with much more than a microwave and a toaster.

The flat felt even smaller than usual with him there. It wasn't that he was particularly big – he wasn't; he was lean and graceful, and only a bit above average height. It was more that moving around the flat, and around him, made me super-conscious of not wanting to touch him accidentally but very much wanting to touch him on purpose. Also, the bed seemed to have increased in size so it loomed hugely, there whenever I turned my head like it was following me around the place saying, 'Come on. You're going to end up here, you know. Get on with it.'

'Beans on toast is my fave,' Jude said. 'So long as you've got chilli sauce to put on it. And you do, don't you?'

'Of course,' I said, and our eyes met and we both smiled the same identical, goofy smile, because it was just too strange and amazing that this was happening.

I told him a bit about the Ginger Cat: how Alice had saved it from being bought and redeveloped by Fabian Flatley (although I didn't mention that it was Fabian who Dani and I had been going to meet); how in the end the pub had been purchased by a co-operative of local people who were running it for the benefit of the community; how Maurice had taught me to play dominoes. Jude told me about the internship he was doing with a homelessness charity in Bedfordshire, even though he was as good as homeless himself, sleeping on a friend's sofa during the week and going back to his parents' place at weekends.

'I told Mum not to expect me back until late tonight,' he said. 'She worries about me like I'm still about fourteen and might fall off my skateboard.'

'Oh my God, I had a skateboard when I was fourteen, too! I was totally crap at it. My knees were always covered in scabs, like they'll be tomorrow.'

'Mine too. Mum kept trying to make me wear pads and a helmet, but I always took them off when I met my mates because I thought it was uncool.'

I laughed, not needing to tell him that I'd done exactly the same.

'But I bet you were one of the edgy kids,' I said. 'Sneaking off to gigs at weekends and getting into pubs with fake ID and smoking weed behind the bike sheds. Weren't you?'

He widened his eyes in fake innocence. 'Of course not! Okay, I was. How do you know? Were you there? Only there was this gorgeous redhead I snogged when I was in my GCSE year. I always felt like she was the one that got away.'

'Lucky her. But it wasn't me – you'd have remembered my braces for sure.'

He laughed. 'I had braces too. They'd have got caught up in yours, and we'd still be trying to untangle ourselves.'

When we'd finished the food and the beers, Jude stood up and said he supposed he'd better get going, if he was going to make the last train, and I hesitated for only a second before saying, 'You can stay if you like.'

'I thought you'd never offer,' he said.

'I thought you'd never ask,' I countered.

'There's a spare toothbrush in the bathroom.' I felt suddenly shy. 'Help yourself.'

'Thanks. It's like being in a five-star hotel.'

He disappeared into the bathroom and I enticed Frazzle out from under the sofa where he'd been hiding, feeling terrible about scaring him but telling myself he just wasn't used to strangers, and Jude was a complete animal lover so of course it would be okay and they'd be friends before long. I gave him some dinner and changed the water in his bowl and cleaned his litter tray and gave him some fuss, all the while listening to the unfamiliar sounds of Jude in my bathroom: water running, the toilet flushing, the tread of his feet on the floorboards. The flat suddenly felt very, very small and I felt very, very shy.

A few minutes later, Jude emerged, wearing only his T-shirt and black cotton boxer shorts. His legs were long and strong and I could see a tan line above his knees. He must spend a lot of time outside in the sun, wearing shorts.

I gestured towards the bed, relieved that I'd remembered to make it that morning. There was a big patch of ginger fur on the duvet cover where Frazzle liked to sleep.

'I can sleep on the floor, if you like,' Jude said. 'I've been up since four and I can sleep anywhere, anyway.'

'It's okay,' I said. 'I'm just going to have a shower.' And get rid of every last scrap of the make-up that had settled into my pores and made my face feel grimy and horrible, and shave my legs for the second time that day, and rub body lotion all over myself, and spend far too long staring at my body in the mirror from all angles wondering if it would do.

'Sure.' Jude stretched out on the pillows, one arm behind his head so I could see a strip of pale skin between his top and his underwear, looking at his phone, as relaxed as if he was in his own bed at home, or wherever he thought of as home. I could see Frazzle's tail sticking out from under the bed, but I didn't think Jude had noticed it.

I showered quickly, worrying stupidly that he might come in. What did it matter if he did, since we were about to sleep together? But still, the idea was unsettling. My hair was already kinking and frizzing, but there was nothing I could do about that. And I wasn't going to put on my lacy pyjamas, because that would be too try-hard. I settled for a T-shirt from a long-ago PETA convention, faded and worn almost see-through, and black pants, because if that was good enough for Jude surely it was good enough for me.

And, after I'd brushed my teeth a second time, I pushed open the bathroom door and approached the bed.

Jude was fast asleep, his head and feet sticking out from either end of the duvet. Frazzle was sitting on the little table where I worked and ate, looking deeply resentful.

So I got into bed and lay there, trying to breathe without making a sound, my mind racing like a poor caged hamster on a wheel. What if I'd read this all wrong, and Jude simply hadn't felt the same sense of connection I had? What if he had genuinely just been knackered and hadn't wanted to trek across London at night to get a train home? What if he simply didn't fancy me? What if no one would ever fancy me again and I was destined to be alone forever and never have sex again?

I tried to relax, to identify points of tension in my body and release them, to distract my brain by counting backwards from three hundred, but nothing worked. Next to me, Jude turned over and flung an arm across the pillow. I looked at his face in the semi-darkness, admiring the swoop of his cheekbones and the clean line of his jaw, but it was still and unreadable in sleep. Eventually, I felt the heavy thud of Frazzle jumping up onto the bed. He didn't get under the duvet with me as usual, though;, he just settled down on my feet in a disgruntled fashion and started to snore, and eventually I must have fallen asleep too.

I woke up at six as usual, and for a second everything felt normal. Then I remembered Jude. I turned over, cautiously, partly not wanting to wake him, partly fearing that he might have vanished in the night, or somehow never have been there at all. But he was. His glossy brown hair was spread out over my pillow, his long body was a Z shape under my duvet, his hand was so close my hair was almost brushing it.

Silently, I sat up. What was the etiquette here? Did I get up and get ready for work as usual, and head out? Did I wake him up and tell him he needed to leave? I didn't have a clue. But I knew I needed to wee and clean my teeth, so I stood up and made my way to the bathroom, Frazzle padding behind me.

When I came out, Jude was awake, sitting up against the pillows.

'Hello,' I said.

'Hello. What time is it?'

'Ten past six.'

'Good, nice and early. Come here.'

I went over and sat on the bed, and Jude took my hand. It was the first time he'd touched me since he'd helped me up from the pavement the previous day, which seemed like about a century ago. His hand was warm and dry and strong, and fitted perfectly around mine. I felt a surge of nervous excitement at his touch, not knowing what would happen next.

'I believe we have some unfinished business,' he said.

'I don't believe we even started.'

'We didn't. Better do something about that, then.'

And he leaned over and kissed me on the lips, very gently. My lips parted and I felt his tongue brush mine, his fingers caress my face. His eyes were so close to mine that they were just a blur, so I let my eyelids close and let myself kiss him back, losing myself in the closeness and newness of him like I was diving into a pool of warm water.

Chapter Thirteen

Today, a tall dark stranger will bring good news – but you may not see it for what it is at first.

I didn't hear from Dani for a couple of days. Since her reply to the message I'd sent when I was on the train with Jude, in which she'd said she was okay, in one piece and about to get on a train herself, there'd been nothing. I'd messaged her a couple more times, but she hadn't replied. In this case, I strongly suspected, no news was bad news.

So I was relieved when I turned up at the gym on Wednesday and she was there, in the plank position on the mat, her legs trembling with the effort of holding her body still.

'Hey,' I said, squatting down next to her. 'How's it going?'

'Zoë!' She flopped down onto the mat, then rolled over on her back. To my surprise, her face was glowing with happiness that definitely wasn't the result of a killer workout. 'Look! Look over there!'

She gestured towards the rack of wire cages that were the closest the Dark Arch had to lockers. I could see her familiar purple nylon backpack squeezed into one of them, and on the floor in front of it was an enormous bouquet of red roses, far too big to have fitted in the locker.

'From Fabian?'

She nodded. 'They were here when I arrived. He doesn't know my home or work address so he sent them to Mike's. How adorable is that? And there was a note with them that just said, "Sorry. Will you consider giving me another chance?" So of course I messaged him right away.'

Of course you did, I thought. 'And what did he say?'

'He said he was really, really sorry about Saturday night. He said there was some cock-up with the guest list and he'd asked for our names to be added but they must've slipped through the cracks somehow, and he was going to sack that snooty blonde woman. He said he tried to text me that evening to ask where we were, but his phone was out of battery. And then he said he was really, really sorry some more, and he's going to come round to mine on Friday night and I'm going to make dinner for him. So it's okay!'

Fabian's story had as many holes in it as a colander, and it was him who should have been making dinner for Dani, by my reckoning, but there was no point saying that to her.

'You're going to have to help me, Zoë. What the hell do I cook for him? I want to impress him but I'm totally crap with food; my signature dish is scrambled eggs. What do I do?'

Chicken a la salmonella, I thought. *Day-old rice insufficiently heated through. Jerusalem artichoke soup that'll blow him right out of your front door with the force of his own farts.*

'Steak,' I said. 'Man like that, a fabulous steak will impress him more than anything. I'll get the organic place we use for beef to add a couple to our order, if you like? And I'll lend you a meat thermometer so you can get it just right.'

'Do you mean bloody? I hate bloody meat – it freaks me right out.'

'Me too. But it won't freak him out, so you'll have to learn to like it, fast.'

'Okay, fine. So steak. And what else?'

'Bacon.'

Dani boggled at me. 'Seriously?'

'Not really. But I bet he'd be made up if you did serve bacon on the side. Or eggs. I've been a chef for a long time and I know my market. But I'll send you some easy recipes for salads and stuff.'

'You're a star. So what happened to you on Saturday, anyway? One minute you were there and the next I looked around and you'd vanished.'

I pulled up my Lycra leggings to show her the impressive scabs that had formed on both my knees. 'I fell over, like a plonker. I'm crap at walking in heels.'

'Oh no! You poor thing! Ouch, that looks really painful. And I wasn't even there to help.'

'It's okay. Someone else helped me.'

Dani's perfectly microbladed eyebrows rose enquiringly, and I spilled out the whole story of how Jude had stopped and looked after me, and how we'd gone back to my flat.

'Oh my God, that's so cool! So romantic! And so did you…?'

'Not that night. He fell asleep. But the next morning.'

'And was it amazing?'

I paused. Part of me wanted to big it up, give Dani the romance she was craving, and myself the reassurance that I longed for just as much. But I couldn't do that – I felt bad enough that I hadn't told her exactly what I thought about Fabian, even though I had tried to warn her and she wouldn't have listened anyway. At least when it came to my own love life I could be straight with her.

'Not really, if I'm honest. But you know how it is, the first time.'

That's what I'd told myself, afterwards. Only about ten minutes after that first kiss, to be exact. Sex with Jude had been perfunctory and clumsy, and quite frankly the best thing about it had been the fact that it hadn't gone on for longer. But there'd still been that connection, that intensity in the way he'd looked at me with his amazing eyes, greeny-brown flecked with gold, like a forest pool in dappled sunlight. The way he'd held me, close and tenderly, until he'd fallen asleep again and I'd had to extract myself from his arms before getting ready for work.

It would get better, I'd assured myself. We'd get used to each other, learn how each other's bodies worked and what made each other tick. Far better, I'd rationalised, to have room for improvement than to start off with a bang and then for it all to go downhill from there. Sex with Seth had been mind-blowing the first time, after all, and where had that got me?

Dani interrupted my musings. 'I wonder if Friday will be my first time with Fabian. God, I'm so nervous. What if I'm crap? I'm going to have to book in for a fanny wax. And an everything-else wax. Just in case. But I'm sorry it wasn't great for you. Was the next time better?'

I sighed. 'There hasn't been a next time.'

'What? Why not?'

'Because when I went up to my flat during my break, he'd gone.'

'Gone?'

I nodded, remembering the feeling of hollow shock I'd felt when I pushed open the door to the empty flat and he'd disappeared, with only the imprint of his head on my pillow reminding me that he'd been there at all.

'That could be okay though, couldn't it? Like, maybe he had to get back to his mum's place or whatever. Maybe there was an emergency and he knew you were working so he didn't want to interrupt you. He's got your number, right?'

'Wrong. He left a note, just saying thanks for the bed and other stuff. I mean, seriously. Like a shag was part of the service that started with beans on toast.'

Gloomily, I remembered what the app had said when I checked it, once I'd finished staring around the empty flat in confusion, like Jude was going to jump out from under the bed and say, 'Ha! Fooled you!'

Clever, curious and charismatic, your Gemini man can charm the birds out of the trees. But the Twins' boredom threshold is notoriously low, and they can be fickle in romantic relationships.

So, after one night, I'd bored him. Which was just fabulous for my ego.

'Okay. I guess that is a bit shit. But he can find you if he wants to. It would take five seconds to get your last name off the pub's website and then you're on social media and he could just reach out, couldn't he?'

'He could. If he wanted to. But I'm not sure he does. Why would he have just fucked off like that if he did?'

'Men!' Dani sighed. 'Honestly, I don't know why we bother.'

'Me neither.'

'They're just shits, aren't they?'

'A total waste of time. Seriously, I wish I was a lesbian.'

'That must be so great. Imagine, you'd be able to borrow each other's clothes.'

'Your flat would always smell amazing.'

'And you'd never have to worry about a condom bursting ever again.'

'Total life goals,' I said. 'Anyway. I'd better get back on Tinder and find my next date.'

'You're not giving up, then?'

'How can I? It's not like anything else is working out that brilliantly for me, is it?'

Dani gave my shoulder a sympathetic squeeze. 'So you're okay to send me some recipes, then? And lend me the meat thermometer thingy?'

So clearly she wasn't quite ready to give up on men yet either.

On my way back to work, I popped into Craft Fever to see if the owner, Archie, had got in the locally made cider we'd ordered, which Robbie had thought would be brilliant in a chicken and leek pie. But there was already a customer in there, buying some of the honey Archie's sister made from the hives on the roof of her nearby apartment.

The guy looked familiar, which was nothing new – lots of the Ginger Cat regulars were customers of Archie's too. But he wasn't a regular. He was – I stared so hard at his back, trying to place him, he must have practically got scorched by the laser beams of my eyes – Adam! Adam, the awkward, monosyllabic cat lover who I'd tried to persuade to be the Ginger Cat's official Dungeon Master, but who had never got in touch and not been in the pub since the first and last time I'd seen him there.

I'd assumed that he had decided against moving to the area, after all, and I was going to have to get my skates on and find another Dungeon Master somehow. But here he was, so clearly that wasn't the case.

'If it crystallises, just stand the jar in hot water for a couple of minutes,' Archie said, handing over a paper bag.

'Cheers,' Adam said, fumbling his phone out of his pocket and tapping it on the card reader. 'Got to try and help bees, right?'

Archie nodded. 'Numbers are falling precipitously all over the world because of pesticide use and disease. Poor little guys – girls, rather. They need us.'

'And so much of the honey you buy in supermarkets is basically industrially produced,' I cut in. 'It's like battery farming only for bees.'

Adam turned around and looked at me, blankly at first and then with dawning recognition.

'Hey, Zoë,' Archie said. 'We've got your cider. I'll drop a crate round later.'

'That would be great, thanks. You'll get a chicken pie on the house as a thank you when Robbie's nailed the recipe. Oh, hello. It's Adam, isn't it?'

'Uh, hi, Zoë,' Adam said, clutching his jar of honey so tightly I worried he might smash it.

The doorbell pinged with the arrival of another customer, and Adam turned to leave. But I wasn't going to let him get away that easily – I followed on his heels, keeping a bright and breezy smile on my face.

'So you're a local now?' I asked.

Reluctantly, Adam nodded. 'I moved in yesterday. The flat was okay, once I got the landlord to agree to paint it.'

'And you'll be needing a local pub,' I said cheerily.

He shook his head. 'I don't go out much, if I'm honest. I work long hours.'

'A local pub with a *cat*,' I continued.

Adam looked around like he was hoping a hole in the ground might open and swallow him, or the hand of God reach from above and scoop him up.

'I'm so happy to have bumped into you,' I carried on, ignoring his discomfort. 'Because the first of the D&D games is in just over a week and we still haven't found a Dungeon Master. I know you expressed an interest and since you're living in the area now, you'll be able to come on board. It's absolutely ideal.'

Adam opened his mouth as if he was going to point out that he hadn't done any such thing; in fact, it was me who'd begged him to say he'd consider giving it a try. So I didn't give him the chance.

'We've got six players involved,' I forged relentlessly on. 'Two of them work at the pub – me and Freddie, who's one of the bar staff – and the others are just young regulars who live locally. Archie's coming with his girlfriend. So it's really very much a family affair.

And none of us have played before so there's no high expectations and no pressure. It's just a bit of fun really. And as the DM, you'll get a free meal, and I expect the players will shout your drinks.'

I had no idea how much Adam earned, but who doesn't like free stuff? I don't know if it was that or just my forceful positivity, but all at once the fight went out of him.

'Okay, fine,' he said, 'I'll do it. But I'm only committing to the first game, and if I'm rubbish I won't do it again.'

'You won't be rubbish.' I gave him what I hoped was an encouraging smile. 'Honestly, this is just such good news. I can't wait to tell Alice. She's the landlady – you'll meet her next time you come in, I'm sure. It's so amazing, my horoscope said today that a dark stranger would bring good news, and look – you're him!'

Adam looked at me like I'd just casually mentioned going along to a Scientology meeting or something.

'You do know that stuff's utter crap, don't you?' he said.

I bristled. 'I know some people think that. But a lot of it is surprisingly accurate, actually. I use this app that—'

'Tells you your star sign – whatever it is – is sometimes insecure, especially with people you don't know well. And that you may appear confident on the surface, but have doubts about your place in the world. And that you always like to see the good in others, and believe the world would be a better place if more people felt free to display their true generosity of spirit?'

It was my turn to look startled. 'What, you've got Stargazer on your phone, too?'

Adam snorted. 'Of course I haven't. It's the way all these things work, coming up with a load of waffle that everyone knows is true about themselves, or wants to be true. It's all a con, like tarot reading or psychics.'

'But that's just not the case. I mean, the other day I went on a date with a man who was literally exactly what his star sign said he'd be.'

'That would be your own cognitive bias. Anyway, here's my number.' He rattled off the eleven digits and I frantically typed them into my phone. 'I'll get cracking planning a game.'

'And I'll look forward to seeing you,' I said, wondering if he ever smiled at anyone who didn't have four legs, whiskers and a tail.

That night, alone again in my flat, I turned back to the apps on my phone: the one that would tell me what man I was to try and date next, and the one that would help me to find him. Like evil twins, I thought bitterly.

Twins. Gemini. Another reminder of Jude. Maybe the sex hadn't been that great for him either and that was why he'd left, giving me no way to contact him. Maybe that was how things worked now. It was how it worked for Robbie, and it was how it had worked for Seth. Maybe I needed to just accept that, learn to enjoy a series of sexual encounters that weren't going to lead to anything, until… What? Until Mr Right suddenly popped up out of nowhere by some magical coincidence?

Online dating was it for me, for now, I realised bitterly. I was just going to have to be persistent and see what the zodiac had in store for me next.

It had better get its act together though, because on its present form, I was not impressed.

'Right then, Cancer man,' I said, with more resignation than enthusiasm. 'Show me what you've got.'

Frazzle hopped up and took his place at my feet, and I started reading.

Your Cancer guy might have ambitions in the workplace, but home is definitely where his heart is. As the crab carries its shell on its back, so Cancer's mind always returns to the domestic sphere. However much he enjoys travel and the company of friends, ultimately home and – in the future – family are where his priorities lie.

Fair do's, I thought. You wouldn't catch Mr Cancer fucking off without a word after I'd made him beans on toast with extra chilli sauce, would you?

For flighty, fickle Aquarius, with her head always more or less in the clouds, this can be frustrating. She craves intellectual adventure and is constantly drawn to the company of like-minded souls and the higher realm of the spirit; he wants to set a rota for taking out the bins. In order for this relationship to work long-term, Cancer needs to cut his lady loose and let her pursue interests outside the home, perhaps even in a true reversal of roles in which the man of the house becomes the main home-maker and caregiver for the couple's children.

Steady on, I told the app. *I haven't even met the man and you're already giving us two kids and a picket fence.*

But I allowed my mind to drift into a fantasy in which I had just that. I came home from work to find my Cancerean husband reading our children their bedtime story. In the morning, he'd be giving the kids their breakfast while I got ready for my day. The house would be clean, the bills paid on time, the dog taken for walks.

Hold on, what dog? How come we've suddenly got a dog? But I was pretty certain that this man, this family-focused homebody, would be a dog person.

'What do you reckon to that, Frazzle?' I asked.

Frazz turned his amber eyes on me, like two traffic lights saying, 'Slow the hell down right now.'

'Okay. Maybe the dog would be up for negotiation,' I told him.

*

A couple of days later on a glorious early summer evening, the Ginger Cat's tiny beer garden heaving with people, Robbie and I were discussing whether it would be worth getting a mobile fish and chips van out there to relieve some of the pressure in the kitchen, while sweating over the deep-fat fryer.

'It would pay for itself in no time,' I said.

'And we could work outside, instead of roasting in here,' he agreed. 'At least, one of us could.'

'That would be you then, I take it?'

'Well, not necessarily.' Robbie ducked his head. 'I mean, it's just that I bet it would attract loads of families, and I'm way better at dealing with kids than you.'

His words reminded me of my impending date and my fantasy of life with a Cancerean husband.

'Have you ever thought about being a father?' I asked.

'I always reckoned I'd be a hell of a lot better at it than my old man,' Robbie said, turning courgette falafels over in the boiling oil. 'But then, your cat would probably be a better dad than him. Walked out when I was twelve and my little sister was three and Mum was up the stick with my brother. Loser.'

'I'm sorry. That must've been hard.'

'Not as hard as it would've been if he'd stayed. He was fuck-all help anyway. But at least when he was around Mum could pretend there was a responsible adult to look after me and Tia when she went to work. After that, it was just me taking care of Tia and Sammy, and my nan when she moved in with us after her dementia got bad.'

'That must have been enough to put you off having caring responsibilities for life.'

'God, no! I love kids. And older folk. I love looking after people. That's why I love cooking. It's nurturing, isn't it?'

My knife stopped in mid-chop over a heap of shallots, garlic and mint. I'd never thought of it that way – ever. To me, it was an intellectual challenge, and a sensory one, ideally with a plate of something tasty at the end. I saw, now, why Robbie had been so eager to take the job at the Ginger Cat – persuaded by the whole community-hub thing, starry-eyed over our vision of it as a local asset, a refuge from hunger and loneliness.

'I suppose it is,' I said. 'But kids? Ones of your own?'

'Well, not now, obviously. But I always thought I would, one day, if I could. Given the obvious logistical challenges.'

'It's just, I've always known I didn't but everyone says it changes when you meet the right person. I'm not sure whether it will for me, though. Not really. Although my mate Nadia says it totally does.'

'Nadia's nailed it. Sorry, Zoë, but she has. Since I met Rex, I've been like, totally, marry me. No word of a lie. He'd make my ovaries twang if I had them. I can just see the two of us, thinning out carrots in our allotment while the doggo lies in the shade and the kiddies make mud pies.'

'*Really?*'

'Really. Obviously it'll never happen, because I'm nowhere near ready to settle down and why would I want to, when there are so many hot men in the world left to bang? But yeah, when I'm ancient – like, your age – and I meet another man like Rex, I might be up for it.'

'Ah, I guess I'm overthinking it,' I said. 'I read all this stuff about Cancer men being perfect dads and I kind of forgot that the app's just meant to be a bit of fun, really. And so's our date. So I'm daft to be so nervous about it.'

'Daft is right,' Robbie said. 'Now pass me those cucumbers and I'll get grating.'

Chapter Fourteen

You've been facing your fears lately, Aquarius. But sometimes it takes true courage to walk away.

'Ooooh, you look nice,' Robbie said when I stuck my head round the kitchen door on my way out, just to check that he had everything under control. 'Off on your date? Love the frock – it's very fifties housewife.'

'Oh God, is it that obvious?' I looked down at my dress. I'd found it in a charity shop and bought it, thinking it ticked the feminine box, and besides, it was only a fiver. But now Robbie mentioned it, the sweetheart neckline, nipped-in waist and full skirt were a bit OTT. 'Shit. I look like Betty Draper, don't I?'

Robbie put his head on one side. 'A bit. But it suits you. Demure. Not your usual style at all.'

'Well, hopefully it'll work for Mr Cancer. Get this – he's called Sheldon.'

Robbie doubled over, almost sending a bottle of olive oil flying. 'No way!'

'Yep. It's going to take some doing to keep a straight face. He's from Chicago, and we're meeting at a burger bar. Which seems like a bit of a cliché, but there you go.'

'I hope they do a vegan option.'

'They do, I checked. And about thirty different flavours of milkshake, which made me rethink my life choices a bit. But there'll be a dairy-free one, I expect.'

'Well, make sure you report back,' Robbie said, and as the door closed behind me I heard him say, 'Sheldon. Oh my word, you couldn't make it up.'

On the train, I checked my phone to remind myself what my date looked like, and the exact location of Dexter's. I was feeling nervous, but nothing like as jittery as I'd been the first time I went to meet a stranger for a date. Give it a couple more goes, I told myself, and I'd be taking all this in my stride. I'd survived so far – how bad could this home-loving, family-minded man actually be?

Dexter's was in a chichi part of West London where I rarely ventured. The street was lined with the kind of boutique that displays just one cashmere jumper in the window, and you know that nothing in there – not even a pair of socks – will cost less than a hundred pounds. There was a florist, an artisan chocolate shop and a place that sold handmade stationery.

Sheldon lived nearby, he'd told me, and worked in finance. Clearly he was making shedloads of cash, to be able to afford a house in an area like this. As I walked, I let myself imagine briefly what his future wife's life would be like – my life, if he turned out to be The One.

I'd have a massive car – one of those Chelsea tractors I disapproved of on environmental grounds – that I'd drop the children

off at their private school in, even though I disapproved equally
of fee-paying schools. Then I'd go to my barre exercise class in my
Lululemon sportswear, before having a massage or a manicure and
meeting a friend for lunch. In the afternoon I'd take the children to
their activities – riding lessons, I supposed, or fencing or Japanese
or something. I'd give them their tea and they'd be in bed by the
time Sheldon got home from work, and I'd be freshly made up and
smiling, with a chilled bottle of Chablis ready for us.

I'd have a massive fuck-off shoe collection and a massive fuck-off
Valium habit.

Shaking my head at my own silliness, I pulled my mind back
to the present. I hadn't even met Sheldon yet, never mind married
him, had his babies and developed a substance-abuse problem as a
result. But I had arrived at our designated meeting spot.

Dexter's was a diner-lover's diner, that was for sure. It had
bright red plastic benches in the booths, metal holders stuffed
with paper napkins on the tables, and stripy red-and-white straws
in the chunky glasses the customers were enthusiastically slurping
milkshakes from. There were 1980s-style airbrushed prints of Coke
bottles, fries, hot dogs and ice-cream sundaes on the walls, complete
with photo-realistic drips of sauce and condensation that made
me hungry just looking at them. The waitresses I could see were
wearing ra-ra skirts in neon colours and tight cropped T-shirts with
the restaurant's name on them in a 3D typeface.

I paused outside, glancing faux-casually over my shoulder
through the plate-glass windows. First prize was for spotting Sheldon
before he spotted me, and not looking like a weirdo in the process.
Only problem was, I couldn't see anyone there who might be him.

The restaurant wasn't large – fifty covers, maybe – and it was full of groups of teenagers, families and one table of ultra-slim, heavily made-up women in designer clothes stuffing food into their faces in a kind of guilty frenzy.

But anyway, I was here even if he wasn't. If he didn't show up, I'd just have to front it out and enjoy a trash-tastic feast on my own. I pushed open the door and stepped in, then hesitated for a second looking for a free table.

'Welcome to Dexter's.' A waitress approached me with an iPad secured to a clipboard. Authentic, I thought. 'Do you have a reservation?'

'No, I'm meeting someone but I'm not sure if he's…'

I stopped, my attention caught by a waving hand across the room. That was Sheldon, I was pretty sure. The man I'd seen in his profile pictures, with crinkly brown hair, straight white teeth and bulky shoulders. I was fairly certain I even recognised the mint-green polo shirt he was wearing. But my first impression of the room had been correct: there were no single men there.

Because sitting opposite Sheldon, craning his neck round to have a good old open-mouthed gawp at me, was a little boy in a shirt just like his dad's with an alligator on the pocket, only coral pink.

Shit. He'd only gone and brought his kid.

His. Kid. On. A. Date.

'Of course, what I should have done is turned right around and left.' Dani and I were conducting a post-date post-mortem in the gym, both of us flopped against the wall, sipping water and waiting for our heart rates to drop back to normal. Across the room from us, Fabian Flatley was doing handstand push-ups against the wall, shirtless, the muscles of his back bunching and rippling as he worked, sweat dripping off him onto the floor and rhythmic grunts issuing from him with every press.

'Yeah, maybe. But you can't just do that, can you?'

'I could have. I'm kicking myself for not doing it. But at the time, it just feels so awkward and you don't want to be rude.'

'And you're all invested in the idea of it and you've got dressed for it and everything.'

'Exactly. He hadn't even mentioned the kid, not in his profile or our messages or anything. Who does that? But then part of me was thinking, I didn't want the kid to think it was something he'd done that had made me bail out, and be upset.'

'Which is ridiculous if you think about it for more than about a nanosecond.'

I nodded. 'If you don't want your kid to be upset by how your date behaves, there's a simple solution.'

'Don't bring your bloody kid on the date in the first place.'

'Correct. But I didn't even have a nanosecond to think about it, because I was already walking in through the door and he was waving at me and the kid was staring and it was like I lost the power of rational thought, so I just kept walking in and sat down. And it went downhill from there – fast.'

'How so?' Dani draped her towel over her neck and took a big gulp of water. Fabian had finished his press-ups and had strolled over to the weights rack where he was loading up the bar for deadlifts, making a lot more crashing sounds than were strictly necessary.

Dani watched him admiringly, and I resisted the urge to ask her if he was this annoying and attention-seeking, like, all the time.

'It started right when I sat down,' I said. 'The kid had put one of those things on my chair that make a huge farting noise when you sit on them. I was so thrown by the whole situation I didn't notice. I just sat, and "paaarp".'

'No way.'

'Yes. And the kid – TJ, he's called – absolutely pissed himself laughing and so did Sheldon and so did the people at the next table and the waitress.'

'And you still didn't leave?'

'How could I? The whole restaurant was staring at me, and Sheldon was looking at me like this was some kind of test. So I had to laugh too.'

'What a bastard! So he knew it was there?'

I nodded, my face flaming as I relived the moment. 'He said, "My little man is quite the comedian." And I was like, "Yes, he certainly is, haha." And then we introduced ourselves like all this was perfectly normal.'

'Oh my God. That's just so weird. What a nutter.'

'He said, "A central part of my dating journey is finding someone who can fit with me and TJ, and play a part in his life as she does in mine." He didn't actually say be a mum but that was so blatantly what he meant. He said how every moment of the time he spent with his boy was precious, which I guess was his way of justifying dragging him along as a kind of wing-child on a Tinder date. And the kid was sitting there the whole time with this massive grin on his face like he was having the best time ever, blowing bubbles into his milkshake.'

'Ugh.'

'I know, right? And then when TJ got up to go to the loo, Sheldon got right in there and started slagging off his ex.'

'I bet he did.'

'He was like, "Of course I cherish Wanda as the mother of my child, but…" and then he launched into this tirade about how she didn't value family life, she was a "career girl" and although he would've been quite happy to support the family because he's a high earner, she was having none of it and had insisted on going back to work after she had TJ.'

'Okaaay. I think I see where this is going.'

'I think you do. Poor Wanda got it from both directions. He was so cross that she didn't want to sacrifice her career to be a mum that he refused to lift a finger in the house and then made it her fault when everything went to shit and his shirts weren't ironed and the grouting between the kitchen tiles wasn't getting bleached three times a day and there wasn't a hot meal on the table when he got in from work.'

'He didn't say that, though, did he?'

'He didn't need to. It was so clear that was what he meant. He said he believes home-making is the most important job a woman can do, and that was one of the reasons he wanted to date me, because of me being a chef.'

'Ha! Like you'd finish a shift at work and want nothing more than to make bangers and mash for him and his child.'

'And he said that was the reason, when he and Wanda split up, that he tried to get full parental responsibility for TJ but had to settle for fifty–fifty, and now he's trying to "reboot his intimate relationships" and "launch family life 2.0". He asked me if I'd read *The Surrendered Wife*.'

Dani cackled. 'Okay, I feel a bit sorry for him now. He so picked the wrong woman. And I'm not talking about Wanda.'

His workout over, Fabian strolled over to us and, blanking me completely, ruffled Dani's hair and said he'd see her later. Seconds later, we heard the roar of his Lexus as he drove away.

'We'd ordered our food by this stage,' I carried on. 'I really don't know why I bothered. I couldn't have eaten a thing sat opposite him. But he hadn't got completely into the misogynist stuff when the waitress came round, so I still thought I could have a burger and say it had been nice to meet them both and then leave.'

'But you couldn't.'

'I couldn't. I went into a massive rant. I just couldn't stop myself. I asked him if he was aware how many single mothers – and their children – live in poverty because they've back-burnered their careers to parent full-time and then the dad's fucked off. I said there's nothing wrong with being a stay-at-home mum, but that if he couldn't see that women have just as much right to a rich and full life outside the home as men do, then he needed to get to Specsavers, stat. And I said that if he thought having a wife and a mother for his child was so important, maybe he should have tried a little harder to make his first marriage work, not be trying to find a younger model who was willing to be his cook, cleaner, nanny and unpaid prostitute.'

'You go, sister!'

'And then I did go. I put twenty quid on the table and wished him and TJ all the best, and stormed out. And you know what? It felt bloody brilliant.'

Chapter Fifteen

You're not imagining it – sometimes fate does conspire to get between you and your goals. When that happens, take a little time out and refresh your spirit.

'Your adventure begins in an inn,' Adam said, just loudly enough for the six of us gathered around the table to make out his words, as the Dungeons & Dragons game began.

It was true, of course – we were in the Ginger Cat, with candles, bottles of merlot and bowls of potato wedges, hot chipolata sausages and spicy tomato sauce in front of us, along with our notepads, players' manuals and dice. But it wasn't quite the inn Adam would have had in mind.

I closed my eyes for a second, trying to transport myself into another time – another world, even. There'd be rough-sawn tables and possibly only hewn logs to sit on. There'd be a fire – here, in a London summer, there was no need for such a thing, even though we did light one on winter nights. There'd be horses tethered outside the door where Tim's motorbike and Lana's bicycle were. There'd be – I wasn't sure – mead, maybe? Roast ox? Acorn soup?

'You're all relieved to have come upon this place, where weary travellers can find a bed for the night and a hot meal, exchange tales of their adventures with their fellows and perhaps put together a party to embark on the next quest. You don't know what the future holds beyond tonight, but you're in a refuge, a place of safety – or so it seems, for now.'

A shiver ran down my spine and my eyes snapped open. The faces around the table were all transfixed, leaning in towards Adam. I reminded myself to stop seeing Freddie and Nat and Archie and all the rest of them, and to stop being myself, too.

For tonight – and for every Tuesday for the foreseeable future, until we got bored and wound up the game, or my character was killed in battle and I had to choose a new one – I wasn't Zoë Meredith, pub cook and unsuccessful serial dater. I was Galena, a skilled fighter with the strength, dexterity and toughness that had been bestowed on me by rolls of a twenty-sided dice. Freddie was Hesketh, a bearded barbarian who could swing a double-headed battle-axe as easily as if it were a toothpick. Archie was Dun, a rogue who could move as silently as a cat and pick a lock in seconds. Nat was a sorcerer called Annella, Nat's friend Lara was a cleric called Lorien, and Freddie's mate Tim was Torvid, a ranger.

'As you drink and eat,' Adam went on, 'you notice a group similar to yourselves, armed and equipped as if for a journey. They, too, are huddled over earthenware bowls, devouring the food as hungrily as if it were the finest roast fowl. And they are also talking among themselves, secretively and urgently. And you notice that the meal they have been served is far superior to the thin stew on your own table. It *is* the finest roast fowl. There are roasted roots, too, rich gravy and a freshly baked loaf. And in their glasses is not weak small beer but vintage red wine.'

'What a rip-off!' Freddie exclaimed, then hastily got back into character. 'I mean, does it not seem strange to you, comrades, that they should sup so finely while we make do with a meal that is barely fit for pigs?'

'I'm going to totally diss this place on TripAdvisor,' said Nat. 'Freddie – I mean Hesketh – should we discuss this matter with our noble hostess and try to learn the reason for this shameful discrepancy?'

'We could do that,' said Archie – or rather, Dun the rogue, 'or we could attempt to relieve them of their meal by stealth when the next course is delivered by yonder serving wench.'

Right on cue, Kelly put a couple of fresh bottles of wine on the table, along with a plate of barbecue pork ribs and one of corn on the cob, charred from the grill. Adam watched in silence as we discussed the matter, slipping in and out of character, taking big gulps of red wine and piling into the food, unlike our poor imaginary characters with their thin stew, and decided that our characters would have a chat with the imaginary landlady.

He glanced down at his notes, which were hidden from our view by a cardboard screen printed with castles, dragons, warriors on horseback and a wizard gazing into a crystal ball. 'The landlady tells you that the nearby fortress, Castle Drakeford, was recently invaded by an evil lord from lands to the east, who has installed his garrison there. Those men are his soldiers, and they descend on the village each evening, plundering and demanding crops, money and food.'

'Bastards! I had them for wrong'uns right from the start,' said Archie.

'Ssshh!' Nat elbowed him in the ribs.

'But there is worse to come,' Adam continued. 'The landlady's only daughter, a beautiful young maiden named Zarah, has been captured by Lord Brandrel. In just twelve days, he intends to take her as his bride. And it is well known in these parts the terrible fates that have befallen his previous wives: one driven mad and plunged to her death from the highest battlement; one given to his soldiers to use as they pleased after she refused to comply with his twisted desires; a third chained in a deep dungeon guarded by a dragon. But that last may merely be a tale told by old men after too long in the tavern.'

I glanced around the table. Everyone was leaning forward, fascinated. It was like the noise of the pub around us had been silenced, like the bright street scene over the mantlepiece had been replaced with a medieval tapestry, as if the polished parquet floor was now covered in bulrushes.

Adam's face was cast into angles and planes of light and shadow by the flickering candlelight. His hands moved as he spoke, like he was drawing pictures in his own head. His shabby corduroy shirt had a sheen like velvet in the dim light. *Holy shit*, I thought. *He's really good at this.*

'Just then, you hear a commotion near the door. The landlady's face turns as white as milk. Her son, a hot-blooded young boy named Darian, is squaring up to Lord Brandrel's men, demanding the return of his sister. Already, the soldiers have drawn their swords and are closing in on him. What will you do?'

Of course, it was obvious what we'd do. The game so far had been a slow burn, character-developing and background-setting, but we all knew we were there for the excitement of hand-to-hand combat. Our characters drew their own weapons, rushed into the fray and won the skirmish. Brandrel's bruisers fled, Darian returned to his mother for a bollocking to end all bollockings, Lorien tended to a cut on Hesketh's jaw.

'A mere flesh wound.' Adam consulted the dice. 'You were lucky. Right, we'll call it there for tonight.'

He folded the screen and started tidying his notes, and Alice turned up the lights in the bar and said, 'Time, please, ladies and gents.'

And straight away, it was just the Ginger Cat again, and I was me, and Adam and Archie and Freddie and the rest of them were just a bunch of dorky people I sort of knew.

We all exhaled in nervous giggles as we settled the bill (with the rest of us picking up Adam's share, as we'd agreed) and gathered our stuff.

'That was brilliant.'

'Awesome fun; thanks, guys.'

'Can't wait for next week.'

'You were ace, Adam.'

'I can't believe I let myself get in the way of that dagger.'

Together, we all headed out into the night. It was still warm, but a light drizzle hung in the air, blurring the headlights of approaching cars and the sign above Archie's shop next door. I watched as he and Nat hurried off down the road, Archie ineffectually holding his hand over her head to keep her dry. Freddie buried his hands in his pockets and headed in the other direction, whistling along with whatever music was on his headphones. Soon, only Adam and I were left.

'Which way are you going?' he asked.

'Just there.' I pointed over my head. 'I live above the pub, remember?'

'Of course. You and Frazzle. But he didn't put in an appearance tonight.'

'He was probably worried about getting run through with a dagger.'

Adam smiled. 'No animals will be harmed in the making of this D&D adventure, I promise.'

'You thought it all up yourself, didn't you? I mean, you didn't use one of the ready-made games.'

'Nah.' He pushed up his glasses. Their lenses were misted with rain so his eyes looked blurry, too. 'I guess I wanted to do it properly.'

'And you did. You were brilliant.'

He gave a kind of 'aw, shucks' shrug. 'It's been fun, planning it all. I'm glad you asked me to do it.'

'I'm glad too. I'm really excited for next time.'

'No pressure then.' He smiled again, a proper grin this time.

I smiled back. 'No pressure.'

Then, both at the same time, we said, 'I should—'

'I should head home,' he said.

'And I should head upstairs.'

'Night, then, Zoë.'

'Night. And thanks.'

We turned away from each other and I pushed open the door and walked back through the almost empty pub, feeling suddenly, hollowly alone. The stairs to my flat were in darkness, and for a second I felt a return of the nervous tension that had gripped me while we were engrossed in the game, like I might be ambushed by a mercenary with a broadsword.

But I told myself not to be stupid. I started up the stairs, then almost fell backwards when I saw a figure sitting on the top stair, hunched over in the gloom, and heard a voice say my name.

'Jesus Christ! You scared the hell out of me!'

It was Jude.

Chapter Sixteen

*It might feel as if love has fallen right into your waiting arms,
Aquarius, but don't cling onto it so hard you squeeze the life
out of it.*

And so, the next morning, I woke up with Jude's head next to mine
on the pillow again. The previous night, I'd been all set to send
him packing after telling him exactly what I thought of men who
slept with women and then fucked off without a word or a trace.
But he'd disarmed me totally right from the moment I'd seen him
on the stairs.

He'd got to his feet, a bit stiffly, like he'd been sitting there for
a long time, and reached right over to give me a hug, pulling me
close and saying, 'Your hair smells amazing. I've been thinking
about you so much.'

So why didn't you call then? I thought. But he answered the
question before I could get the words out.

'I'm such a muppet, I completely forgot the name of the pub. And
I don't know your last name so I couldn't find you on social media.
I tried and tried. And then I came up to London for a Labour Party

meeting today and when it finished I thought, I'm going to find her. And I did. I kind of remembered where the pub was in relation to the station and I just walked around until I saw it. And then I saw you, but you were busy and I didn't want to interrupt so I just snuck in here and waited for you to finish. My God, it's good to see you.'

Such was the sweetness of his smile and the comforting strength of his arms around me that all my resolve melted away, and I found myself hugging him back.

'Why didn't you get in touch with me?' he murmured into my hair. 'Every time I got a new email or a missed call or a connection on LinkedIn, I hoped it would be you. But it never was.'

'I don't know. I guess I thought that because you'd just left that morning, you didn't want to see me again.'

'As if!' He cupped my face between his palms and kissed my lips, and I could feel his smile meeting my own. 'I've been thinking about you all the time. I even dreamed one night that I was here with you and your cat was sleeping on my face so I couldn't breathe, but when I woke up it was only my pillow.'

I couldn't help laughing. 'That must have been quite a relief.'

'It should have been.' He smiled down at me. 'But it wasn't. I even smelled the smell of your hair in my dream, and the whole day afterwards. It was like being haunted by a ginger ghost.'

Normally, when people described me as ginger, I bristled at the reminder of being teased at school. But I couldn't muster even the slightest resentment now.

'Come in,' I said.

He stepped aside and I unlocked the door. He dumped his bag by the bed and headed for the bathroom while I sorted out Frazzle's food and water and litter tray, and when I finished cleaning my teeth and washing my face, there he was in bed, waiting for me.

This time, we didn't wait until the morning. As soon as I got under the duvet, Jude's arms closed around me and we kissed, with an urgency that hadn't been there the first time. Then, it had felt tentative and uncertain – *Are we really going to do this? Oh, okay, looks like we are. Oh wait, we just did.*

But now, my relief at seeing him and the confidence his words had given me allowed me to take the lead. I explored his body with my fingertips, running my hands over his chest beneath his T-shirt, discovering the arches of his ribs, the ridges of his stomach muscles, the silky hair running down his belly.

I pulled his T-shirt off over his head and knelt there above him, my legs either side of his thighs. He looked up at me, smiling.

'Hey.'

'Fancy seeing you here.'

We both laughed, and I lowered myself over him, kissing him again. Now, his hands were on my body, too, stroking my back, sliding under the waistband of my jeans to cup my bottom.

'Come on, let's get these off,' he said.

I stood up and unbuttoned my jeans, thankful that I'd only been wearing flip-flops so there was no embarrassing sock-removal moment to negotiate. I had a moment of panic wondering whether I was wearing particularly old, ratty underwear, but it was okay – my bright red boy shorts were at least free of holes, if not the sexiest garment ever. I eased my jeans down over my hips, slowly, watching his eyes follow my hands down my legs.

I stepped out of my jeans and then, still slowly, pulled my vest top over my head. Annoyingly, there was no sexy way of doing that. I joined him on the bed again in just my bra and pants, trying to remember what the app – which had its risqué moments – had said about what Gemini men liked in bed. Hopefully not twin sisters, because I wouldn't be able to stretch to those.

Jude took me in his arms again, holding me the way he had before, like I was something precious and fragile. His touch was feather-light, almost ticklish on my skin. He reached for the clasp of my bra and fumbled with one hand, before undoing it with two. No biggie – one-handed bra removal was expert-level undressing, I thought. The awkwardness that had been there last time was almost gone – almost, if not completely – blotted from my mind by my happiness and relief at seeing him.

And what was going on inside his boxer shorts distracted me from that, anyway – because that was a biggie. I reached down and touched his cock, running my palm over the bulge then sliding my fingers inside his pants to hold his warm hardness, loving the way he felt in my hand.

He touched my breasts, his fingers finding my nipples and then his mouth following them to kiss and suck. I heard him groan with pleasure and an answering gasp from me as his lips and tongue teased my flesh. I felt myself getting swept into a whirlpool of pleasure – his hands on my body, the feel of his skin against my palms and fingers, the gorgeous man-smell of him. I was desperate for him to carry on, to give me more and more and more, but at the same time, I wanted this moment of pure perfection to last forever. His other hand was inside my knickers now, touching me, reaching for me, finding almost the right place. So close. Almost there.

And then I felt a flood of hot wetness on my hand.

'Oh shit.' Jude pulled a pillow up over his face, like he was blushing and trying to hide it. 'Sorry about that.'

'That's okay.' I mean, what the hell else are you supposed to say?

'It's just, you're so sexy. Too sexy. And it's been…'

'Sshh. Don't worry.'

I pulled him close and held him, trying to ignore the cooling wetness of his pants against my thigh and subdue my disappointment. He kissed me again.

'You're amazing. Next time, I promise…'

'It's okay. It really is.'

He turned away from me, and I spooned myself against his warm back, feeling his breathing slow until, within minutes, he started to snore softly. Then Frazzle jumped up and settled into the crook of my knees and I knew I'd spend the night that way, wet patch on my sheets and all, unable to move for fear of disturbing these two sleeping boys.

When I woke up the next morning, though, Jude wasn't there. When I opened my eyes, expecting to see him sleeping there, there was only the empty pillow and the duvet scrunched up to one side. Frazzle was sitting next to the closed bathroom door, looking deeply pissed off.

I sat up. *Oh God, he hasn't upped and left again, has he?*

The thought lasered through my sleep-fogged brain. But no. His bag was still there, next to the bed where he'd left it, and I could hear the shower running. I got up, pulled on yesterday's vest and pants, gave Frazzle his breakfast and switched the kettle on. A few minutes later, Jude emerged from the bathroom wrapped in my towel. He'd shaved, he smelled of toothpaste and my lemon-and-poppy-seed soap and his smile was like the sun coming out.

He folded me in a hug, and I pressed myself against the warm hardness of his body. 'Good morning, beautiful. I didn't want to wake you.'

'I wouldn't have minded. I'm just pleased you're here.'

'Makes two of us.' He kissed the tip of my nose.

'Coffee? There's only instant, I'm afraid. I usually use the proper machine downstairs in the bar.'

'That would be amazing. And some toast?'

'Help yourself. There's bread in the cupboard, and some nut butter and stuff. I'd better get ready for work.'

Reluctantly, I loosened my arms and moved away from Jude's bare chest, but he pulled me close again.

'We'll be able to see each other much more, now,' he said.

I felt my lips curve into a smile against his skin. 'Why's that?'

'Because I want to see lots more of you. And also, because I've got a job in London now. Well, an internship, at a trade union.'

'Oh, that's amazing! Congratulations.'

'I just felt, you know, I should do something. Working with homeless people is important, vital work, and I'll probably go back to it in the future, but first you've got to dismantle the structural inequalities that have allowed the situation to get so bad in the first place. There's so much energy, so much hope. It's incredible to be a part of it.'

I felt almost humbled by his passion, his zeal to change the world for the better. I shared his ideals, I truly did – but he was doing something about it, whereas I was just working as a cook in a pub.

'It feels like there's a real impetus, right now, to achieving a fairer world,' I said. 'It must be incredible to be a part of it.'

He grinned. 'That's one of the reasons I love you, Zoë. We care about the same things.'

He pulled off the towel and handed it to me, and I let myself admire his lean, naked body for a few seconds, until he pulled on his underwear and jeans. Then I reluctantly turned and went to have my own shower, my mind whirring as it registered what I'd just heard.

Did he just say he loved me?

Chapter Seventeen

As Venus enters Gemini, things are looking good for you on the love front. But are the stars in your eyes making you lose track of where you're going?

After that, things with me and Jude went from zero to a hundred in, like, a day. Or not even a day, because after that first night, he never really left. He kept saying he needed to go back to his mum's place to pick up some stuff, but if he did, he must have gone during the day, because every evening when I got home, there he was.

After about a week, I stopped feeling anxious that when I pushed open the door, the flat would be empty and he would somehow have vanished again. And even if for some reason he was out – like one time when he developed a craving for chips and headed to the local late-night kebab shop – I didn't have to worry, because now I had his number.

And he texted me throughout the day: little jokes and memes, notes to say that he was thinking of me, even a semi-regular countdown to how long it would be until we saw each other again.

Sharing the flat with him after living alone for so long was kind of weird, but I told myself I'd get used to it – and I promised Frazzle he would, too. I didn't want to put Jude under any pressure, so I never asked how long he planned to stay. He was a Gemini, a bohemian, a free spirit like me. If I made him feel crowded or rushed, he might change his mind about us.

And anyway, things were so good when we were together, there was no reason to change anything. Although the time we had with each other was limited by my long working hours, we made the most of it. Like me, he loved watching old reruns of *Buffy* and *The Big Bang Theory*. The Spotify playlists we had on our phones were almost identical. He was rereading his way through the complete works of Terry Pratchett, and the bits he read aloud to me to make me laugh were all my favourite lines from when I'd read the series.

If we were often too tired to do anything more than snuggle into each other's arms in bed, and if when anything more did happen it was often over really quickly, that didn't seem to matter. After all, we were still new to each other, still discovering each other, and he was so considerate and sweet in so many other, more important ways.

Like one Wednesday after work, when I trudged up the stairs to the flat, my feet aching after an evening in the kitchen that had seemed like it would never end. Everything had gone wrong that night. Robbie had forgotten to take a batch of soup out of the freezer and it had caught and burned when we tried to defrost it on the hob. The grass-fed beef mince we'd ordered for the burgers hadn't turned up. A big table celebrating a birthday had neglected to mention when they booked that three of their party were gluten intolerant, five couldn't eat dairy and one had a severe allergy that would land them in hospital if they so much as sniffed a peanut, and with the best will in the world I hadn't been able to cater safely for them all. No matter how nice Alice had been about it, I knew the loss of revenue was the last thing the Ginger Cat needed.

I felt my face almost split in half with a huge yawn, and Frazzle, following me up the stairs, yawned in sympathy. He'd been working the room all night, doing his best to charm the punters and make up for the failings of the kitchen, and it wasn't his fault that the person with the nut allergy was allergic to cats too and had threatened to report us to the local authority's environmental health department.

'Oh well, Frazz,' I said, fitting my key into the lock, 'that's tonight over, at least, Onwards and upwards, right?'

Frazzle rubbed against my legs to remind me that tonight was far from over, and wouldn't be until he'd had his late-night snack and I'd cleaned out his litter tray.

The flat wasn't in darkness as I'd expected. Jude had said that he was going back to his mum's place that evening after work, and I'd assumed he'd stay over there. But he was sitting on the sofa, surrounded by the golden glow of what looked like about a thousand tea lights, dotted all around the flat like a flickering galaxy. Music was playing softly and there was an unfamiliar scent in the air, which I realised came from a reed diffuser perched on the counter next to the kettle.

'Surprise!' Jude jumped up and folded me into a hug.

'Wow.' I gazed around the room. There was a new throw on the bed, a vintage Indian blanket with little mirrors embroidered onto its surface, a seventies-style lava lamp in one corner and a fleshy-leaved plant in a brass pot by the bed. 'You've gone full hippie chic. What is all this stuff?'

Jude laughed. 'Mate of mine is doing house clearances for some extra cash. He came across a load of stuff in some old woman's place in Dalston and gave me first dibs. What do you reckon? Adds a certain *je ne sais quoi*, right?'

'It's awesome.' I'd never got around to buying anything much for the flat myself – I was too busy, too skint and didn't have enough confidence in my own taste in interior décor. Besides, I was so used to feeling like everything in my life was temporary and any second I might be uprooted – or uproot myself – that the idea that this place was home still hadn't properly sunk in, even after almost half a year.

'Glad you like it. I thought, if I was going to stay here for a bit, I should probably contribute a bit more than just a warm body in your bed.'

I pressed myself against him, feeling his strong arms around me, his chin resting on my head. He was going to be staying here for a bit. I didn't want to ask how long 'a bit' was; I worried that, if I tried to hold on to him, he might slip through my fingers like quicksilver, disappear just like he had that first morning.

'You didn't have to do this. Thank you.'

'But that's not all.' Gently, he released me and turned towards my makeshift kitchen. 'Romantic dinner for two coming right up.'

He produced a bottle of red wine and splashed some into two glasses, handing one to me. I hadn't the heart to say that I'd already had dinner earlier, in the pub, and that, at nearly midnight, the only thing I wanted to drink was a cup of tea, ideally in bed.

'Cheers,' I said, clinking my glass against his and taking a sip. The wine was almost amber coloured and I could see dust on the bottle.

'The old dear had quite the collection, and my mate let me liberate a couple of bottles,' Jude said proudly. 'This is a nineteen ninety something. Only the finest vintages to go with our midnight feast.'

'I can't believe you did all this. I thought you were going back to Bedford.'

'I wanted to surprise you.'

'Consider me surprised.'

He flicked on the kettle and tipped a sachet of instant noodles into two bowls. As always when someone was cooking for me, I felt the urge to dive in and help, but I resisted. This was Jude's treat. I sat down, sipped my wine and watched as he opened a can of sweetcorn, tore open a pack of tofu with his teeth, splashed soy sauce over the noodles, then poured boiling water over it all.

'I'm no chef,' he said apologetically. 'But I just wanted to… you know… treat you. Just a bit.'

'I don't care whether you're a chef or not,' I said. 'You're a bloody sweetheart to have done all this.'

He joined me on the carpet, our backs against the sofa, and we slurped noodles out of the bowls, washing them down with gulps of the slightly musty-tasting red wine. I didn't want any of it, really, but I wanted to not disappoint Jude more. I managed to suppress a huge yawn and tried not to think about needing to be up at six the next morning.

After we'd finished our noodles, Jude took our plates and left them on the table – again, I had to suppress the urge to jump to my feet and wash them up – and produced a pack of Oreo cookies.

'Vegan-friendly dessert,' he said proudly.

I laughed. 'How did you know I love Oreos?'

Jude took my hand. 'Isn't it obvious?'

'Is it?'

'Of course. Because I love them, too.'

I took two and ate them the proper way, levering off one half of the biscuit, eating that, then scraping off the white frosting with my teeth before crunching the other half. Kind of gross, I know, but I didn't have to worry because Jude was eating his in exactly the same way. When we noticed, our eyes met and we both laughed.

The wine and the sugar had given me a much-needed surge of energy, and I dragged myself to my feet and sorted out Frazzle's litter tray and water for the night. Then I went to the bathroom to clean my teeth. I caught sight of my face in the mirror, pale and hollow-eyed – but then I laughed. With a soapy finger, Jude had written on the glass: 'World's Sexiest Woman'.

'Now,' he said, when I returned. 'Get your kit off.'

'What?'

'You heard. You've had a hard day and I'm going to give you a massage.'

'Seriously?'

'Seriously. I'm good at it – I have healing hands. You'll like it.'

I didn't need telling again. After a day hunched over the chopping board and a brutal overhead press session in the gym that afternoon, my back and shoulders felt creaky with tension. I peeled off my jeans, T-shirt and bra and sat on the bed.

'Lie down on your front,' Jude instructed, and I obeyed. I heard the snap of a bottle top opening and smelled patchouli oil, before

Jude's warm, slippery hands began to glide over my back, gently at first, then more firmly, his thumbs easing out the tight knots in my shoulders.

'Oh God, that feels good,' I said, my words muffled by the pillow.

'Hard enough?'

'Just right.'

He carried on, his hands working their way down my back, knowing exactly where to press, for how long and how firmly. I felt a warm wave of relaxation and tiredness wash over me, and barely felt him ease down my pants to massage my buttocks. By the time his fingers slid between my legs to caress me there, it was too late – I was fast asleep.

But Jude didn't fall asleep straight away, I realised the next morning. Because when I went to the bathroom, up before him as usual, the note on the mirror had been cleaned off and replaced with a new one: 'Good morning, beautiful'.

And my reflection, smiling back at me, surrounded by my tangled hair, did look beautiful.

'So he's basically moved in with you?' Dani asked, her eyebrows disappearing behind the smooth curtain of her fringe.

'Well, kind of. But not really. I mean, it would be far too soon for that, right?'

'I'll say.' Dani sipped her cappuccino.

It was one of those summer days that manage to be both overcast and stiflingly hot, and we were in a new coffee shop that had opened on the high street where the greasy spoon used to be. Alice had mourned its passing, saying it was yet another piece of the fabric of the area that was being stripped away by gentrification, and I knew Jude would have taken the same view. But this was still a local business that deserved support, and besides, there were red velvet cupcakes that had tiny doughnuts perched on top of the swirls of dairy-free frosting.

'It's just that he's working here for the time being, and he's got nowhere to live. And because he's an unpaid volunteer, he can't really stretch to London rent, can he?'

'So he's staying in London for how long?'

'Well, potentially until the end of the year, I guess. Depending on what happens with politics and stuff. Maybe longer, if they offer him a permanent job.'

'Wow. So an indefinite period then.' Dani carefully lifted the tiny doughnut off her cupcake, raked it through the icing and took a bite. 'Oh my fucking God, total sugar rush. So good. You must feel really sure about each other, then.'

I peeled the paper case off my cupcake and looked at it. Ideally, in order to get the full flavour experience, you'd want to bite through all three layers: red velvet sponge, frosting and doughnut, in one go. But if I tried that I'd dislocate my jaw for sure. I broke a piece of crimson cake off the bottom and ate it to reduce the overall height of the structure.

'He's an amazing person,' I said. 'He has incredibly strong morals and ethics. I really admire his commitment to the causes he believes in. It's all the same things I care about, only I've never really been arsed to do anything about it.'

I wondered guiltily whether the red colouring in the cupcake had come from the crushed shells of poor little cochineal beetles.

Surely not – not when it had a big 'V' next to it on the menu. But I should have asked, and I hadn't, because I didn't want the waitress to think I was a wanker.

Jude would've asked, though.

'That's all well and good,' Dani said. 'But what's he like in the sack?'

I almost choked on my coconut chai latte. 'Really nice. Really kind of gentle and sweet.'

'Hmmm. That's good. Better than him being a tree-hugging leftie.'

I tried to look disapproving but couldn't help laughing. 'I'm a tree-hugging leftie too. And he's a feminist. How many blokes are willing to admit that?'

'Not that many,' Dani admitted. 'Certainly none of the ones I've dated.'

'How about Fabian?' I asked.

'Ah, you know what? I couldn't care less if he's a feminist or not, to be honest with you. He treats me decently, he takes me to nice places, he's hot, he makes me laugh and he's a fabulous fuck. We never talk about politics and stuff, anyway. He's not that interested and nor am I.'

I tried to imagine Fabian on an Extinction Rebellion demo, or wearing a 'This is What a Feminist Looks Like' T-shirt, and failed totally.

'No, I guess he's not. But things are going well with him?'

'Really, really well. He sends me flowers, like, every other day. Whenever we can't see each other. He's really romantic, but not in an over-the-top kind of way. Just a gentleman. Opens the car door for me and stuff.'

I wasn't sure opening the car door was chivalrous enough to make up for ignoring Dani's calls and texts, but maybe Fabian had mended his ways. Jude didn't have a car, of course. He even objected to using Uber, on the basis that it didn't offer sufficiently robust safeguards for workers' rights.

'Isn't it weird,' I said, 'how you and I have both found boyfriends at the same time? I mean, Jude and I haven't actually had the exclusivity talk, but he's been staying at my place for ten days and he's said he loves me, so that must mean it's serious, right?'

Dani licked her spoon. 'It must do. Did you say it back?'

'Not that first time. To be honest, I was so surprised, and the way he said it was kind of casual, so I wasn't even sure if he really meant it and I didn't want to be clingy. But since then, yeah.'

It had felt so strange, forming my mouth around those words for the first time since I'd said them to Joe. But the smile on Jude's face, the way he'd held me close afterwards, reassured me. He didn't think I was clingy or needy – or if he did, he felt clingy and needy, too, so that was all right.

'If Fabian said he loved me I think I'd faint with shock,' Dani said.

'But they're so totally different. I mean, we're not that different from each other – we're mates and everything. I can't imagine Jude and Fabian having a beer together, can you?'

'We could try going out, all four of us together.' Dani chewed a cuticle. 'Just to see what happened.'

'We could,' I agreed, thinking that actually, we both knew that would never, ever happen. 'What star sign is Fabian, anyway?'

'Aries, of course. I didn't ask him directly, though. I just kind of quizzed him about when his last birthday was. But he's totally textbook. Driven, fiery, ambitious, stubborn.'

'He must spend shedloads of time at work,' I said, 'with all his start-ups and everything.'

Dani sighed and ate the rest of her cupcake in one enormous bite. 'You know what, I almost envy you, Jude being there every night. You're right, Fabian's so busy. Last week he was in Bermuda and the week before he was in Malta, and he's constantly having these business meetings that go on until, like, ten at night. He wants to see me – I know he does; he says so all the time – but there's no point me hanging around at his waiting for him to get home, because there'd be nothing for me to do except mess around on my phone.'

'Of course not. Jude doesn't spend much time round mine, either, when I'm not there. He's got other stuff to do, working late and meetings and stuff. Which is just as well, because we're crazy busy and I'm on split shifts most days. So we only really see each other in the mornings and last thing at night.'

'I see Fabian at the gym, though.' Dani brightened. She had changed the time of her workouts to coincide with Fabian's rather than with mine. I missed her company, but at least it meant we got to do other things together instead.

'He's there a lot, isn't he?'

'Yeah, just about every day. It takes hard work to get a body like his. He says it takes hard work to succeed in any avenue in life, and he's right, of course. Maybe if I'd worked harder at uni I wouldn't be stuck in a dead-end job I hate. But sometimes I wish he'd be just a bit less bloody driven, so we could do normal stuff together like watch *Love Island* and go to the pub and stuff. When we do go out it's always to these flash restaurants and I never know what to wear or what to order or what knife to use. And his mates are always there and they talk across me about business and I feel like a right twat.'

Her words had come out in a massive rush.

I said, 'On my last night off, Jude and I were meant to go out for a curry. Only there was this homeless guy sitting outside the restaurant, and Jude stopped to chat to him, and by the time he'd sorted out a hot meal for him and a bed for the night in a shelter, and somewhere for his dog to stay, it was too late, so we just went home and had toast.'

I remembered how respectfully Jude had spoken to Andrei, how he'd squatted down and shaken his hand and asked what his dog was called, and known exactly what he needed to do to help him. I'd felt the hugest rush of admiration for him then, and wished that I could be as capable and compassionate as him, as willing to abandon my plans when I saw someone in need. Never mind being able to speak a few words of Romanian. And how not being able to have the pea and potato samosas I'd been craving had faded into insignificance when I considered how fortunate I was to have a home and a toaster.

I remembered how, afterwards, Jude and I had gone back to mine, and he'd told me he loved me, and it had felt quite natural to say that I loved him too, and we'd had sex and it had lasted much longer that time. Although it hadn't been quite there, not for me, the closeness to Jude had felt so precious and important that my lack of an orgasm had mattered about as much as my lack of samosas. We loved each other. It would get even better – we just needed practice.

I ate the last of my cupcake in one, enormous bite, and Dani finished her cappuccino.

'Isn't it amazing, having a boyfriend?' she said. 'Mum sent me a load of photos of my ex Jamie's wedding the other day. I know she meant me to feel gutted that he'd got someone else and now he'll never marry me, but I didn't feel even a bit sad. I mean, I felt sad about her wanting to do that to me, but not about Jamie.'

'I get it. Who the hell needs Jamie?'

'Exactly! And best of all, now I've got Fabian, I'll never, ever have to date again. I love that feeling.'

'Oh my God, me too,' I said.

Chapter Eighteen

Today a rival has an eye on your prize, Aquarius. If good fortune was yours for the taking, remember that it can be snatched from you just as easily.

'This is our stop.'

I followed Jude down the steps to the lower deck of the bus, clinging tightly to the handrails, because the vehicle was still moving. We were in a part of East London I'd never visited before, part of the old docklands, except, unlike most of the area, this bit hadn't been redeveloped and taken over by shiny glass skyscrapers. Here, it looked as if nothing had changed for forty years: the grubby high-rise apartment blocks, the scrubby patches of grass where children kicked footballs between swathes of broken glass, the washing lines strung haphazardly across balconies, the cars parked on the grass verges on the rims of their wheels, rusting quietly to death.

'Wow,' I said. 'How long has your friend lived here?'

'Only a couple of months. It's not permanent – she's acting as a property guardian, looking after a flat in a building that's due to be knocked down. It would have happened years ago, but the residents put up a fight, and rightly so. They'll be moved out to God knows where, the whole community ripped apart.'

I noticed the sun glinting off a pile of used nitrous-oxide canisters outside a boarded-up pub and wondered whether, if it'd had an Alice to rescue it, breathe new life into it like the Ginger Cat, it would have changed anything at all. Somehow I couldn't picture it.

'It's a shame,' I said. 'So much underinvestment in infrastructure for so long. How sad.'

'It's become a dumping ground for forgotten people,' Jude agreed. 'Refugees, the long-term-unemployed, people with substance abuse and mental health problems. I've worked in communities like this, volunteering at food banks and stuff, and you never get used to the hardship.'

'But this is a social call, right?' I tried my best to lighten the mood. 'We've brought wine and everything.'

'And Indigo can't wait to meet you.' Jude looked down at me and smiled, his face softening. 'You two will get on really well, I just know it.'

'Are you sure I look okay?'

I felt woefully unprepared for my first official outing as Jude's girlfriend and first introduction to one of his friends. Just the night before, I'd mentioned that I had the evening off, and he'd said, 'Cool! We can go and see Indigo,' and before I'd been able to gain much more intel than that they'd been at university together and she lived not that far away, he'd whipped out his phone and WhatsApped her, and now here we were.

'It's this one, I think,' Jude said. 'Pettigrew Tower.'

We looked up at the sign on one of the concrete walkways, which was missing all its letters bar the 'T's and 'E's, and could just about make out the less-stained shadows where the others had been.

'Must be,' I said.

'There's no lift. Well, there was, back in the day, but not any more. So we're walking up to the eighth floor.'

I laughed. 'Just as well I'm wearing flat shoes. That, and I hit the gym almost every day.'

Even so, I was properly out of breath by the time we reached our destination, and had to stop and wipe sweat off my top lip. Meeting Jude's oldest friend was nerve-wracking enough without being a panting, perspiring mess.

'Are you sure I look okay?' I asked.

'You look gorgeous. You couldn't look any other way if you tried.'

Reassured by his words and his hand gripping mine, I fixed a friendly smile on my face as Jude tapped on the door of Flat 805. But I felt it waver as soon as Indigo answered the door. It wasn't so much that she was attractive – although she was properly, knock-out beautiful – it was the particular type she was.

She was tall, slender almost to the point of gauntness, with pearl-pale skin and long, poker-straight black hair that matched her all-black, trailing clothes. She had enormous bluey-green eyes fringed with lashes so thick and dark they looked false, although I was ninety-nine per cent sure they weren't. See also her full, perfectly curved lips that I was willing to bet had never been near an aesthetician's needle. She looked exactly the way fourteen-years-ago emo me had dreamed of waking up looking, through some random overnight miracle that would transform a short, curvy ginger girl into a tall, slender dark one. It had never happened, of course (barring the one time, best forgotten, when I'd attempted to dye my hair black using a kit in a box from Boots) and I'd long since grown to accept and even like the way I looked. But still, Indigo awakened teenage insecurities I'd thought were long gone.

'Hello!' She reached out and hugged Jude, then hugged me too. She smelled of fags and musky perfume. 'Come in! Welcome to my humble abode! You're my first visitors.'

'We brought a bottle of cava,' I said, humbly offering it.

'Lovely.' Indigo led the way into the flat. Although the day was bright and sunny, in here it was almost dark. Only thin slivers of light managed to slip through the edges of the windows, which were hung with heavy drapes in various mismatched pieces of fabric. There was no furniture apart from a single upright wooden chair, a pile of cushions on the floor and an easel holding a portrait of a woman with a green face, who bore a passing resemblance to Indigo herself.

'Make yourselves comfortable,' she said. 'I'll just get some glasses.'

Jude and I sat down on the floor, our backs against the wall, and he put his hand on my knee and squeezed it reassuringly. After a couple of moments Indigo reappeared with the open bottle and three empty jam jars.

'I've used these for paint water,' she said. 'But they should be reasonably clean. I've cold running water but no hot, so I have to borrow friends' showers.'

I almost said politely that she was welcome to add me to the roster, then thought better of it. The last thing I wanted was this woman floating alluringly round my flat in nothing but a towel.

'So how did you two meet?' She lowered herself gracefully down onto a cushion without using her hands, splashed wine into the jars and passed one to each of us.

'At the climate-change demo a few weeks back,' Jude said. 'It was love at first sight, wasn't it, Zoë?'

I laughed. 'Lust, maybe. But then I'd just fallen over and taken all the skin off my knees and I wasn't myself. Jude rescued me.'

'And Zoë insisted on knowing my star sign before she'd get on the train with me,' Jude said.

'And we've been together ever since,' I said, omitting to mention the four-week hiatus when I'd neither seen nor heard from Jude.

It was the first time we'd talked about this to anyone apart from each other, and I could imagine the story becoming a familiar one, which we'd embellish and improve over time – part of the mythology of us. The thought was an odd mixture of thrilling and comforting, and I guess Jude must have felt it too, because we met each other's eyes with a smile that was as intimate as a caress.

'Cute,' Indigo said, not very enthusiastically. 'So you believe then? In the science of the stars?'

'Well… kind of. I mean, I've got an app on my phone and I was doing online dating and I thought it would be kind of interesting to see what happened if I went out with guys with different star signs.'

She raised an eyebrow, a skill I'd never mastered and always envied. 'An app on your phone. That's not very scientific, is it?'

'It uses data provided by NASA,' I said defensively. 'And it's actually been surprisingly accurate. In fact, on the day I met Jude, it said…' I tailed off, because I couldn't actually remember what

Stargazer had said on that particular day, only that, with hindsight, it appeared to have foretold exactly what had happened.

'Indigo's all over that stuff,' Jude said. 'She reads tarot cards and does palmistry and everything. She used to do readings at parties to earn extra cash at uni.'

'Until I realised that I shouldn't cheapen my gifts in that way. Now I just practise occasionally, as a favour to friends. I could do your charts, if you like? See how compatible you are on a deeper level?'

'I… thanks for offering,' I said.

I wasn't sure why, but suddenly the dark room, Indigo's shadowy face and the stifling air was making me feel slightly sick and definitely unsettled. I sipped my fizzy wine and tried to fix the bright smile on my face again.

'That would be amazing,' Jude said. 'Come on, Zoë, you're up for it, aren't you?'

'Of course.' It was nothing, I assured myself – just a bit of fun. What did that matter? Jude and I were together. He'd told me he loved me and I'd told him back.

Indigo did the same trick she'd done when she sat down, only in reverse. It was like there was a string running from the top of her head to the ceiling, allowing her to raise and lower herself without any apparent effort. That, or she did shedloads of yoga or Pilates or something that made her both enviably strong and enviably bendy. She drifted over to a teetering pile of books in a corner and ran her finger down the spines, before pulling one out. The rest of the pile wavered and fell, but she ignored that, returning to her place on the cushions.

'Now, Zoë, the date, time and place of your birth,' she said.

I told her, although I wasn't sure exactly what time I'd been born and had to make it up.

'And you're the twenty-ninth of May, ten minutes past one, in Bristol,' she said, with a smile at Jude.

Bloody hell, how did she know that? Presumably she'd done his horoscope before. They'd known each other for years, after all, and it was clearly a bit of a party trick of hers. But how had she remembered? Was there more between them than friendship? But I wasn't going to be jealous – I wasn't going to allow myself to be the insecure girlfriend who quizzed her man about his past relationships and his current friendships and made myself miserable over comparisons that were only in my own head.

Even if she did look like Christina Ricci.

'Okay?' Jude whispered, giving my thigh a reassuring squeeze.

I nodded and squeezed his in return. Indigo was flicking through the pages of her book, her head bent so her black hair touched the page, cigarette smoke curling up around her head. She paused and ran a not-very-clean fingernail down a page. *Don't judge,* I told myself, *your fingernails probably wouldn't be all that clean either if you were living in a place with no hot water. She's Jude's friend – you're meant to like her, not feel all defensive and resentful.*

'Well, this is interesting,' she said. 'Of course, as you know, Gemini and Aquarius are normally an excellent match. Your shared curiosity about the world, your passion for causes you care about, your quirkiness and willingness to turn your backs on convention make you well suited. But there are some strange things in this particular chart.'

Jude laughed. 'Go on then, Ind, hit us with it. Stop being all mysterious. We're not a hen party you're trying to impress.'

'I won't go into detail. But, Zoë, your chart has some anomalies. It's Saturn in your rising sign. It suggests that, in fact, you have a yearning for stability and a leaning towards convention that's unusual in an Aquarian. Unusual in any air sign, in fact.'

I remembered the words on my app. *It's okay to admit that you're a bird who'd be happier in a cage.* Most of the messages it sent me I'd forgotten almost as soon as I read them, but that had stuck with me for some reason – possibly because whenever I thought about it, it reminded me of poor battery chickens, and made me feel guilty about every single fried egg I'd ever eaten. And then thinking about fried eggs made me really crave one, which made me feel guiltier still.

Indigo might have said she didn't intend to go into detail, but detail was exactly what she went into. Smoke curling up around her face between her curtains of dark hair, her finger tracing the lines on the page, she proceeded to tell Jude and me what the stars had in store for us.

'Your need for security can lead you to stifle those you love, Zoë,' she said, her voice low and solemn. 'Do you ever find yourself driving people away because you consider your own needs above their own? I thought so. You see, Jude, like most Geminis, needs an escape from the mundane. And for him, with that Libra ascendant, it's even more important to strike a balance. A relationship such as yours, which has burned so hot and intensely at first, can easily be smothered to nothing, if you don't keep on fanning the flames.'

'That doesn't sound too bad, does it?' Jude said. 'Zoë can be my stability, and I can fan her flames. Win–win.'

Indigo did the eyebrow thing again. 'Then there's nothing to worry about, is there? Unless you'd like a tarot reading, just to be sure?'

'Maybe next time,' I said. 'But I'd love to hear more about your art. That painting is amazing – you're seriously talented.'

And that was the end of the mysticism talk, thank heavens. Indigo chatted away, a lot more normally, about how she sold her paintings online and at car boot sales, and even asked me a bit about my work, and Jude listened and occasionally made a flattering comment about one or the other of us. We finished the cava, Indigo opened a bottle of red wine and Jude suggested ordering a takeaway, but it turned out Indigo was on one of her fast days, so we didn't.

And at about nine o'clock we finally said goodbye and left.

'Do you think she was right, about us not really being compatible? In terms of astrology, I mean?' I asked Jude, as we started the long descent of the stairs.

He laughed. 'Oh God, don't give it a second thought. Ind loves a bit of drama. Besides, it's…'

'All bollocks really?'

'Exactly! Although I'd never say that to her, because she's a mate and stuff. But the main thing is, you and me, we're good, right?'

'Well, I will be, once I've had something to eat.'

So we stopped off at a Turkish restaurant on the way home and had loads of falafel and chips and salad, and then we went back to my flat and were both too knackered to do anything other than fall into bed and hold each other close.

But once Jude was asleep, I found myself wondering what Indigo had really meant. Maybe she genuinely believed what she'd said was true. But I doubted that, somehow. I'd noticed her looking at Jude with something like hunger, which might of course have been down to the fast day. (I mean, really. The longest I'd ever gone without food had been twenty-four hours, when I'd had a killer stomach bug, and by the end of that I'd practically been climbing the walls.) I couldn't shake the feeling that she was as suspicious of me as I was of her, and for the same reason.

That only strengthened my resolve. Jude and I were together. I was going to make this work. I was going to keep the flame of passion burning in our relationship, whatever it took. I had a boyfriend, and I wasn't going to let some eyebrow-raising, tarot-reading, high-cheekboned rival come between us.

Chapter Nineteen

Peace and happiness may be found today in nature, but don't forget that the tides have power and tigers have teeth.

It was ten o'clock and I was still in bed – my first morning off in ages and, crucially, what felt like the first free time in ages that I didn't have to spend combing the internet for potential dates. It had been three weeks since Jude had… not moved in, exactly. But moved in. And I still hadn't quite got my head around the fact that I was no longer single.

It seemed Jude had moved in with me permanently. His laptop was on my coffee table, his guitar was propped up against the wall, his clothes were… well, pretty much everywhere. Task one for my morning off was going to have to be putting on a load of washing – or more like three, judging by the amount of stuff there was draped over the sofa, half under the bed and covering most of the floor.

When I'd suggested to Jude that we do a bit of cleaning together, he'd said that he had work to do and wasn't housework a ridiculously bourgeois construct, anyway? And to be fair to him, he was working brutally long hours, often leaving the flat before seven and not returning until nine or ten at night. And it was all for virtually no pay – as an intern, his transport costs were covered and he got an allowance for lunch, but that was it.

His commitment to the cause impressed me, but I couldn't help wondering what it would be like to have a live-in boyfriend who I actually saw sometimes, as opposed to just seeing his stuff.

At the window behind me, open to the warm, breezy morning, I heard Frazzle give his familiar chirrup of longing. The blackbirds that had been nesting in the beer garden had kept him fascinated for days: he perched on the windowsill, his fluffy orange tail twitching with frustration, his whiskers bristling, as he watched the parents fly back and forth to their nest. As I watched, he stretched his jaw open in an enormous yawn, then started the little clicking cries again.

'You're on a hiding to nothing, Frazz,' I told him. 'Those birds can fly, and you can't. You've got claws; they've got wings. Deal with it.'

Frazzle turned and gave me a hard stare. Clearly he expected his human servant to go out and bring him a bird to play with. Telling him to stop being so ridiculous, I heaved myself out of bed and pulled on a pair of frayed denim shorts and an old T-shirt. My shower could wait – by the time I'd finished cleaning the flat, I certainly wouldn't be clean myself.

How, I wondered, could Jude have accumulated so much stuff in just a few weeks? There were newspapers everywhere – the *Guardian*, the *New Statesman*, the *Morning Star*, the *Daily Mirror* – most of them unread because Jude, like everyone else, got the news from Twitter. There was a teetering stack of vinyl LPs that he'd picked up from the side of the road where someone had left them after a clear-out. The same person had been getting rid of a load of old cookery books – Delia Smith, Marguerite Patten and *The Microwave Gourmet* – and Jude had brought them home because they'd have ended up in landfill otherwise and he thought I might want them. I hadn't had the heart to tell him I really, really didn't.

'We've got a hoarder on our hands,' I told Frazzle. 'You won't be able to get to your catnip mice at this rate.'

But I suspected that if I did what I so longed to do and took the whole lot out to the recycling, Jude would be hurt and annoyed. So I put a load of washing on and started the arduous task of sorting everything into more or less orderly piles.

From his spot on the windowsill, Frazzle gave another frantic chatter. I turned to see what was going on, and froze. There, on the ledge less than four inches from his nose, was a small, newly fledged blackbird. Frazz had gone quiet, frozen, clearly unable to believe his good fortune. Helpless, immobile prey didn't just land under cats' noses, I could imagine him thinking, *Surely this must be some kind of trick?*

But he didn't freeze for long. Before I could cross the room, he'd pounced. The bird gave a frantic flap of its wings and managed, just in time, to take off – only instead of flying to safety, it flew into the flat, closely pursued by my cat.

'Shit! Frazzle, come here. Leave the bird alone!'

But Frazzle wasn't listening. He wanted to investigate this gift from the cat gods further. The bird had landed on the carpet and Frazzle was watching it, transfixed, as if he knew that just one more pounce would do the trick. I tried to grab him but, for the first time ever, he growled at me and darted underneath the bed.

It was fair enough, I suppose. In that moment, I wasn't his loving human, provider of food, fuss, warmth and exciting games involving a sparkly fishing-rod toy. I was a deadly rival, intent on stealing his prey. And that was exactly what I was going to do. But I was too slow. The fledgling ran a few uncertain steps, then found the use of its wings and flapped frantically, managing a brief flight that took it to the top of the bathroom door, where it perched, hunched over in terror.

'Fuck, fuck, fuck. Frazzle, you are such a naughty cat. What the hell do I do now?'

I was no ornithologist, but I knew that cats' teeth and claws could be lethal to this tiny creature. Just because it had managed a short maiden flight didn't mean it would be able to find its way back out through the window. And besides, Frazzle had emerged from under the bed and was crouched on the floor, waiting for the bird to leave its precarious perch.

I'm here for the long game, he seemed to be saying. *One of us is going to give up first and it isn't going to be me.*

I needed to shut the cat away, but I couldn't, because the only door inside my small flat was the one the bird was using as a temporary refuge. I needed to rescue the bird, but I wasn't tall enough to reach it.

I needed help.

Scooping Frazzle up in my arms, ignoring his wriggling protests, I hurried out of the flat and down the stairs to the pub. Someone would be there who could rescue the bird – someone taller than me, which meant practically anyone.

But Robbie would be alone in the kitchen, with hot pans on the stovetop that couldn't be left. Alice was sitting at a table with Maurice and the rest of the pub's committee, deep in conversation. Fat Don was at his usual place at the bar, no doubt already on his third pint of the day, and would be absolutely no help to me.

I hesitated for a second. Even though Alice wasn't much taller than me, she was sensible, and so were all the others – Maurice and various worthy people drawn from the local community. One of them would know what to do.

But then Frazzle started to squirm even more determinedly in my arms, his claws raking across my bare shoulder. He freed himself from my grasp, jumped down to the floor with an affronted meow and trotted off towards one of the corner tables.

I hadn't noticed Adam there. He had the D&D set open on the table and was drawing what looked like a massively complex map on a pad of graph paper. There was a pack of coloured felt-tip pens in front of him, pencils, a ruler and a book called *The Mega Monster Companion*, which I'd never seen before.

I followed Frazzle towards him, and he raised his head, clocked me and hastily flipped the pad closed. Frazz jumped up on his lap and started to purr.

'I'm sorry, I wasn't trying to spy on you,' I said.

'I didn't think you were. I just didn't want to spoil anything for our next game. I've got the day off work and I thought I'd come and do some planning here – it feels like I'm in the zone. How's Frazzle?'

'He's a cold-blooded murderer. Do you know anything about birds?'

I blurted out an explanation of the situation, and Adam got up, scooping Frazzle back onto his chair.

'You keep that chair warm,' he instructed the cat. 'And stay here until you're called. Understand?'

Frazzle looked at him and blinked, like whatever Adam wanted was fine with him.

'Thanks so much. I honestly don't know what to do. It's up on top of a door and I can't reach it and I don't know if it's hurt.'

'Come on then,' Adam said. 'Rescue mission under way.'

We hurried up the stairs to my flat, and I opened the door cautiously, half expecting the bird to fly out into the stairwell and create a whole new set of problems. But it was still huddled where I had left it.

'Right.' Adam glanced around and picked up a T-shirt from the floor. 'Okay if I use this?'

I nodded and stammered out an apology for the mess, which Adam ignored.

He approached the bird slowly, reached up and lifted it down, wrapped safely in the soft cotton.

'Wow,' I said, 'you just picked it up.'

'It doesn't know yet to be afraid of people,' Adam said. 'It's just a baby. Now, have you got a box with a lid?'

I passed him the cardboard crate Jude's LP records had come in, and he carefully lowered the bird into it.

'Hot-water bottle?'

'I've got one of those microwave wheat-bag things. I use it after the gym sometimes.'

'That'll do, if we wrap it up in something.'

Another T-shirt was pressed into service.

'He looks okay, doesn't he?' I peered into the box, but the baby bird didn't look back at me; it was hunched down, its newly grown feathers looking ruffled and unkempt. 'I mean, not like its wing is broken or anything? It seemed to be flying okay.'

'Yeah, but I think it's more worrying if Frazzle clawed it.' Adam's head leaned over the box, close to mine. He smelled of coffee and shampoo. 'It's got no immune resistance to that, and it could get infected and… well…'

'Die.'

He nodded. 'There's a local wildlife rescue place. Want me to call them?'

I nodded. Suddenly I felt like I wouldn't be able to explain the situation to anyone without starting to cry. It was just a bird – just a blackbird, not even something rare or endangered (other than by my cat), but I was flooded with awareness, all at once, of the fragility of life. How easily that little bird's first flight could be its last; how everywhere, all the time, lives were being snuffed out like candles on a birthday cake.

I waited as Adam called, talked and listened.

'Right,' he said, tucking his phone back in his pocket. 'We've done the right thing, keeping him warm. They say to bring him in and they'll check him out, and if he seems okay there's a chance we can bring him back here and the mum and dad might carry on feeding him.'

'You can hear them now,' I said. 'I've got so used to the noise outside my window I hardly notice it. But listen.'

We stood there together in my messy flat. I could hear the traffic on the street outside, the rattle of a delivery of beer to Archie's shop next door, a child crying. But above it all, closer, were the urgent cheeps of the blackbird parents, trying in vain to summon their little one back to safety.

'They're worried about their baby,' I said, my voice going a bit hoarse.

'Just as well he's in good hands, then.'

'He won't die, will he?'

Adam looked down at the box cradled against his chest. 'I don't know. But I hope not.'

'It's just… if he does, it'll be my fault.' I felt a tear inching down my cheek and brushed it away.

'Hey, Zoë. It won't be your fault. Or Frazzle's even. You did everything you could. And Frazzle – well, you can't expect a cat to appreciate the sanctity of life, can you?'

I managed a laugh. 'I guess not.'

Adam unwrapped one arm from around the box, and for a second I wondered if he was going to reach out to put his hand on my shoulder. I could have totally done with a hug right then. But there was a rustle from inside the box as the baby bird lurched from one side to the other, no doubt beginning to wonder why it was trapped in this dark, weird-smelling space, and Adam hastily steadied it in both arms.

'I guess we should get him looked at,' I said.

'Shall we go together?' Adam agreed. 'We can get an Uber.'

'Yes. Let's go together.'

Chapter Twenty

What you want to feel is a bit different from what you're actually feeling, isn't it, Aquarius?

'So it was fine in the end,' I said. 'We took the little bird to the wildlife place and a vet looked at him – actually, it turned out he was a her, so that told me with my male-centred view of wildlife – and he gave her antibiotics even though he couldn't see any puncture wounds or anything. And he said we did the right thing by keeping her warm, and the trip in the Uber was actually a good thing because it gave her a chance to recover from the shock.'

Jude looked up from his phone and took a gulp of beer. 'That's good.'

Then his eyes returned to the screen.

We were – at least in theory – on a date. But the location of the date was my flat, and the meal and booze had both been liberated by me from the pub downstairs. I'd paid, of course, using my staff discount, and it made sense for us not to go out, out, given that neither of us could really afford to eat anywhere other than the

Ginger Cat – certainly not anywhere that would do food and drink of the same quality.

But still, it did feel a bit discouraging, somehow, to be eating food on my night off that I'd cooked for the customers the night before, and which was destined for the staff dinner that evening. Not that there was anything wrong with it – it was my special bean chilli, made with no less than four different sorts of hot peppers and loads of other secret spices, and there were flatbreads and rice and guacamole and cashew cream on the side. Thanks to my delayed housework, the flat was clean and tidy and there were candles glowing on the coffee table. Jude had even written on the bathroom mirror in soap, 'D8 NITE', with a massive heart underneath.

Frazzle, however, was still sulking over the removal of his prey and had taken himself off downstairs to the bar like a stroppy husband to scrounge bits of Robbie's lamb tagine off anyone who'd indulge him.

I drank some of my red wine. 'And we brought her back and put her back in the garden like the vet said, and I definitely saw the parents feeding her. Apparently it's a myth that birds will abandon their chicks if they've been handled by humans. They don't even know, because they hardly have any sense of smell. Which makes sense, doesn't it?'

'What?' Jude said.

'The baby bird. And she's not there now, so she must have flown away, either back to the nest or somewhere else, I'm not sure. But Frazz definitely hasn't eaten her because he's been in the pub all afternoon. Anyway, how was your day?'

'Amazing,' he said. 'I sat in on a consultation with a group of factory workers who were going to be laid off, and it looks like we'll reach a compromise to save their jobs. That's fourteen families who'll still be bringing in an income. I feel like I'm really making a difference, and I'm learning all the time. I just can't wait to be able to get my teeth into some actual work, if that makes sense, rather than just observing and shadowing.'

'And you must be making useful contacts,' I suggested, pouring myself some more wine. 'I mean, I know it shouldn't be who you know rather than what you know, but it's like that everywhere, isn't it?'

Jude brightened. 'I've been invited to a meeting of the Alliance for Labour Liberty tomorrow and a meeting of the Workers' Liberty League the next day. And I'm having a beer with some guys from the Revolutionary Workers' Alliance next week.'

I couldn't help giggling. 'Isn't that just like the scene in the Monty Python film, with the Judean People's Front and the People's Front of Judea?'

'I don't watch that film any more,' Jude said. 'It's horribly transphobic.'

'Oh. I suppose it is. But they do sound just the same, don't they? How do you know which is which?'

'It's perfectly simple. The Alliance for Labour Liberty is a socialist collective, aimed at changing the party machinery from within. The Workers' Liberty League is a grassroots Marxist organisation and the RWA are – obviously – revolutionary Maoists.'

He carried on explaining, and I listened carefully. I knew that what he was saying was important, and I ought to know this stuff already. But I couldn't stop my mind wandering a bit. I remembered how panicked I'd felt about the baby bird, and how calmly Adam had dealt with the situation. I wondered what would have happened if he hadn't been there – it didn't bear thinking about. I imagined the little fledgling, out there somewhere in the night, hopefully safe in the nest with its parents.

'So you should come along,' Jude was saying, snapping my mind back to the present. 'There's a speaker from the Green Party and someone from the Climate Coalition. It should be really interesting.'

'Uh… sorry, when was this again? I'll have to check if I can get time off.'

'Next Wednesday. Indigo's going to be there. She was just texting me now.'

So that was what he'd been doing, staring so intently at his phone. Texting Indigo. I felt a hollow pit of anxiety forming in my stomach, and had to remind myself that I was meant to be fanning the flames of passion between us and not stifling him.

'Sure, I'd love to come.' If I was honest, I'd rather have done something with just Jude and me. But if the options on offer were Jude, Indigo and me or just Jude and Indigo, I knew what I was going to pick. 'Would you like more chilli?'

Jude drained his beer and yawned. 'I'm all good. And shattered. I'm going to shower and hit the sack.'

I cleared up our plates and went to collect Frazzle from the bar, gave him his dinner (which he was unenthusiastic about, whether because he was still sulking about the baby bird or because he'd been fed scraps by too many of the pub regulars, I couldn't tell) and hung the final load of washing on the airer to dry. When Jude had finished in the bathroom I got ready for bed and slid under the duvet next to him.

'Come here.' He held out his arms and I edged closer, leaning my head against his chest and breathing in the clean smell of him. He kissed me and I felt the now-familiar beginnings of caresses as his fingers moved from my back around to my breasts. But instead of the flickering of desire that would ignite and grow until it consumed me completely, I felt something else.

I couldn't put a name to it at first. It was like although my skin was warm under the bedcovers and warmer where Jude's hands were, inside me was all cold. I remembered the last time we'd had sex, two or three nights before, and how, like almost every time, it had been over almost before it had even begun. I remembered taking Jude's hand afterwards and guiding it gently between my legs, and waiting. And how he'd stroked me for a few seconds, casually, not really taking any notice of my response, before kissing me, telling me he loved me and I was beautiful and amazing, and then rolling over and going to sleep.

I knew that was what would happen again this time. I knew I had to talk to him about it, but I didn't want to hurt his feelings, and how on earth could you tell a man that sex with him wasn't working without hurting his feelings, exactly? If I hurt him, I might lose him, and then what? But the thought of what was going to happen in the next few minutes – the growing surge of desire and then the disappointment and resentment I'd feel when it was over for him and also for me, way before I was ready for it to be – and the prospect of that happening over and over and over again, and me being powerless to ever change it, was awful.

I knew what I was feeling, I realised, as he moved on top of me. It was dread. I remembered the message the Stargazer app had sent to me that morning, and I felt totally seen.

'Jude, I'm too tired,' I said. 'Not tonight, okay?'

*

The next morning, feeling horrendously guilty for some reason I didn't quite want to pin down, I got up early and silently, careful not to wake Jude, showered and went downstairs to the dark, silent pub. The cleaners had recently left, I could tell, because the smell of bleach was still hanging in the air, overlaying the smells of long-dead fires, beer and varnished wood, which were so familiar to me now I barely noticed them.

I let Frazzle out into the garden, then glanced into the kitchen and saw that everything was in order, ready for Robbie and me to start the day. There was the bread to prove, the breakfast pastries to bake, a vegetable delivery coming at nine and a vat of stock to reduce. But there was no hurry for any of that; no urgency. It was only six thirty and I could enjoy half an hour of blissful solitude with a coffee.

Every day used to be like this, I remembered, back when it was just me and Frazzle. I'd imagined that the rest of my life might end up being the same way, and even embraced the idea. But now, I'd got used to sharing my space with Jude – well, used-ish. However crowded the tiny flat might sometimes feel, whatever doubts were threatening to grow in my mind, there was no doubt that having another person in bed with me was reassuring; that I was only starting to realise that I hadn't just been alone, but also lonely.

I carried my mug over to a table by the window, pulled up the cheerful orange-and-green-striped blind and sat down. The street outside was just beginning to get busy. Early commuters hurried past on their way to the station, laptop bags slung over their shoulders and phones clamped to their ears. A lorry rumbled by on its way to deliver an order to the Sainsbury's supermarket down the road. The woman who owned the florist a few doors down parked her neon-pink van on a double yellow line, jumped out and began unloading armfuls of blooms and foliage. As I watched, the sun emerged over the rooftops opposite, and the street was suddenly flooded with light.

I noticed a man standing outside the pub, stock-still, staring up at my flat. He was wearing jeans, an open-necked white shirt and a leather jacket, and he, too, was carrying a laptop bag and a phone. A totally normal-looking guy on his way to work – so why was he staring up at my window like that?

It was only when the sunlight illuminated him that I realised it was Adam.

I put down my half-finished coffee and opened the door, stepping out into the bright morning. The sound alerted him to my presence and he spun around. He didn't look surprised to see me, or guilty about having been caught loitering in the street outside the pub, though. He smiled and beckoned me over.

'Look, Zoë. Look up there.'

I took the few steps over to join him and followed his pointing finger. High up in the tree were four blackbirds, all chirping their heads off. It might have been their song that had woken me so early.

'Do you think one of them's our one?'

He pushed back his sunglasses. 'Hard to tell. See the brownish-coloured one? That's the mum.'

'And the one with the bright yellow beak is the dad, right? I wish I'd paid attention to how many babies there were originally. They both look the same.'

We craned our necks upwards, trying to make out the two dusty-looking black-brown chicks up in the tree.

'They're not the prettiest birds ever, are they?' Adam said.

'How can you even say that about our baby bird? They're adorable.'

He looked at me and we both laughed. Laughter changed his whole face, showing off his straight white teeth and making him look almost handsome.

'We could feed them, I guess,' he suggested. 'Or leave food for the parents to give them.'

'What do blackbirds even eat?'

'Didn't the rescue place say worms yesterday?'

'Yeah, that's right. We can't exactly hunt worms to give them, can we?'

'Well, we could, but…'

'I'm a vegan. Mostly, anyway. I can't go around murdering worms, even if it is to feed a bird.'

'Hold on.' Adam tapped at his phone a bit. 'They like fat balls, apparently. But they can't eat off hanging bird feeders because they're too big. We could set up a bird table for them in the pub garden if your boss wouldn't mind.'

'Alice loves animals – she'll be dead keen on that. But won't Frazzle think it's a cat table, with an all-you-can-eat bird buffet?'

'All-you-can-eat buffets can't fly.'

'Good point.'

'So why don't I order one? I'll get it delivered here and swing by tomorrow morning and we can set it up.'

'Deal,' I said. 'Thanks, Adam.'

Adam shook his head. 'It's nothing. I'd better dash, I've got an eight a.m. meeting.'

And before I could properly say goodbye, or even thank him again, he'd strode off down the road, his legs long and strong in his dark grey jeans and his fingers flying over the face of his phone as he walked.

I don't know where Adam shopped, but it must have been the bird equivalent of Harrods, because the feeding table that arrived later that day was the poshest thing ever. It came in an enormous, glossy cardboard box with a picture of the finished article printed on it: painted pale green, it had a little pillared fence thing around the edge like a fancy colonial house might have and was mounted on a tall pole that I reckoned would make it almost Frazzle-proof. Along with it was another, plain box that I presumed contained food to put in it, and, together, they filled every inch of available space in Alice's tiny office.

Throughout the afternoon, I kept glancing out of the windows at the front of the pub and the door at the back, checking that the birds were still there.

'Hang in there,' I told them. 'Tomorrow your life of luxury will begin.'

As good as his word, Adam turned up before seven the next morning, yawning and smelling freshly showered, his hair still damp. He followed me through the empty, silent pub and I showed him the boxes.

'Blimey.'

'Blimey is right. They're huge. Shall we get them outside?'

Together, we heaved the boxes out through the back door and into the garden, Frazzle watching us warily from the top of the fence. I fetched a knife from the kitchen and carefully slit open the tape that sealed the bigger box. Adam tipped it up, and about a million pieces of glossy green-painted wood slid out onto the grass, together with a little bag containing dozens of screws, nuts, bolts and Allen keys of varying sizes and, finally, a single A4 sheet of printed instructions.

'Okay,' Adam said. 'I'm not sure I'm qualified for this.'

'How hard can it be? I've put together enough Ikea chests of drawers in my time.'

'You're in charge, then.'

I picked up the assembly sheet and looked at it, then turned it the other way and looked at it again. Adam peered over my shoulder, so close I could feel his warm breath on my neck.

'Uh… Maybe this is a bit more complicated than I thought.'

'It looks like we've got to make the base first,' he said. 'Then that long pole thing fixes onto it. Then we put together the main bird-house bit, and that gets mounted on the top.'

'Do all those fancy little balustrade things have to be screwed on individually? Seriously?'

'Hey, I thought you only wanted the best for our birds.'

I laughed. 'I'd best get screwing then.'

Half an hour later, we were almost done. The main post had toppled over and landed on Adam's foot. The instruction sheet had blown away and I'd only just managed to catch it before it flew over the fence and was gone forever. Frazzle had come to help and carried one of the Allen keys away in his mouth. And we were almost helpless with laughter.

'Oh my God, we are so crap at this,' I said, inspecting a scrape on my knuckle and a corresponding smear of blood on the pale-green wood.

'Those birds need to get some competent staff.'

'As opposed to Tweedledum and Tweedledumber here.'

'What do you suppose we do with that bit?'

'No idea. Shall we just put the roof on and hope for the best?'

'Let's. And then I should probably get to work; I'm already going to be late.'

We finished the assembly as best we could, loaded up the bird feeder with fat balls, peanuts and even a whole sunflower head, then stood back to admire our handiwork, watched by Frazzle and an inquisitive squirrel.

Then Adam said reluctantly that he really needed to go and dashed off through the bar before I could even thank him properly.

All morning, Robbie and I kept sticking our heads out from the kitchen to see if any birds had arrived. We didn't spot any that day, only the squirrel and a few of his mates, but the next morning there was totally, definitely a blackbird there, feasting away, and soon it was joined by another. I took a photo and sent it to Adam, and he replied with a heart emoji.

Chapter Twenty-One

You know what they say about boredom, Aquarius? It only ever affects boring people.

After that, I started having a coffee in the bar each morning, keeping an eye out for Adam on his way to work. A couple of times, in the beginning, I didn't see him before I had to go into the kitchen to begin my work. But on Friday, after I'd sent another bird pic the previous day, I saw him walking down the road before seven, with his laptop bag and his sunglasses, which I'd noticed were well classy vintage Ray-Bans. In the darkness of the bar, I watched as he paused, stopped, looked up into the tree, then looked at the window where I was sitting.

I raised a hand and waved, and his face broke out into a grin and he hurried to the door.

'Come in,' I said. 'We're not open yet, obviously, but still.'

I hustled him through the pub, lit only by the early sunshine, and out of the back door, opening it cautiously with a finger to my lips.

Adam nodded and stepped silently outside behind me.

On the bird table were three blackbirds: the mum and two of the coal-feathered youngsters. As we watched, a robin flew down hopefully, but the mum flapped her wings aggressively at it and it departed, looking as pissed off as it's possible for a common garden bird to look. We could see Frazzle crouched under one of the wooden picnic tables, just as transfixed as we were. On the roof of Archie's shop next door, a squirrel was hopefully waiting its turn.

'Like trying to get a table at the Chiltern Firehouse. Apparently it can take months, and that's just if you're a celebrity,' I whispered.

Adam laughed. 'I'm going there for lunch, actually, with work. It's not all that. I'd rather have sausages and wedges here.'

'Wow. That's quite the work lunch. What is it you do?'

'Nothing exciting. I just work in cyber security for a hedge fund. But my boss likes splashing the cash on lunches and stuff. He's really old-school like that.'

If I'd ever thought of what Adam might do for a living – which I hadn't really – I'd have assumed it was something IT-related. It was all of a piece with the algebra equation T-shirt I'd seen him wear and the laptop bag that seemed to be permanently attached to his shoulder. But I'd never have associated that with something as full-on fabulous as lunch at one of Mayfair's most exclusive restaurants.

'Lucky you. You'll have to tell me all about it. Maybe over a coffee and some bird-watching tomorrow?'

'Maybe,' Adam said, but his face had kind of closed up. 'I'd best be on my way. Thanks for showing me the birds.'

'Thanks for bringing the bird table,' I said, but I had to say it to his departing back, because he'd already hurried off back into the pub, and by the time I got inside myself, the front door was already swinging shut behind him.

*

The next Thursday was pizza night at the Ginger Cat, so my presence wasn't required and Dani and I were *out*-out. I couldn't remember the last time I'd been able to get dressed up and go for cocktails with a mate, and I was practically giddy with excitement, especially as I hadn't seen her at the gym for over a week. I was wearing a strappy black satin shift dress and, although I'd drawn the lines at heels, I was in one of my less battered pairs of Converse. My hair was behaving itself and I'd put on bright red lipstick which made me feel like I didn't know what to do with my mouth.

However pleased I might have felt with my appearance when I left the flat, I knew no one would ever look twice at me with Dani around, though. She was wearing a black velvet bodysuit, high-necked but sleeveless, a tiny leather miniskirt and black suede shoe boots with massive heels that made her tower over me.

But comparisons didn't matter – neither of us was interested in pulling, obviously; we were just there to get totally shitfaced on brightly coloured, too-sweet cocktails, and maybe even dance.

We were already on our second round of drinks that involved pink gin, lychee juice and sherbet, and we'd ordered a bowl of spicy Bombay mix that came, for some reason I couldn't fathom, with chopsticks. But everything here was both complicated and fabulous – even the drinks were served in two parts, with a tiny copper bucket hanging off the side of the glass so you mixed them yourself and watched them fizz up spectacularly.

The room was lit by neon tubing, Madonna's 'Like a Virgin' was playing and I knew that I was going to get to spend the evening not thinking about work, or Jude, or even how much the bill would be at the end of the night.

But Dani seemed preoccupied. I'd asked her whether she'd been to the gym recently, and she'd said she wasn't really feeling it right now, but she was sure she'd get back into it soon. I'd asked her how work was going, and instead of launching into a tirade about her boss messing her about, patients not turning up for appointments and then blaming it on the text-message reminder system not working, and people expecting refunds for tooth-whitening systems that had already spent several nights literally in their mouths, she'd just said, 'Okay.'

Clearly, much more alcohol was going to be required for her to open up to me about what was wrong.

'Look, they do strawberry milkshakes with vodka in them!' I said. 'I can't have one because of the dairy but you can. Go on, take one for the team.'

'Only if you have the lemonade that's basically fizzy rum.'

'With a stick of rock in it. Sold.'

Our drinks came, and we ordered a bowl of fries that came with ketchup in one of those squeezy red plastic tomatoes, and we sipped and ate, stuffing our mouths with crunchy saltiness until our lips puckered and we had to drink even more.

And after a bit, Dani said, 'Zoë, do you mind if I ask you something?'

'Course not.'

'Have you ever been to a sex club?'

I tried very hard not to let shock register on my face. I mean, not that I thought there was anything wrong with stuff like that. Far from it. I wasn't going to shame or blame anyone for their bedroom goings-on. But it was so far outside my experience as to be almost unimaginable. She might as well have asked me if I'd ever snogged Russell Brand – although, if what I'd read about Russell's love life was true, that was far more likely.

'Can't say I have,' I admitted. 'In fact, to be perfectly honest, I've slept with six people in my entire life. If I went to a sex club I could double that in one evening, couldn't I?'

I hoped that Dani would return the courtesy of me not judging her by not judging me, because I felt horribly naïve and vanilla in comparison to her.

'I haven't either,' she assured me hastily. 'But Fabian wants us to. He says it's a massive thing now, everyone does it, it's no big deal and it'll make our relationship so much stronger.'

'Okay…' That sounded like typical Fabian. 'But do you actually want to do it?'

'I don't know. Part of me thinks it's just the most cringe thing ever, and I can't get past imagining wipe-clean pleather sofas and bowls of condoms and being hit on by sleazy guys I wouldn't ever shag in a million years. But also, Fabian's got me to try other things I haven't been sure about and some of them have ended up being kind of hot.'

And the ones that haven't? I thought.

I said, 'Honestly, if it were me, I'd be completely freaked out. I'd be worried about how I'd feel if my boyfriend shagged someone else in front of me, and about how he'd feel if I did. And I'd be all self-conscious about being the only person there with ginger pubes. Or any pubes. But maybe it's different once you're there, if you get into it.'

Dani took the straw out of her drink and chewed it, then grimaced and stopped. 'Yuck. It's one of those paper ones, and it's disintegrating in my mouth.'

'But you're helping to save the planet, right?'

She laughed. 'I guess a mouth full of paper is a price worth paying. But the thing is, Fabian's way more experienced than me. He's been with loads of girls and he watches loads of porn and I kind of feel like there's this massive expectation that I'll be into the same stuff.'

'Like what?' I couldn't help asking, even though the thought of Fabian knocking one out to a porno gave me the literal shivers.

'Like some poor woman having a load of men spunking all over her face until she looks like a plasterer's radio. But other stuff, too. He likes me to dress up.'

'An ex of mine tried that once,' I remembered. 'I don't know what got into his head. I was in bed and he came into the room with an eyepatch on and a stripy jumper, and a breadknife stuck into his belt, and he was like, "Yarrr, a fine filly we have here, me hearties."'

'What?' Dani spluttered. 'He dressed up as a pirate?'

'He did. But I don't think he'd really thought it through. I tried to play along. I said, "No, sir, I am an innocent girl. Do not defile me!" and I pretended to cry, and he went, "Oh my God, Zoë, I'm so sorry," and got into bed with me and gave me a massive hug, and that was the end of that. Well, the end of the pirate thing. We had sex, obviously, once I'd explained that I hadn't really been scared.'

And that had been the end of any kind of fantasy role-playing sex games with Joe. We hadn't needed to spice things up, not really – sex with him had always been amazing. But maybe it would be better with Jude if I made more of an effort? Maybe I should invest in stripper heels and cut-out bras and thong knickers that would get stuck up my bum crack and give me thrush? Maybe I was too boring, and that was why it wasn't working out like I'd hoped?

'Fabian keeps telling me about stuff he got up to with his exes,' Dani said, when we'd ordered another round of drinks. 'Threesomes with other girls, and even with other blokes. It just makes me feel so inadequate, like I should be up for all that stuff, when really I'm just not. But I want to be good enough for him. The sex club thing… he says we don't have to even do anything – we can just go along and watch. But I don't know if I want to watch a bunch of strangers getting it on.'

'Honestly, I can't think of anything worse. Like watching other people play computer games or something. Wouldn't you be like, "No, don't do it that way!" Or you'd be worried that you were staring and it was rude.'

'I know, right? But then he tells me I'm so hot, and he wants to show me off, and that's nice, isn't it?'

'It's only nice if it's what you want to do, surely?'

'I know – you're right really. But when we're actually having sex and he talks about this stuff, I kind of go along with it. Maybe it's just fantasy, and all he wants to do is talk about it?'

'I wish there was more of that with Jude,' I admitted. 'Not sex clubs, obviously. But it's… well, I wouldn't say it's crap. But when we shag, it's always over in, like, a few seconds and I worry it's because he doesn't fancy me enough and he just wants to get it over with. I don't know what to do.'

'Of course he fancies you! Why wouldn't he? Maybe you've just got into a rut. Maybe you need to spice things up a bit.'

Surely two months isn't long enough to be in a rut, I thought. 'Spice things up how?'

'Like, buy some saucy new underwear. Light candles. Stuff like that. Nothing major. Just – you know – let him know you're up for it.'

'I guess,' I said, thinking without much enthusiasm about scratchy lacy knickers that would be a case of thrush waiting to happen.

'And talk to him,' Dani went on. 'Tell him what you're into. Guys love that. They're dead eager to please, really.'

'You need to be honest with Fabian, too,' I advised. 'Maybe have a proper talk about it, when you've both got your clothes on, and tell him what your boundaries are. Isn't that how it's supposed to work, with safe words and stuff? And if he suggests anything you're not into, just say no.'

'That's all very well.' Dani sighed. 'But with Fabian, it's just not as easy as that.'

Chapter Twenty-Two

When opportunity knocks, will you open the door or stay under the covers? Take control of your destiny and you might notice your luck beginning to change.

It was almost a week before I saw Adam again. I still checked up on the birds every morning, and Robbie made a point of leaving bacon rind out for them instead of putting it in the kitchen food-waste bin. The blackbirds and the robin seemed to have made peace, and most mornings I saw them together, feasting at the bird table, joined by a couple of nondescript little brown birds I couldn't identify.

Then, on the morning of our next Dungeons & Dragons game, I spotted Adam walking down the street on his way to the station, and almost without thinking I found myself opening the door of the Ginger Cat and stepping out to intercept him.

'Morning,' I said.

Adam's eyes flicked beyond me for a second, like he was considering blanking me and hurrying on past. But, to my relief, he didn't.

'Hi, Zoë.'

'Fancy a coffee?'

'I should really… oh, go on, then.'

'Come in.'

We walked into the empty pub and I switched on the coffee machine, its roar sounding even louder than usual in the early-morning silence. The heady smell of fresh coffee filled the pub as I opened the canister of organic, fair-trade Rwandan beans.

'Double espresso?' I asked.

'How did you guess?'

I laughed. 'Come on. You're clearly an espresso drinker. I've been a cook for long enough to have a kind of sixth sense of what people are going to order. I guess it helps that I'm Aquarius, and we're highly intuitive.'

The Stargazer app, I realised, had been upping the ante lately. Its push notifications, which had often been acerbic, were now sometimes downright vicious – so it was just as well, I told myself, that I didn't take any of this stuff too seriously. But mentioning it was a good way to needle Adam, and it worked.

'You do know that's—' he began.

'A load of rubbish? So you said before. But I knew how you like your coffee, without having to ask, didn't I?'

Adam grinned and shook his head, but he accepted a perfect espresso from me gratefully, and I pushed open the door to the garden.

'Let's see how those fledglings are getting on, then,' he said.

We stood in the doorway and looked out at the garden. It wasn't up to much, really – just a little square of paving stones with weeds growing up between some of them, a couple of wooden picnic tables, the giant barbecue under its canvas cover, and a few hanging baskets that Alice had planted with geraniums and pansies, a bit bedraggled-looking now that summer was coming to an end, and of course the bird table. But in the cool morning, with a bright bar of golden sunlight falling across it and birdsong filling the air, it felt almost magical.

I could feel the warmth of Adam's arm next to my shoulder, hear him breathing and smell the fragrant steam from his coffee and whatever shower gel he'd used – the scent was as fresh as a gin and tonic on a hot evening.

As we watched, the male and female blackbirds fluttered down and started helping themselves to mealworms. The robin joined in, too, and a couple of fat pigeons pecked around below, snapping up any bits that got dropped.

'Where are the babies, though?' I fretted.

'Maybe they'll come,' Adam said, 'if we wait.'

We waited, but there were no baby blackbirds. In the past few days, I'd found it harder and harder to tell which were the fledglings and which the parents, but I'd been watching them for long enough to just about know the difference, and I was sure that only the adults were there for breakfast.

'What if something's happened to them?' I asked. 'What if Frazzle…'

'You'd have known,' Adam said. 'He'd have presented you with a body, wouldn't he? Or have feathers in his whiskers or something.'

I shuddered. 'Yes, I suppose so. But then where are they?'

Adam hesitated, then he said, 'I expect they've gone.'

'Gone?'

'I was reading about it online. They stay with the parents for a couple of weeks after they learn to fly, and then they go off to find their own territory, and the adults start a new family.'

'But…' Absurdly, I felt tears stinging my eyes. 'But what will they do, without us to look after them? What if, wherever they've gone, there's no food for them?'

'They'll be okay,' Adam said. 'Their instinct will help them find a good place to live. At least, I hope so.'

We looked at each other for a second. Adam's face was as full of doubt as I knew mine was, and I felt a tear trickle down my cheek.

'Are you sure?'

'Positive.' But he didn't sound very sure.

I dug in my pocket for a tissue. 'I know I'm being ridiculous. I just hate thinking of them out there all alone in the world, with no one to look out for them.'

'I get it.' Adam cleared his throat. 'I felt the same way about Freezer, our neighbours' cat. I think I told you about him.'

'White, with one blue eye and one green?'

'Yeah. When Luke and Hannah moved, I knew he would be fine and safe, and they love him and Hannah would be home all day while she was on maternity leave. But I still thought, what if he missed me and didn't understand why he never saw me any more.'

I blew my nose, feeling the threat of tears growing closer, but I managed to force them away.

'We're a right pair of dicks, aren't we?' I said.

'Yup.' Adam was wearing his retro shades so I couldn't see his eyes, but I was willing to bet he was struggling not to cry, too. That was what my intuition was telling me, anyway.

'You really think the fledglings will be okay?' I asked, briefly serious again.

'Of course they will. So long as you keep that cat of yours in line.'

'I do my best. But, you know…'

'Cats gonna cat. And I have to get to work.'

He handed me his empty coffee mug, thanked me, and – as he had before – shot out through the bar before I had a chance to properly say goodbye, or wish him a nice day or anything. As I pushed open the door to the kitchen, Jude came clattering down the stairs and enfolded me in a hug, kissing the top of my head and saying he'd see me later, and my working day began.

But the whole time, as I chopped and stirred and sat with Alice over coffee to plan the following week's menu, my thoughts kept returning to Adam. I reminded myself that I had a boyfriend. I wasn't sure whether I had a type, unlike Dani, who'd said that Fabian was totally hers, but I was fairly sure I didn't fancy Adam. So there was nothing to worry about – no need for Jude to feel jealous or insecure.

Adam and I could be friends. I could offer him some sort of time-share in Frazzle, to make up for the cat he used to fuss and feed, and maybe when – if – Jude and I ever went on holiday together, Adam could stay in my flat and keep Frazz company. Although, I realised, if he had the kind of job that involved working lunches at the Chiltern Firehouse, he probably lived in such luxury at his own apartment that my poky studio would seem a hovel in comparison.

Anyway, I felt there had been something there – a connection, a meeting of minds. I hoped that now the baby birds had embarked on their independent lives, in the manner of millennial boomerang children who finally get turfed out of the family home in their thirties, Adam might still pop in in the mornings on his way to the station to see what exciting bird-feeder action I had to share. Maybe Mr and Mrs Blackbird would raise another family for us to watch and stress over.

But, at the Dungeons & Dragons game that evening, Adam didn't mention the birds, or Freezer the cat, or give any indication that anything at all had passed between us. He greeted me with just the same awkward semi-formality as everyone else, accepted a mint julep, which Freddie had discovered was his favourite cocktail, arranged his screen and notepads and coloured pens on the table, and said, 'Right, shall we get started?'

In the game, our party had reached the castle where the young girl was being held prisoner, but had no way of gaining entrance. The previous week had ended with us trying to buy our way in by bribing one of the shifty guards who patrolled the perimeter.

Adam rolled the dice. 'The guard accepts your bribe, and you return under cover of darkness to gain entrance to Castle Drakeford. The night is stormy, with gusts of wind ruffling your cloaks and whistling through the battlements above your heads. The sky is overcast, but occasionally scudding clouds part to reveal a sliver of moon, thin as the blade of a sickle. You can hear the hoot of an owl swooping overhead, and there are other creatures hunting in the darkness above you, too. You think they may be bats – at least, you hope that is what they are.'

I shivered and took a gulp of my red wine. Around me, Freddie, Archie, Nat, Tim and Lara's faces were still and intent. The candles on the table flickered. The pub was full, but the tables around us were silent as they, too, listened to Adam's voice.

Over the past few weeks, the Dungeons & Dragons game had become quite the spectator sport, with a huge waiting list of people who wanted to join as soon as one of our characters came to a sticky end. But so far we had all survived, and Adam had refused numerous requests to start games with other groups – planning our adventure was taking up almost all his spare time, he said. I wondered what he did with the rest of it – aside from saving local wildlife – if he had very much time outside his impressive-sounding job at the hedge fund.

'The guard greets you with a grunt, carefully unhooking a heavy bunch of keys from his belt,' he carried on. 'The clink of metal on metal resounds in the still night air, and you hope that it will not alert other guards to your presence. He fits a key into the iron lock, and you hear the grinding of the mechanism within as he slowly turns it. The door swings open with a creak, and beyond you see only darkness.'

'We should kill the guard,' Dun said, with a coldness that I couldn't imagine being there if he was still cheerful, smiley Archie. 'Now that he's let us in. It's too risky. He knows that we're here; he could tell anyone and we'd be screwed.'

'It's a good point,' said Hesketh. 'Secrecy is the only defence we have once we're in there.'

'I cannot countenance the murder of an innocent man,' said Lorien.

'But he's one of Brandrel's men,' I pointed out. 'That's not exactly innocent, is it? He'll have been pillaging all over the place most of his life.'

Adam watched in silence as we argued the toss. Once we'd made a decision, a couple of rolls of the dice would determine what happened next – whether we succeeded in doing away with the guard; whether, if we decided not to try, he alerted his colleagues to our presence; whether they found us in the darkness underneath the castle.

'I could cast a spell of silence on him,' Annella said. Under her blunt dark fringe, Nat's eyes were bright. 'It would render him speechless for twenty-four hours, by which time we'd be safely inside. If it works.'

'I say we do that,' I said.

'Agreed,' said Annella.

'I still think it would be safer…' Dun began, but he was outvoted.

'Very well.' Adam rolled the dice. 'An eight. Annella's spell is successful.'

'We'd better get our skates on, then,' Freddie said, then segued back into being Hesketh. 'I mean, we should make haste, and explore as much of this dungeon as we can whilst we have the cover of darkness and secrecy.'

'We could split up,' suggested Lorien. 'Half of us go to the heart of the castle to find and rescue Zarah and the rest explore a bit and look for treasure.'

'What? Have you never seen a horror movie, ever? Split up? That's crazy talk.'

'It does make sense though. When the guard gets his speech back he'll sing like a canary, and if we're in two parties at least that reduces their chances of finding all of us.'

'We might not have the same fighting power in smaller groups but we could move more quickly and more silently.'

'And if we split our skills appropriately we'd all be safe enough.'

'So long as we agree that if we find treasure, we'll share it equally.'

'Equal won't mean a row of beans if we're all dead.'

We argued a bit, drinking our wine and eating the sausages, buns and potato wedges that Robbie had sent us from the kitchen. I knew that if I was me, I'd want our party to stick together. Cautious, risk-averse Zoë would look for safety in numbers. But I wasn't me. I was Galena, who barely knew what fear meant.

As we ate and drank and talked, I watched Adam's face, looking for a hint of what he thought was the right or wrong course of action. But he was impassive, glancing down occasionally at his maps and notes, then looking back at us, half-smiling. His smile was strangely sweet and gentle, at odds with the sharp angles of his face, exaggerated by the candlelight. If Adam was a Dungeons & Dragons character, I thought, he'd be a wizard – wise and kind and a bit mysterious, able to weave magic through the words he spoke.

As Adam described the scene inside the imaginary castle, I could hear – almost like it was in my imagination and the game was real – the background noise of the pub, the clink of glasses and the hum of conversation and laughter. I could smell the food on our table, and taste the red wine in my glass. It was like I was in two places at once, and the bridge between them – the portal, as I guessed Adam might say – was the click of the dice on the wooden table as it decided the outcome of the battle that followed.

'Without Annella, you are unable to use magic against the undead warriors,' Adam said softly. 'Your swords are mere earthly metal, while theirs are forged from materials harder than steel. It is only your skill and courage that allows you to prevail, but at grievous cost. Dun and Hesketh are both wounded, Dun seriously.

Lorien must try to tend to their wounds, while performing rites over the fallen ghoul soldiers that will allow them to return at last to the realm of the dead.

'Next week, we'll see whether the two of you survive, and how Galena and the others get on in their search for Zarah.'

He stopped and smiled, the spell of his voice broken. I felt like I'd been holding my breath for a long time, and I think the others did too – all at once, we started laughing and chatting, the tension Adam had created dissipating as we returned to reality.

I hurried to the bar and asked Alice to make him a cocktail, and brought it back to him, hoping that he would stay and chat. He took his time sliding his notes and maps together behind the screen, carefully slotting the multifaceted dice into their places in the box and tidying his coloured felt-tip pens away into their case, seemingly oblivious of Alice tidying up around him, the lights in the bar having been turned up, and the last of the punters finishing their drinks and heading out into the night.

I left him to it, giving Alice a hand with the last tasks of the night, feeling the excitement of having been in that other world for three hours gradually seep away and be replaced by tiredness. I was leaning up against the bar, yawning hugely, glancing at my phone, when Adam came up to me, all his stuff now stashed away in his laptop bag.

'Zoë?'

'Mmmhmm.'

'Mind if I ask you something?'

'Sure.'

'Does the Ginger Cat do private hire? Like, for parties and stuff?'

'Yeah. I mean, like, in theory we do. But the last one was a while back, when Maurice and Wesley got married.'

I couldn't help smiling remembering that day: the pub newly reopened, rainbow bunting strung across the ceiling, Maurice and Wesley glowing with happiness with carnations in their buttonholes. And then I remembered, too, how my own heart had ached when I saw Alice and Joe together, how it had seemed like everyone in the world could be happy, could have someone for their own, except for me.

But now I had Jude. I didn't have to be lonely, ever again. So why did it feel as if I was?

Adam's voice jerked me out of my thoughts. 'My friend's been travelling with her other half. She's been in Australia for almost a year and now they're back, and I wanted to organise something. Like a welcome-home thing. Josh and me organised a surprise birthday party for her a while back, and she loved it. So I thought it would be kind of traditional, you know?'

It had never occurred to me that Adam might have friends. I mean, obviously he had a life outside of the world of the game, and a job and everything, but he'd never struck me as a person who'd book out an entire pub for a party. I didn't have that many friends myself, I thought.

'You'll need to ask Alice. She's in charge of that kind of thing. Well, she's in charge of everything really. But I'm sure it will be fine. She'll give you a price per head or a minimum spend or whatever.'

'Great.' Adam hesitated, and then he went on, 'Could we do, like, an Australian theme? With the food and stuff?'

'I don't see why not. Shrimp on the barbie, and…' That was pretty much the extent of my knowledge.

'Lamingtons?' Adam suggested.

'Shrimp on the barbie and Lamingtons. Whatever those are. Got you.'

Our eyes met and we laughed.

'Pies and gravy?' Adam suggested. 'That's a thing, isn't it?'

'I've got no idea. I'll have to google. But we'll come up with something, don't worry.'

'Great,' Adam said again.

There was a pause, and I thought he might be about to say something else – I even saw him take a deep breath like he was going to. But he just said he'd see me next week, slung his bag over his shoulder and strolled out into the night, and I had a final check of the kitchen and went upstairs to the flat to find Jude.

He was on the sofa, slouched down low so his hips were right on the edge of the cushions and his chin on his chest, his long legs stretched out in front of him, reading a book called *Engines of Privilege*. Frazzle was on the bed, one eye open, waiting to see if there was any chance of a last and final snack before bed.

'Hey, beautiful,' Jude said, not raising his eyes from the page. 'Okay day?'

'Yeah, it was good,' I replied brightly. 'How was yours?'

'Bloody knackering. I was just about to call it a night.'

I thought longingly of bed – and sleep. But I'd promised Dani – and, more importantly, myself – that I was going to do this. One last throw of the dice: the idea made me think of Adam, his long fingers dropping the many-sided dice on the table, determining our fate. If he was rolling now, would it be a one, a twenty, or something in between?

But this wasn't up to Adam or a dice. It was up to me.

'I'm just going to jump in the shower,' I said. 'How about lighting some candles?'

'Candles?' Jude looked at me blankly, like I'd suggested summoning a string quartet to entertain us for what was left of the evening.

'Sure. You know, ambience.'

'And a fire hazard,' Jude grumbled, but he got up from the sofa and I heard him rummaging around on a shelf looking for matches as I closed the bathroom door behind me, having snatched up the ASOS carrier bag I'd stashed behind the door that morning.

Ten minutes later, I was standing in front of the slightly fogged-up bathroom mirror, looking at my reflection with a mixture of wonder and embarrassment. I was a bralette and boy shorts kind of person. I'd hardly ever in my life owned anything you could describe as lingerie. Perhaps I could have started off slowly, with something tasteful in oyster-coloured silk, but I'd decided that if I was going to do this thing, I was going to do it properly.

The result was a black, multi-strapped bra (although whether it was actually worthy of the name – given its cups comprised three strips of elastic that criss-crossed my breasts, meeting in the middle and just about covering my nipples but leaving nothing else to the imagination – was another matter), and a matching thong that left my nether regions similarly exposed.

I looked bizarre, yet also sexy, in a totally in-your-face kind of way. And I felt absolutely terrified, far more nervous than the first time I'd brought Jude back to the flat. What would he do? Would this overt display of my assets drive him wild with desire and transform him into a lover of Seth-like enthusiasm and skill, as I hoped? Or would he be horrified, assuming that his girlfriend had somehow transformed into Mistress Whiplash in the course of a fifteen-minute shower? Or maybe my new kit would have the opposite of the desired effect, turning him on so much that our usual perfunctory sex didn't even get that far?

I had no idea, but there was only one way to find out.

I opened the bathroom door and stepped out as tentatively as a Victorian virgin on her wedding night, although rather less modestly dressed.

Jude looked up from the sofa and for a second he gawped at me, his jaw literally falling open.

And then he burst out laughing.

Chapter Twenty-Three

Today presents you with questions, Aquarius: why are you so afraid to be alone? What are you willing to sacrifice for love? And why is your closet full of odd socks?

In the gym the next afternoon, I pushed myself relentlessly, lifting heavier weights than I ever had before, carrying on until my muscles were burning and trembling and Mike came over and stood by me, his face impassive, his hands ready to support my arms if they gave up altogether.

'You were giving it some today,' he commented when I got up off the bench, leaving behind the sweaty imprint of my arms and shoulders.

I nodded, for a few moments enjoying the sensation of there being nothing else in the world except my screaming muscles and my pounding heart. There was no space to think, and that was what I wanted.

'Missing your training buddy?' he asked.

'Yeah. Was Dani in earlier?'

'Nah. I haven't seen her all week. I sent her a message but she didn't read it.'

'We went for drinks a few days ago. She's okay, but she didn't say anything about having a break from training. And she didn't read the last message I sent her either.'

'Sometimes people need a break,' he said. 'And sometimes they just quit. You get used to people being around, you think they're part of the furniture, and then they just don't turn up one day and that's it.'

'I'm sure that won't happen with Dani, though. She loves it here.'

'She's made great progress. You too.'

His words gave me a glow of pride, but that wasn't enough to dispel the shadow of worry I felt over Dani. She wouldn't just quit. Not out of the blue like that. Something was wrong. I made my way back to work with various scenarios jostling around in my head like unwelcome house guests, resolving to go round to Dani's as soon as I could and check she was okay.

The pub was busy that night, and Robbie had the evening off, so I had work to keep me occupied at least. I turned out plate after plate of food, the rhythm of a busy service as compelling and all-encompassing as that of a workout in the gym. Alone in the kitchen, at least I didn't have to smile or pretend that everything was okay. I plugged in my headphones, I worked flat out until ten, and then I cleaned everything down, said a brief goodnight to Kelly and Freddie, and dragged myself wearily up the stairs to the flat.

I found myself half-hoping that Jude wouldn't be there, although I knew he would be.

I still burned with shame, remembering the previous night – how he'd totally corpsed at the sight of me, laughing so hard he'd barely been able to speak, and then, when at last he could, he'd asked me what the hell I was doing in that hooker's get-up.

'I thought you were a feminist, Zoë,' he'd said, gasping for breath. 'Never realised you moonlighted as a *Playboy* centrefold.'

'I… I just wanted to do something different. Something nice. For us.'

'Different is right. Good grief. I haven't seen anything like that since I was knocking one out over Babestation when I was sixteen.'

'Don't you like it?' I folded my arms over my chest, not feeling even a bit sexy any more, only embarrassed and exposed.

'Come here.' He crossed the room and folded me in his arms. 'You don't need shit like that to be beautiful. No one does. You're lovely as you are.'

But his words couldn't take away the sting of his laughter.

'I just…' I tried again, but my throat was closing up and I knew if I carried on, I'd start to cry.

'Come on, let's get you out of that nonsense.'

He unhooked the bra – easily enough, because there was just one tiny clasp – and tugged the stretchy elastic thong down over my hips, tossing it into the corner of the room, where Frazzle leaped on it and started to savage it ferociously. Even if I was dishonest enough to try and return it, I thought, my cat had put paid to any chance of that.

'If you're in the mood, you only have to say, you know,' Jude went on.

I'd never, ever, been less in the mood in my life. But still, I felt I had to go through with it, and I did. Knowing it would be over in just a few short minutes, which it was.

I'd lain awake for what felt like hours afterwards, cold with misery. And now I was going to have to spend the evening with him, with that between us.

Jude was in the flat, lying on the bed, his shoes still on, his laptop on his knees.

He glanced up when I came in. 'Evening, babe. Busy day?'

'Crazy.' I leaned over to fuss Frazzle hello, and so I didn't have to meet Jude's eyes. 'Has he had his dinner? Have you?'

Jude shook his head. 'I literally just walked in. I'm starving, actually.'

And he and Frazzle both looked at me hopefully, expecting me to magic up their dinner. Well, Frazzle was entitled to, of course – he was a cat and if I didn't provide regular meals, he would decimate the local wildlife and probably leave home. But I couldn't help feeling slightly resentful that Jude, knowing I'd spent almost all day cooking for other people, now expected me to cook for him, too.

'I ate earlier,' I reminded him. 'Family meal in the pub, remember? Five every evening.'

'Oh, right.' Jude looked crestfallen. 'Haven't we got anything in, then?'

'There's some bread,' I said. 'And some porridge oats. And the twenty-four-hour Tesco down the road. And Uber Eats.'

I opened the fridge and found a pack of the special raw cat food I'd started buying for Frazzle, on the basis that it was organic and ethically produced and apparently identical to cats' natural diet, even though it cost a fortune and every time I ordered it I felt like the manufacturer, and my cat, had seen me coming. Frazz wound himself around my legs, meowing urgently as he always did, like he was quite sure that if he didn't keep reminding me, I'd change my mind and do something else instead of feeding him.

'I wouldn't mind some ramen,' Jude said. 'Fancy any?'

I shook my head. 'Like I said, I ate earlier.'

'Okay. Only, do you mind ordering on your account? I'm kind of skint, to be honest.'

I felt resentment flare inside me. He'd been living here rent free for three months and never paid a penny towards the bills, and now he expected me to bankroll his takeaway as well? He'd laughed at me when I'd tried to make our sex life better by pushing my own boundaries.

But was any of that his fault?

He couldn't have expected my clumsy attempt at seduction. The Zoë he'd met lived in trainers and was on a year-long shopping ban. I'd never said that there was anything amiss with our sex life; I'd just expected him to understand that what was okay for him wasn't for me.

I'd known when he moved in that he wasn't earning a proper wage. It was unfair to judge him for that. But was it unfair to expect him to go to the supermarket on his way home and sort out some food for himself to eat, like an adult? Or eat toast and peanut butter, like I'd done on more occasions than I cared to remember, when my finances had been even more perilous than usual?

But Jude was lying there on the bed, looking at me with wide pleading eyes just like Frazzle's, and I found I didn't have the energy to point any of that out to him.

'Sure. Where do you want to order from?'

'Blessing Bowl?' he said immediately. 'White natural with shiitake broth, crispy tofu, bamboo shoots and seaweed? And a side of edamame, and maybe some pumpkin gyoza? And a couple of bottles of lager. Thanks babe.'

I couldn't help wondering if he'd had the menu already open on his laptop, waiting for me to come home so he could place his order with me, and I could place it with the noodle place. That lot would set me back almost thirty quid, I calculated, tapping it all into the app. But it was churlish to point that out – churlish and mean. It wasn't fair to take my worry over Dani out on Jude, when he was doing nothing he didn't normally do.

'It'll be about thirty minutes,' I said.

'Great.' Jude got up off the bed and stretched. 'I'll have a shower while I wait, then. And do you know where my jeans are? I couldn't find any clean ones this morning.'

'I should imagine they're in the washing machine,' I said, 'with the rest of your stuff that I put in this morning.'

'Damn it,' he said, 'I'll have to hang them out now, and they probably won't be dry by the morning.'

'They probably won't. There's a twenty-four-hour launderette down the road; I expect they have dryers, if you're desperate.'

Finally, Jude looked sheepish. 'Look, I'm sorry, okay? I've had a total fucker of a day and I'm tired and cranky and work's just like a bloody pressure cooker at the moment with all these factions squabbling with one another, and I know I'm going to have to take a side but I don't know which one to take. But that's no excuse to be a bastard to you. Believe me, I appreciate everything you do for me, because ultimately that helps me to fight for what's right. Okay?'

There was so much to unpick there I didn't know where to start. And I suddenly felt desperately weary. Wasn't this the kind of conversation you were meant to have in a ten-year marriage that had begun to go sour, not in a relationship that was still brand new, still meant to be in its honeymoon period? I needed someone to confide in, someone to comfort me, someone who had my back and right now – actually, always – Jude wasn't that person. Frazzle gave me more emotional support than Jude did and just about as much practical help.

But I was too tired to think about it, too tired to argue about it, and definitely, categorically too tired to get myself into a row that might need make-up sex to resolve itself.

'I know,' I said. 'Just sort out your own clothes tonight, okay? I'm going to sleep.'

And so I found myself, a few minutes later, lying rigid in my bed, with all the lights still on and Jude next to me, scrolling on his phone while he waited for his food, a half-smile on his face. Glancing at the screen over his shoulder, I could see he was on Indigo's Instagram feed; I'd have recognised those abstract canvasses and that messy apartment anywhere. She was his friend, I reminded myself. There was no reason for him not to engage with her social media. But still, I felt like the four walls of the flat were closing in on me, the space getting smaller and smaller. I knew that if I managed to drift into sleep, I'd be woken immediately by the buzz of the entry phone and Jude crashing around finding plates and cutlery, probably asking me where the salt and hot sauce were, and possibly opening the washing machine to try and dry his jeans with my hairdryer.

I was furious, exhausted and desperately sad, but I had no idea what to do. I could tell him to pack his stuff and leave, but I wasn't capable of that. It felt too cruel, too final. I could leave myself, just for the night, to get some head space, but I had nowhere to go. Or, of course, I could just lie here, seething with resentment, and hope that eventually I'd fall asleep and maybe in the morning a solution would magically present itself.

But I didn't fall asleep, because after just a few minutes the door buzzer sounded, jerking me out of my thoughts. It wasn't just one buzz, either – it was three or four, strung rapidly together.

'Jesus Christ,' Jude said, 'take it easy, mate. You're a fucking pizza delivery monkey not an air raid warden.'

I sat up and looked at him, and he added hastily, 'The pressure these guys work under on zero-hours contracts is a bloody disgrace. Got any change?'

I hadn't, but I got up and handed him a fiver out of my purse, and he hurried out. I heard his bare feet pattering on the stairs, then the click of the outside door opening.

And then I realised I hadn't heard what I would have expected: the rumble of a moped engine turning from the street into the alleyway that led to my flat, then cutting out. And now I heard something I totally wasn't expecting: a woman's voice, high with panic and tears.

'Is Zoë here?'

Chapter Twenty-Four

When you compare yourself to your friends, you do everyone a disservice. Especially yourself, if you come out second best. Focus on what makes you special, even if no one else agrees.

Although the night was mild, Dani was wrapped in a long woollen coat, and she was shivering. When I folded her into a hug, I could hear her teeth chattering above my ear.

'It's all right,' I said. 'Whatever's happened, it's going to be okay. Here, come on in.'

I hesitated for a second, about to guide her up the stairs to the flat. But then I thought, whatever it was that had happened, she probably wouldn't want to tell me about it with Jude there.

'Wait here just a second. I'll be right back.'

I ran up the stairs, grabbed my bunch of keys and hurried down again, Frazzle trailing curiously at my heels as I unlocked the door to the pub. Dani followed me inside. The Ginger Cat was empty: the last guests had gone home for the night and the cleaner wouldn't arrive for her early-morning round for another four hours. I flicked the light switch and the spotlights over the bar came on, but the rest of the pub remained in soft darkness.

It could have felt eerie and spooky, but it didn't. The room was warm and the dim light created a little circle of intimacy just big enough for the two of us to sit at a table.

'Cup of tea? Or something stronger?'

'I'm half pissed already,' Dani said. 'Guess there's no point stopping now.'

I found a bottle of red wine and two glasses, promising myself that I'd put money for it in the till and wash the glasses before I went home, and we sat down. Frazzle prowled off into the shadows, hopeful of mice scavenging for dropped crumbs under the tables.

'What's happened? Is it Fabian?'

Dani nodded, taking a big gulp of wine.

'Did you have a row?'

She shook her head, pulling the collar of her coat close around her neck.

'It's okay,' I said. 'Whatever's happened, you'll be fine here. You can stay with me tonight if you like. Jude can sleep on the floor – he won't mind. You don't even have to tell me anything if you don't want to.'

Dani took another swallow of wine, then gave a little choking gasp and started to cry. I grabbed some paper napkins and scooted my chair closer so I could put my arm round her heaving shoulders.

'Shit,' she said. 'I can't even bloody cry. It hurts too much.'

'What hurts? Did he finish with you? It's awful, if he did, but you'll be okay. I totally one hundred per cent promise you will.'

'Not that.' She released her tight grip on her coat collar and it fell open. 'This.'

'Jesus.' The warm golden light fell on the smooth golden skin of her neck, and I could see, as clearly as if they'd been painted on with make-up, the livid red marks on her throat. Four of them, just below her ear, and a fifth stretching around underneath her jaw. She didn't have to turn around for me to know that there would be the same marks on the other side, because Fabian had two hands.

'Fucking hurts,' she said.

I realised I was trembling too. 'We should call the police. Report him for assault.'

'We can't do that. There's literally no point.'

'Why not? He tried to fucking strangle you.'

'Only because I let him.'

'You *what*?'

'It's a thing he's into. Breath play, he calls it. He's done it before and it was okay – I mean, like, kind of scary and everything, but it made him happy so I went along with it and I was turned on and…' She tailed off and drank more wine.

'But this time was different?'

'Yeah. He'd had a bad day and he was really stressed and he didn't want to talk to me about what was wrong, and he didn't want to go out or anything. When he's like that it feels like sex is the only thing I can do to make him feel better. I can't give him advice about his job or be any help at all, really. But I can do that.'

That's all kinds of wrong, I thought. But I just said, 'Go on.'

'And I knew that he'd be in a better mood after a good old session. So I got dressed – he'd bought a load of stuff for me to wear, that I keep at his place – and he put on some porn and… well, you know.'

I didn't really know. I wasn't sure I wanted to know.

'And he said he wanted to choke me, and I said yes, because like I said, he'd done it before and I was okay after, just a bit bruised. That's why I haven't been in the gym for a while, because I thought you and Mike might be freaked out, and anyway it was a bit too sore for me to want to get massively out of breath.'

Too sore for you to breathe for a week? And you thought that was okay? my mind screamed.

'But this time he did it harder. I was so scared, Zoë, I felt like I was going to die. There were dots swimming in front of my eyes and I couldn't breathe at all. I tried to get him off me, but he's so much bigger than me and really strong. And then I guess I must've passed out because when I came round again he'd finished.'

'Dani. Oh my God. You must know how dangerous that is.'

She nodded, wincing a bit. 'The last thing I remember was thinking about that girl, that backpacker in New Zealand, who died from the same thing. And I thought how grim it would be everyone knowing about it, if my name was in the newspapers, and how ashamed Mum would be of me, and how I could never make things right with her if I was dead.'

'Don't be silly – no one would have been ashamed. He's the one who should be ashamed. But you're okay. Thank God, you're okay.'

'Fabian was really nice. He tried to give me a cuddle and stuff, but I just wanted to get out of there. So I put on my coat and I got an Uber here. I didn't want my flatmates to see me like this.'

Now that Dani's coat had fallen open, I could see what she was wearing underneath: a leather corset, suspenders and stockings and the kind of stripper shoes I'd imagined buying to wear for Jude, before immediately rejecting the idea.

'I'll lend you something to wear tomorrow,' I promised. 'Something of mine will fit you, I'm sure. And if not, we'll ask Alice. It'll be fine. But I still think you need to report him to the police.'

'How can I? They'd see me in this get-up and they wouldn't believe a word I said. And Fabian would tell them I consented, I said it was fine, and he'd be right. I did.'

'But you can't consent to that. Not to being hurt like that.'

'You can. I did. And I did before. I said yes to all the stuff he did to me. I even enjoyed lots of it. It's just – he kept pushing and pushing, you know? It's like he was trying to find where my boundaries were, only I didn't know. Not until tonight.'

Being strangled until you blacked out would pretty much be beyond anyone's boundaries, I thought.

'It's going to be fine,' I said. 'You never have to see him again. You never have to do anything you're not comfortable with again – ever. You've got this.'

Dani drank more wine. She'd stopped crying now, and her face was strangely blank under what was left of her heavy make-up.

'I thought he was so great,' she said. 'I literally couldn't believe my luck, that this hot, rich, successful man wanted to go out with me. I thought that was it, as long as I didn't put a foot wrong, I was sorted. Mum would be proud of me. My life would be perfect. But it wasn't true, was it?'

'Fabian's a creep. He always was and he always will be. You're way too good for him. And there are plenty of other guys out there who are normal and decent and kind and won't make you do weird shit you don't want to do, and won't hurt you, and won't endanger your fucking life for kicks. Really there are.'

'Like Jude?'

It was my turn to take a big gulp of wine. 'Jude's never done anything like that. But all the same, I've been thinking, lately, that maybe it's not going to work. I thought having a boyfriend would make me happy, but it hasn't. And I think it's because he doesn't really want to make me happy. He's not a bad person. But maybe "not a bad person" is setting the bar way, way too low.'

'So it's back to the drawing board, then? Back to online dating?'

'I don't know.' I thought of Jude, upstairs in my flat, eating the takeaway I'd paid for, maybe commenting on Indigo's Insta feed. It had been a long time, I realised, since I'd looked at him and felt that rush of excitement, admired the curve of his lips when he smiled and the flicker of his eyes when he laughed. It had been a while since I'd even seen him laugh, except when he'd laughed at me.

'So "not a bad person" is enough, then? I'm worth more than Fabian, but you're not worth more than that?'

'I don't know,' I said again.

Chapter Twenty-Five

You know what to do with your excess baggage, Aquarius. Ditch it, or pay the price.

Over the next few days, I kept remembering my unequivocal advice to Dani. *Dump his sorry arse. Don't put yourself in danger for a man. No guy is worth this. You deserve so much more.*

I remembered it, and I knew it was right. But when I chatted to Dani over coffee and cake at a pavement table after our workout, both of us wrapped up with our hoodies zipped to our chins against the chilly afternoon, and she told me that she had ended it with Fabian – *Thank God*, I said to myself – there was still something almost wistful in the way she talked about him.

'I called him and told him it was over,' she said, her words coming out in a rush. 'It was horrible, Zoë. He begged me to forgive him. He said he'd never hurt me again, he hadn't meant to, he'd only done it because he thought it was what I wanted – all that stuff. He sounded almost like he was crying. And then I had to go round to his place to pick up my things and he'd put this massive fuck-off diamond bracelet in with them and it was just as well I noticed and gave it back, otherwise I'd have had to see him again.'

'You never have to see him again,' I tried to reassure her, not mentioning that, of course, he could turn up at the gym any time he wanted.

'You don't think I overreacted, do you? I mean, if I told him I didn't like what he was doing, maybe he'd have just stopped, and it would've been okay?'

'Maybe,' I said. 'But maybe he wouldn't. Maybe next time he could have hurt you really badly. Maybe he'd have stopped doing that one thing but carried on pushing your boundaries in other ways.'

She sighed. 'I suppose you're right. I do miss him, though, in some ways.'

'What do you miss, though?'

'Being able to go out to nice places with a handsome man. Not having to worry about being the only person without a plus-one at weddings for the rest of my life. Not having to worry about never having a wedding of my own. Being able to go home with him and introduce him to Mum, and all my friends back in Liverpool seeing that it was the right thing to have split up with Jamie and made my own way in life. And now I'm back to worrying about all that shit.'

'But just think about it for a second.' I waved my fork a bit too vigorously, and a bit of carrot cake flew off it and immediately got devoured by a passing pigeon. 'If Fabian had been your plus-one at a wedding, what would be the chances of him not turning up? How many times when you went to nice places with him did you end up feeling bored and anxious while he ignored you and talked to his important friends? Would he actually ever have asked you to marry him, even if you put up with his shitty behaviour and dodgy kinks for years and years?'

'I know, you're right. Of course you're right. I'll just have to get used to being single again,' Dani said gloomily.

'Being single's not so bad. Come on! I was single for years and years and I was fine about it. It's good to be at peace with yourself, have your own space, no one to answer to but yourself.'

'It's easy for you to say that now,' she pointed out, 'you've got a boyfriend.'

And that shut me up, good and proper. Because I knew that the advice I was so generously dishing out to my friend wasn't necessarily advice I'd follow myself. Sometimes, when the direct debit for the gas bill came out of my account and left me staring queasily at my bank balance wondering where Frazzle's next consignment of posh raw food pouches was going to come from, or when I looked at the bathroom mirror and tried to remember the last time Jude had left me a note written with a soapy finger, or when I lay in bed after we'd had sex, sleepless and unsatisfied, I wondered what advice I'd give someone in my situation.

And I knew exactly what it was. *Kick him to the kerb.* Or maybe, if I was feeling charitable, *Tell him to shape up or ship out. He's just a cocklodger.*

But, somehow, I couldn't do it. It wasn't Jude's fault he wasn't earning much and was working such long hours. It wasn't fair that I had a job that paid me a decent wage and he didn't. I got to swan off to the gym in the middle of the day, while he was stuck at work in an office, or walking the streets pushing leaflets through letterboxes, or getting a train to a rally somewhere at six in the morning. And he couldn't help that sex wasn't always satisfying for me. (Wasn't *ever* satisfying, said the brutally honest voice in my head.) He always held me and told me he loved me afterwards, before he fell asleep, and often he said he was sorry it had been over so quickly. Before, I'd told him I loved him, too, but now I couldn't bring myself to say the words.

Maybe, I decided, I should talk to him. I'd pick a moment and have a proper chat, like the grown-ups we both were, and point out ways in which we could make our relationship better.

Over the next few days, I had conversation after conversation with Jude in my head. They all ended the same way: with him saying that of course I was right, he couldn't believe it had taken him so long to see my point of view. He'd make a contribution to the rent on the flat. He'd make sure he got in early from work at least once a week, on my night off, so we could go out for a meal together. He'd make time over the weekend to help me give the place a good clean.

I never quite worked out what I imagined he would say about how to make things better in bed, because however many times I considered raising that particular issue, I couldn't find any words at all.

Finally, my moment came. It was Sunday, lunch service at the Ginger Cat was over and for once Jude hadn't had to go to work, or to a rally, or to some obscure meeting of political people in a pub. So we packed a bottle of wine and a picnic blanket and stopped off at Craft Fever and bought a pack of swanky truffle-flavoured crisps, and walked up the hill to the park. I spread out the blanket and sat down, opening the wine and pouring it into the glasses I'd brought from home, carefully wrapped in the blanket so they wouldn't chip.

It was a glorious afternoon – one of the last we'd have that year, I thought. The sky was such a deep blue it looked almost purple, and the leaves clashed against it in their early-autumn oranges and golds. Jude spread himself out next to me and put his head in my lap, and I stroked his long hair back from his face, looking down at him and wishing things were simple but knowing they weren't.

'So how's your week been?' I began tentatively.

'Fucking horrible,' Jude said. 'Relentless. But there's a proper job vacancy come up, and I've been told there's a decent chance I might get it if I apply.'

This was my moment – or was it? Shouldn't I wait and, if he did get the job and was earning money, he'd offer to make more of a contribution?

'That would be amazing,' I said. I stopped, almost bottling it, but then forced myself to carry on. 'Because, you see, I've been feeling lately that things between us are a bit kind of uneven. Like, in terms of who pays for stuff and who does stuff around the flat, and… you know.'

Jude opened his eyes and stared at me, his face full of reproach. 'What do you mean?'

'It's just… I mean, when was the last time you bought any groceries, or did any washing or cleaning?'

He sat up, splashing wine into his glass. 'Are you saying I'm not pulling my weight?'

'No, of course not. Not exactly. Well, yes, I suppose I am a bit.'

'You're saying I should be paying you rent, to sleep with you? Is that it?'

I said, 'Not rent, obviously. But I don't get the flat for free. Alice offered, but if I wasn't living there it could be done up and used for functions and stuff, and so I said I should pay for it.'

'More fool you,' Jude said. 'It's not all that, anyway, is it? You could find somewhere much better for the same money.'

'Maybe. But it wouldn't be right above work, and that's really convenient for me and Frazzle loves being a pub cat. But that's not the point. The point is—'

'You think I'm freeloading. When I earn about ten per cent of what you do, and most of that goes on travel and lunches.'

'I don't think you're freeloading,' I objected. Although, I realised, that was exactly what I was beginning to think, and Jude's defensive reaction made me suspect he knew it too. 'I just feel, sometimes, like the way things are between us isn't exactly fair.'

Jude looked at me, his expression changing from anger to hurt. 'I didn't realise that was what this was about. I thought we had something special, a real connection. Something that could transcend all this stuff. I thought we were both free spirits. I thought you cared about the big issues, just like I do – about justice, and equality, and the planet.'

'I do care about those things. But it doesn't feel very just or equal when I'm washing about seventeen of your T-shirts every week. Or particularly great for the planet, for that matter.'

He was still staring at me with those sad eyes. 'I can't believe we're having this conversation. This should be a romantic afternoon and you're nagging at me like we've been married forty years and can't even remember what romance was.'

'Pointing out that you haven't been doing your fair share isn't nagging. And having to say it doesn't make me feel particularly romantic, either.'

'Well, you have now,' Jude said. 'Fine. You've made your point. We can go back to the flat right now and I'll put a wash on, if that'll make you feel better.'

I sipped some of my wine. We hadn't brought a cooler and it was already losing its chill, the bottle streaming with condensation. All at once, I felt a deep weariness. How easy it would be, I thought, to apologise, thank Jude for offering, say we'd stay here and we could give the flat a bit of a tidy-round together in the evening. How easy it would be to just let things return to how they'd been – how Jude clearly wanted and expected them to be.

But I remembered what the app had said: *You know what to do with your excess baggage, Aquarius. Ditch it, or pay the price.*

Why was I letting this happen? What was I being taken for a mug? What had happened to fierce, feminist, independent Zoë who'd never be anyone's doormat?

'Look, I know you don't want to hear this,' I said, 'but I'm not happy being treated like your chief cook and bottle-washer while you live in my flat without paying a penny. Spiritual connections are all very well, and I really felt – I really feel – like that's what we have – what we had. But that doesn't give you the right to treat me like a combination of a 1950s housewife and your mum. And what's more—'

I stopped. I was full of righteous anger, but not quite full enough to go on to say, 'Sex with you isn't all that, either.'

'Are you saying you don't want us to be together any more?' Jude asked. 'I thought you loved me.'

'No! Of course I'm not.' And then I realised that that wasn't actually the case. He wasn't going to change. It had been clear from the start: he wanted a free place to stay and a comfortable life, and, like a mug, I'd given it to him, because I'd believed he loved me and wanted to believe I loved him back. I wasn't sure any more whether he did, but to be totally honest, when it came to me, all I felt was sadness and annoyance. I'd thought we had so much in common, because we liked the same things and believed the same things and cared about the same things. But, I realised, there was one important exception to that: Jude didn't care about me.

I was going to end it. I was going to have to, if I was to retain even a shred of self-respect. The only question was when, and how. And then I said to myself, *Come on, Zoë! Grow a pair! You know this thing's dead in the water. Do it now.*

In my mind, I heard Mike urging me on when I was ready to quit a workout. I remembered myself telling Alice that we'd fight to keep the Ginger Cat alive and open, when it had been under threat of closure by Fabian. I even summoned the picture of Frazzle's cross, disappointed face whenever he jumped up on the bed and found Jude there.

I could do it. I would do it. I opened my mouth to speak – but Jude got there first.

'Good!' he said triumphantly. 'You can't dump me. Want to know why?'

'Why?' I asked stupidly.

'Because I'm ending it first.' His gleeful smile faded away, replaced again with the tragic, hangdog look. 'I'm sorry, but I can't be with a woman who doesn't support me one hundred per cent, doesn't have my back when I need her, doesn't get me as a person. I thought you were that woman, but hey, we all make mistakes. Indigo says…'

I listened, half outraged and half amused. I knew, now, what he expected me to do. I was supposed to grovel and apologise. I was supposed to insist that he had it wrong, I was the special one, his soulmate. I was the one who was going to try harder, be better, kinder, more accommodating and admiring of this unique and wonderful person who had deigned to allow me to wash his socks, put a roof over his head and be a receptacle for his spunk for three months.

But I wasn't following the script. Somehow, I'd found my anger – but I wasn't going to give him the satisfaction of seeing how furious he had made me. That would mean I still cared and, I found, I didn't any more. Not one bit. Not even about what Indigo said.

'Okay,' I said. 'I'm glad we're on the same page, and we can end this without any acrimony. Why don't we head back to the flat and you can pack up your stuff?'

Jude looked at me, then at the half-finished bottle of wine and the unopened pack of crisps. They'd cost me three pounds, even though Archie had given me a discount. This wasn't the script either, clearly – I was meant to let him stay for one last night, which would turn into two, then three, then the thin end of the wedge.

'You mean, like, now?' he asked, his eyes widening in dismay.

'Yes,' I said. 'I think I do.'

And I stood up, waited for him to do the same, then picked up the blanket and shook it vigorously. It felt like I was getting rid of a whole lot more than just grass clippings.

Chapter Twenty-Six

If you get your head out of the sand, Aquarius, you might be able to see things as they are, not as you want them to be.

'So I guess neither of us have boyfriends any more,' I said to Dani as we left the gym a couple of weeks later, sweaty and out of breath. Summer was truly over now; although evening wasn't yet falling, the sky was a threatening leaden grey and a thin drizzle misted our skin, making me shiver with cold and the prospect of what it would do to my hair.

Dani sighed. 'Not for want of trying, on Fabian's part.'

'Really?'

'Really. He's sent flowers to my flat and to work, and he keeps calling and texting.'

'Why don't you block his number?'

'I should, I know. It just seems too kind of final. I think about it sometimes and I'm... not tempted to take him back, exactly, but I just wonder whether if I'd done things differently, it could all have worked out.'

'Differently how? He hurt you, remember? What are you meant to have done differently?'

'I don't know. Been more assertive, maybe? Set boundaries? All the shit you're meant to do in relationships but I didn't do because I was so scared of losing him. And now I've lost him anyway.'

'You dumped him. That's totally different from losing him.'

'Oh God. I know you're right. I need to give my head a wobble and move on. Like you've moved on.'

'I wouldn't put it quite that strongly. I've got back on Tinder and been on two dates.'

'Two dates! Strong work, Zoë.'

'Not really. First guy was a Capricorn. They're meant to be all strong and dependable. Which was why I was surprised when he was half an hour late and then spilled a pint of lager over me.'

'Oh no!'

'Oh yes. And he was blatantly at least five years older than his profile said and four inches shorter. I mean, I'm not tall. I don't mind dating short men. I know the whole thing about wanting a guy to be taller than you is patriarchal bullshit. But…'

'Don't tell porkies in your profile?'

'Exactly. Then the Leo guy – apparently they're fun to be around, super-sociable but a bit egotistical – turned out to be not much fun to be around and super-egotistical. He literally talked about himself non-stop for two hours.'

'God, there's nothing worse than an I specialist.'

'Yeah. If I'd told him I'd been on holiday to Tenerife, he'd have been to Elevenerife. So I said I wasn't feeling it.'

'But you've got another date this evening. I'd call that getting straight back on the horse.'

'That would have to be Sagittarius, though. This one's Taurus.'

'Shame. Sagittarius is half man, half horse, right? Imagine shagging one of those.'

We giggled.

'I wonder how it would work?' I said. 'Like, with all the extra legs and stuff.'

'Bloody hell, I thought I was too boring in bed for Fabian and here I am discussing horse sex.'

'Enough of that. What should I expect from Mr Taurus?'

'He'll be full of bull?'

Still laughing, we parted: Dani turning up the high street to the dental surgery, and I returning to the Ginger Cat to get ready for my date with Brett. Mysterious Brett, who might or might not be a spy.

As I walked, I opened the Stargazer app on my phone and glanced at my horoscope for the day, not for the first time.

Things are not always what they seem, Aquarius. You might not be regretting decisions you've made, but if you let your natural impulsiveness come to the fore, you could soon be regretting other ones.

By the app's recent standards, this was pretty tame stuff. I'd begun to wonder, recently, whether there was something strange going on with it – some glitch in the algorithm or something. Just that morning, I'd had a push notification flash up on my screen that had said, *The camera doesn't lie, Aquarius. You really do look ridiculous when you smile.*

I'd dashed to the mirror and grinned at my reflection like a mentaller. I didn't look any different from normal, but I'd spent the rest of the morning so glum-faced that Robbie asked me if someone had died. I'd forgotten about it pretty quickly, obviously, and gone back to smiling a normal amount.

But then another notification had told me, *You might think you can trust your friends, but what are they saying about you when your back is turned?* and I'd felt myself getting all paranoid again and wondering, when I heard a shout of laughter come from the table where Maurice and his mates were playing dominoes, whether they were talking about me.

I hurried up to the flat and showered and changed ready for my date, pleased that I'd gone to the effort of having my nails and eyelashes done, telling myself that if I was going to be back in the dating game, it was quicker than doing them myself and an investment in my future.

'Okay, Frazz,' I said to my cat, who was lounging on the back of the sofa looking deeply pissed off that I should have the bare-faced cheek to go out on my evening off, rather than staying in with him and maybe playing an exciting game of pounce with my toes under the duvet. 'I'm off. You're in charge here.'

Frazzle blinked crossly.

'I know, I know. But at least Jude isn't here any more, and you ought to be relieved about that, because you never liked him much, did you?'

Frazz blinked again, then stood up, yawned hugely, stretched his back and then each of his four legs, and followed me out, trotting down the stairs and into the bar, where he'd spend the evening socialising and staring pleadingly at the customers until they gave him scraps of food off their plates.

'I won't be late,' I said. 'Mind you be a good cat, okay?'

I hadn't bargained for just how not-late I would be, however. It was before eight when I returned to the Ginger Cat, strangely rattled by the revelation I'd had about Brett. I hadn't felt unsafe at any point. Nothing bad had happened. But still, the whole experience had been the worst of my dating life thus far – a new low. One day, I hoped, I'd be able to look back on the time I thought I was on a date with a spy, only he turned out to have been recently released from gaol, and have a good laugh about it. But I wasn't there yet – not by a long shot. And the prospect of going up to the flat and spending the evening alone made me feel weirdly insecure.

So instead of climbing the stairs and going home, I pushed open the door to the pub. I could sit on my own and have a drink, or help Alice out behind the bar, or maybe Archie and Nat would be there and I could join them for a bit. Or, if all else failed, I'd go into the kitchen, pull rank on Robbie and tell him that I could decide to cancel my evening off any time I liked.

But the first person I noticed was Adam. He was sitting alone at a table, not working on the Dungeons & Dragons game or tapping busily at his laptop but reading a book, a half-finished plate of food in front of him, Frazzle snoozing on his lap.

I needed company, and he was going to have to put up with me.

Alice poured me a glass of red wine and I asked for a mint julep as well, and took the two drinks over to Adam's table.

'Hi,' he said, glancing up from his book.

'Hi. Mind if I join you? I brought you a cocktail.'

Adam shook his head and closed his book, putting a paper napkin inside to mark the place. 'Thanks.'

I sat down and took a sip of wine, and noticed that my hands were shaking so hard my teeth rattled against the glass.

'Are you okay, Zoë?'

'Yes. Yes, I am. I'm fine. I just had a really weird experience and I'm not sure what I think about it.'

Adam raised an eyebrow. 'Want to talk about it? I'm good at telling people what they should think about things.'

I took another big gulp of wine and found myself blurting out the whole story of my date with Brett.

'I'd kind of persuaded myself that him being all weird and secretive about his life was a good thing. Like it made him more interesting, mysterious and stuff. I'd even half-convinced myself that he was a secret agent. And then when I saw the tag on his ankle, I realised how wrong I'd been.'

'Must've come as a bit of a shock, realising he'd been doing porridge instead of sending undercover messages to his fellow spooks.'

I managed a shaky laugh. 'Exactly. Less of the designer dinner jacket and more of the orange jumpsuit. Except they don't wear orange jumpsuits in prison here, do they?'

'I have no idea. Never having done time in one.'

'But then part of me is like, was I being really harsh and judgemental? I mean, I always think of myself as being super open-minded, and here I am completely writing someone off as a date because of something that happened in their past. And I don't even know what he'd done. It could've been murder or it could have been – I don't know, committing some sort of victimless white-collar crime to pay for his grandmother's life-saving surgery or something.'

'Zoë, there's being open-minded and then there's being so open-minded you let your brain fall out. You're allowed to decide who you date and who you don't, for whatever reason. It's not an equal-opportunity situation. If you don't like someone's face or they give you bad vibes or you're just not feeling it, you can walk away and you don't have to feel bad about it. And I bet you were getting bad vibes before you even noticed the tag thing, right?'

'I… yeah, to be fair, I was. Not least because he smelled like he'd had a bath in tequila before he came.'

Adam grimaced. 'Oh no.'

'Oh yes. Right then, I should have called it a day and told him I was leaving. But I didn't.'

Adam sipped his drink and pushed his glasses up his nose. 'Why do you think that was?'

'I just… I don't know, I suppose I didn't want to be rude. And I didn't want him to think I was a horrible person. And I didn't want myself to think I was a horrible person.'

'Oh, Zoë.' He shook his head pityingly. 'Just as well you left, otherwise you'd probably be marrying the guy in two weeks, because he asked and you didn't want to offend him.'

'Oh God. I know – you're right. Worried about offending an offender, what am I like?'

'Still, you got out of there in the nick of time,' Adam said.

It took me a second, then I got his joke. 'Just as well I didn't let my guard down.'

'Or you could have ended up shackled to him for life.'

'It's because I over-cell myself.'

'You need to be more fuzz-y.'

'I'm just bad at thinking off the cuff.'

Adam paused, and I could see his brain working overtime as he tried to think of more crime-and-punishment-related puns.

'Another drink?' he said, and headed for the bar before I could even properly accept. A few moments later he was back with two glasses.

'Thanks, Adam.'

'Know what we have to do now?'

'What?'

'Clink.'

I groaned and we both laughed, relishing our shared silliness. My sense of anxiety had faded, and I knew that it wouldn't be long until I'd forgotten all about the date, except as a funny story to tell.

'Anyway—' I began, but Adam spoke at exactly the same moment.

'Zoë, I was—'

'After you,' I said.

'No, you go first.'

'Anyway, I've been thinking, and that's me done. I've given dating my best shot and it just hasn't worked for me. I'm going to go back to being single, and if I die surrounded by cats I don't care. There are worse things, right?'

'I guess,' he said slowly. 'I mean, you must do whatever makes you happy.'

'Exactly. And dating hasn't. And therefore, I'm out. Now what was it you were going to say before you were so rudely interrupted?'

'Nothing,' Adam said.

Chapter Twenty-Seven

Don't be afraid to speak your mind. Do be afraid of how others will react when you do.

From behind the kitchen door, I could hear the beat of music and the hum of voices talking and laughing. The pub seemed to be alive to a different rhythm than usual. Its normal routine varied a little from morning to evening, from day to day and from week to week, but essentially it was the same. If you walked in through the door and saw the mums and babies finishing off their coffee and muffins, Maurice and his friends just getting started on their game of dominoes, Fat Don propping up the bar and a pay-what-you-can curry lunch advertised on the blackboard, you knew it was around eleven fifteen on a Wednesday morning.

That was how it was: consistent and predictable. There had been huge changes when Alice took over, of course, but it had been like the old place had given itself a shake, got some new clothes and then settled down into a new routine.

Tonight felt different, though. It was like the poetry evenings Drew organised occasionally, or like Maurice and Wesley's wedding day had been. Although there were lots of disparate groups of people in the bar, together they made up one group, because they were all there for the same reason. And the reason was a celebratory one. No one was there because they were going to dump their boyfriend and thought they might as well do it over a drink. No one was drowning their sorrows after losing a job or a bet. No one was working, hunched intently over their laptop.

Over the course of the evening, the noise beyond the door had gradually built up, from the first hum of voices, the tap of a hammer stringing bunting over the beams and the rattle of crates of prosecco being delivered, to a buzz of conversation and laughter and the beat of music.

And Robbie and I were working to a rhythm of our own. Outside in the beer garden, which was littered now with fallen leaves and horse chestnuts that were keeping the squirrels busy, he was manning the barbecue, cooking not just shrimp but burgers and chicken and halloumi cheese and vegetable skewers, served with the salads and bread I'd made. In the kitchen, I was putting the finishing touches to a tray of chocolate and coconut cakes and four huge pavlovas, which Google had assured me were a New Zealand thing not an Australian one, but still a feature of just about any Antipodean celebration.

I was interrupted by a tap on the door, and before I could respond it swung open, and Adam's face appeared in the gap.

'Sorry to bother you, Zoë.'

'That's okay. Although strictly speaking you're not allowed in here, you know. "Staff Only" – it says right there on the door.'

'I know. But the Ginger Cat's Dungeon Master kind of counts as staff, right?'

Adam looked more relaxed than I'd ever seen him. His denim shirt was undone an extra button, showing a tan line where it normally closed. His hair was sticking up a bit, like he or someone else had run their hands through it and mussed it. He had a beer in his hand and a big grin on his face.

'I don't know about that,' I said, but I couldn't help smiling back.

'Everyone says the food is fantastic. They want to buy the chef a drink.'

'What if the chef's busy?'

'She's got backup.' Robbie whisked into the kitchen. 'The barbecue's all done. You take a break, Zoë, and I'll serve up dessert in a bit.'

'Sure?'

'Sure. Seriously, there's nothing more for me to do out there. Freddie's clearing up and the coals are dead even if there was more food to cook, which there isn't.'

'Okay. Give me a second.'

Adam let the door swing shut behind him and I pulled off my apron, grabbed my bag off its hook on the back of the door and ducked into the ladies' loo, where I ran my fingers through my frizzing hair and slapped a bit of mattifying powder on my face, which was all shiny from the heat of the kitchen. As I was considering whether to put on some lipstick or not bother, a woman emerged from the cubicle behind me.

She looked like a Victoria's Secret Angel, no word of a lie. She was tall and slender, but curvy too. Her hair was sun-kissed honey blonde and tumbled down her lightly tanned back. She was wearing

ripped mom jeans, a cropped white broderie anglaise top and trainers, but she was so stunning she made it all look like haute couture.

She looked at me curiously and said, 'Hello.'

'Hi. I'm Zoë. I'm the chef; I haven't gatecrashed the party. But
Adam said I should look in for a drink, so I'm just trying to make
myself look a bit more presentable.'

'It was you who made all that incredible food! I'm so grateful
– it's all been totally amazing.' She folded me into a hug, smelling
of some sort of expensive floral perfume and a bit of prosecco. 'I'm
Tansy; it's me the party's for. Well, me and my boyfriend Josh.'

'Hi. Welcome home, I guess.'

Her beauty was downright intimidating, but her smile was
warm and genuine.

'Adam told us all about this place, and now we're all getting to see
it. It's just incredible; I love it!' she gushed, and then she fixed me with
a beady stare. 'So you play Dungeons & Dragons with him, right?'

'That's right. Well, me and a few others. Adam's our Dungeon
Master.'

'He must be good at that.'

'He is. He's awesome. It's like he's got this whole world inside
his head and while we're playing, we're all completely engrossed in
it. Total suspension of disbelief. It's great.'

Again, she smiled that lovely smile, but followed it up with a hard
stare. 'He's a very special person. Come on, why don't you have a
drink, if you're done working? And thanks again for everything – it's
been such a brilliant evening.'

I followed her out into the bar. It was strange to be in the Ginger
Cat as a guest, and even stranger to be the guest of people I didn't

know. The pub was crowded. Everyone had drinks in their hands, a few people were still eating, everyone was talking and laughing. Frazzle was working the room, his fluffy tail held high, accepting admiration and fuss from all and sundry.

Tansy introduced me to her boyfriend Josh and a few other people whose names I couldn't remember. Everyone was friendly and said nice things about the pub and the food. Tansy and Josh were so relaxed together, laughing and meeting each other's eyes in a way that made me think wistfully how fabulous it would be to be properly in love. And then, with every single person I talked to, the same thing happened.

Someone would say, 'So you know Adam through this place?' And I'd explain about the D&D games.

Then they'd say, 'I only know Adam through Tansy really, but…' or, 'I've known Adam for years – we used to share a house, and…' or, 'I don't know how well you know Adam, but…'

And then all of them, every single one, went on to say more or less the same thing. Did I know that Adam had made a fortune mining Bitcoin and sold his position right at the top of the market? Did I know Adam had a first-class degree from Cambridge? Did I know Adam had been the lead developer on the first ever ride-hailing app in Iran? Had Adam met my cat, because Adam loved cats – in fact he loved all animals. Wasn't it amazing of Adam to have organised this surprise for Tansy and Josh – but it was just typical of him, really because he was such a good friend and an all-round fantastic person. Adam might seem cold at first but really he was the most loyal, funny, wonderful guy you could ever hope to meet, didn't I agree?

It was like I'd accidentally wandered into a convention organised by some culty pyramid scheme, only the product everyone was trying to promote was Adam.

At first I thought it was weird, because usually what strangers wanted to talk to me about when they found out I was a pub cook was food: what their favourite restaurants were and whether I'd been to them (generally I hadn't), what my best secret recipe was (as if I'd tell them, if I had one, because then it wouldn't be a secret any more) and why I hadn't mentioned being a vegan in the first five seconds of us talking, because that's what vegans do, right?

Then I started thinking it was sweet, really, that Adam had so many friends who thought he was wonderful, and it made me question how I hadn't known this, and why I'd assumed that he was some kind of hermit, spending every night alone in his flat drawing treasure maps for our D&D game, and I began to wonder if I had underestimated him.

And then I thought, *Hold on, are they trying to tell me something? Me specifically? Are they trying to get me to like Adam?* Not as a friend – I was totally open to that, of course – but as… well, more than a friend? And if so, did it mean that Adam had said something to one of them, or more than one of them, about wanting to be more than a friend to me?

While I was circulating, being introduced to one person after another, having my glass of prosecco filled up over and over, being brought a plate of food by Robbie, who asked if I was sure I didn't want to sit down after being on my feet all day, like I was his nan or something, I noticed that Adam stayed in one place, by the bar, in the spot where Fat Don usually sat. (He'd turned up as usual in the morning, claiming to have forgotten the pub was closed for a private function, and stood mournfully outside the door like a cat waiting to be let in.) Adam didn't have to circulate; people were coming up to him, chatting to him, probably thanking him for the party. He was almost as much the centre of attention as Tansy and Josh were.

And I noticed another thing. Whenever anyone came over to chat to Adam, they glanced around the room and their eyes found me. And once I'd noticed it, I couldn't un-notice it – all those curious glances in my direction, those little smiles and nods. I felt like I was being assessed – in a perfectly nice way, but assessed all the same.

It was getting late now; Robbie had stopped bringing out plates of food and the speed with which Alice was opening bottles of prosecco had slowed down a bit. But no one was showing any signs of leaving just yet. Adam leaned over the bar and said something to Alice, and she smiled, then dimmed the lights a bit, and someone turned the music up.

The Ginger Cat wasn't really a pub designed for dancing. There were tables and chairs in the way, and we'd signed a pledge to be considerate of our neighbours and not play loud music. But it was loud enough to bring couples and groups to their feet, awkward and shuffling at first, then more enthusiastic as they started to get into it, carried away by the Arctic Monkeys singing about how they bet we looked good on the dance floor.

I didn't make a conscious decision to put my glass down and join in. I just did it. My feet, tired from being in the kitchen all day and clumsy in my trainers, seemed to have a will of their own. I pulled the curly telephone-wire tie out of my hair and let it loose down my back, not caring that it probably smelled of frying and was almost certainly frizzing like a bastard.

I watched Tansy and Josh together, a golden couple, tall and tanned and happy to be home among their friends. I saw Alice, looking less tired than she had for ages, laughing and wiping the top of the bar in time to the music. I saw Joe push open the door, raise his eyebrows in surprise, then burst into a huge grin and go over to give Alice a hug and a kiss, and it didn't even hurt any more, seeing them together.

But then I stopped noticing anything else, because Adam came over to me and started to dance.

I was so used to seeing him still, only his hands and his eyes moving, that for a second he seemed like a stranger. He wasn't stooped over any more, the way he often seemed to be, as if he didn't know what to do with his long legs and arms and his shoulders that were so broad and lean he looked like he'd left the coat hanger in his shirt.

He didn't look like that now. He was moving quickly, fluidly, confidently. I realised I'd never seen him smile so much – his teeth were bright white against his beard and his blue eyes were sparkling. I felt an answering smile spread over my face as I moved towards him.

Let me be clear about this: I'm a crap dancer. Compared to Adam, I had none of the moves. But I didn't actually care – I was having fun, just being in my body the way I was in the gym, enjoying the feeling of being strong and happy and alive. The track changed and I paused, expecting him to move away, but he didn't and so I didn't either. We just carried on, grinning at each other like loons and throwing shapes, on and on through that song and the next and the ones after that. He wasn't taking himself seriously and nor was I (which was just as well, because I'd have looked like someone about to be kicked off *Strictly Come Dancing* if I'd tried), and I cracked up completely when at one point he dropped down to the floor and did a full-on worm.

We carried on until Alice turned the music down, saying apologetically that it was eleven thirty and we didn't want to upset the neighbours, and Adam threw one final floss and stopped dancing.

People started to leave after that, drifting off into the night in little clusters to go into town to a club or back to someone's house to carry on drinking there, or just home to bed. Alice was moving around the bar, clearing up for the night as she always did, but I noticed that she was almost rocking on her feet with tiredness.

'Go home,' I said to her. 'Freddie and I will clear up. It's fine.'

'Are you sure?'

'I'll help,' Adam said. 'I kind of feel like this is my mess too, and I should own it.'

'Don't be daft,' Alice said. 'You're a paying customer.'

'Doesn't mean I'm not part of the team,' Adam argued.

'You… Okay. That's really kind. Thank you.'

Alice gathered up her things and moved towards the door, hesitating there for a second and looking protectively around at her pub. But then she broke into a huge yawn that just about split her face in half, and reluctantly pushed open the door and headed for home.

I'd have expected Adam to get in the way, ask annoying questions about what he was meant to do and where things were supposed to go, or just sit down and watch Freddie and me while we worked. But he didn't. He moved around the room methodically, piling glasses up on the bar, bussing plates through to the kitchen, bagging up cans and bottles ready for the recycling.

'Aren't you full of surprises?' I said. 'You're an ace Dungeon Master, a fab dancer and you can tidy a pub like you've been doing it for years.'

'Tidying's not exactly rocket science, is it?' Adam asked, his hands full of glasses that he was holding between his fingers by their stems.

'You probably do rocket science as well.'

'That's not exactly complex either, to be honest. It's just mechanical engineering with a bit of extra calculus. Not like cooking – that's hard.'

I heard the back door open and close and the rattle and smash as Freddie heaved the huge bags of bottles into the recycling bin. Then he stuck his head back into the bar and said he'd head off, if I didn't mind, because the last train was in five minutes and he'd be stuck on a night bus for ages otherwise.

'But aren't you…' I began. As far as I knew, Freddie lived about ten minutes' walk away. But who knew – maybe he'd moved and not said anything. Maybe he was staying at a girlfriend's place or something. It was none of my business and the work was almost done, anyway, so I said goodnight and he hurried out of the door, leaving Adam and me alone.

I stacked the dishwasher and restored everything to order in the kitchen, while Adam wiped the tables and bar top. Frazzle perched on the chaise longue, supervising and getting scratches behind the ears whenever Adam passed him. As we worked, we chatted, having to raise our voices to be heard through the propped-open kitchen door. At last, we were done, the dishwasher humming, the lights dim, Frazzle's eyes closing and his head sinking down onto his paws – the whole pub settled down for the night.

'Thanks, Adam. You've been a massive help.'

'It's been a pleasure.'

'How about a final drink?'

Adam put the bottle of cleaning fluid away in its cupboard and dropped the cloths in the bag ready for the laundry.

'Seems a shame, after we've got the place all sorted.'

I hesitated for just a second, then said, 'You could come up to my flat?'

Adam didn't reply straight away, and I filled the silence by saying, 'You know, it was really funny, all your mates kept coming up to me tonight and telling me how great you are. You've got quite the fan club going there. Either that, or there was some hidden agenda going on. Or not so hidden, haha.'

And then, all at once, everything changed. The friendly intimacy that had been there while we'd worked together was gone. The electric hint of... something, that had been there while we were dancing, was extinguished so totally I knew I must have imagined it. Adam was just Adam again, his shoulders slightly hunched under his jumper, his face expressionless, apart from a flush of bright red spreading upwards from his collar.

'Nah,' he said. 'I should go.'

Chapter Twenty-Eight

You had your chance and you blew it, Aquarius. Better luck next time.

'So that was it,' I said. 'He said goodnight and he'd see me at the next D&D game, and fucked off.'

'That's so weird!' Dani sat up on the weights bench, wiping her face with her towel. 'To just leave? To say no to an offer of a drink in your flat? When there'd been all that chemistry between you two.'

'I guess I must just have imagined it. Maybe he was a bit more pissed than I realised, and while we were cleaning up and stuff he sobered up.'

'But what about all his mates bigging him up to you?'

'Maybe they weren't. Maybe they're just nice people and they like Adam and they talk about him like that to anyone who'll listen.'

'Hmmm.' Dani moved off the bench and I took her place. 'It doesn't sound that way to me. It sounds like it was the biggest wingman – wingwoman, whatever – operation ever. And it worked, didn't it?'

'How do you mean?'

'They made you fancy him.'

I didn't say anything for a bit, because I was moving the weight up and down, to my chest and then up as far as my arms could reach, then back again. It felt a lot heavier than usual.

'They didn't make me fancy him,' I said, once I'd finished.

'No? Then how come you…?'

'Adam did that,' I said. '*He* made me fancy him. But there's no point thinking about it, because clearly he's not interested.'

'Not necessarily. Maybe he's just shy. Some blokes get that way around a woman they like. They're fine until crunch time and then suddenly they get all awkward.'

We swapped places again.

'He wasn't acting shy though. Not at all. Pulling his MC Hammer moves on the dance floor.'

'That's different. If dancing's something he's good at, then he could just crack on and let you admire him. It's like you – you cooked up a storm, right? And I bet he admired that. But you didn't feel shy doing it, did you?'

'Of course not. Adam wasn't even there when I was cooking. And I wasn't there when he was eating. So it's not the same at all. But anyway, I'm over it now. It was just a one-off thing, heat of the moment, had a few drinks, and I thought something might be going to happen. But it didn't, and I'm cool with that.'

Dani raised her eyebrows. 'Course you are.'

I pushed the weight up and lowered it again, then tried to raise it back up, but my arms were having none of it. I felt them start to tremble and wobble and the bar got all unbalanced, threatening to drop back down onto my chest. But Dani was there to lift it and replace it safely back on the rack.

'Okay,' I said. 'I'm not.'

I sat up, and suddenly my eyes were burning not just with sweat but with tears, too. I thought of everything I'd been through since that spring morning when I'd woken up, suddenly and inexplicably free of the yearning for Joe that I'd carried with me for so many years it had long since felt more like a labour than like love. I'd tried. I really, really had. I'd put myself out there. I'd dated lots. I'd had sex with a near-stranger. I'd had a relationship and given it my best shot and ended it when it wasn't working, like grown-ups are meant to do.

And at the end of all that, there should have been a reward for me. Some sort of prize, like the way Mike high-fived me when I did a perfect press-up, or the time a table at the Ginger Cat asked for the chef to come out into the bar so they could tell me personally how great their meal was, or even the imaginary treasure we were hoping to find in the D&D game.

But there had been nothing. Only my friendship with Adam, which I'd fleetingly thought might become something else. Until it hadn't.

'Hey.' Dani slipped her arm round my shoulder. 'It's only a bench-press.'

I choked out a half-laugh. 'It's not that. It's me. No one is ever going to love me and it's all my fault.'

'Wait, what? Zoë, you know that isn't true.'

I let out a sound that I'm sure hadn't ever been heard in the gym before, not even the time Fabian tried to deadlift double his body weight and pulled a hamstring.

'It is.' I'd buried my face in my towel, so I was pretty sure Dani couldn't hear my words, but she kept on stroking my heaving, sweating back anyway.

'Shhh.' Dani helped me to my feet. 'Come on, we mustn't hog the equipment if we're not using it or Mike will tell us off.'

She guided me to a corner of the gym, behind the racks where the plates were stacked neatly in order of weight, sat me down on the rubber mat and passed me my water bottle and a wad of blue paper towel.

I couldn't say anything for a while. I didn't know where the tears had come from or why they'd picked this moment to come, but I found I couldn't stop them. My shoulders heaved with sobs and my nose and eyes streamed, and Dani sat there patiently, rubbing my shoulder and shushing me, while I cried on and on.

But you can't cry forever, even when it feels like you're going to, and eventually I felt the sobs easing in my aching throat, and I looked up and blew my nose.

'Sorry,' I said. 'I'm such a dick.'

'You're not,' Dani said gently. 'But you can tell me what's wrong, if you like.'

'I feel like I've wasted all this time. I've dated all these men that were wrong for me, and when I met Jude I thought he was right, and I did everything I possibly could to make it work, and then I realised he was wrong too.'

'That's good though, right? I mean, at least you realised and kicked him to the kerb before you got in too deep.'

Dani had told me a while back that work had sent her on a customer relations course, and that one of the things they'd been taught was active listening. That was what she was doing now, I reckoned – not really knowing what I was so upset about but trying to encourage me to keep talking until I told her.

'The thing is, I told Adam I was done with dating. I told him I'm cool with being single and dying alone surrounded by cats. And clearly he's taken that on board, even if he was interested in me in the first place.'

'So talk to him! Tell him you've changed your mind. How hard can it be?'

'I wish I could. But the app – I have this app on my phone that sends me horoscopes every day – it's been getting really weird lately. Really dark. And the other day it said that some choices can't be unmade and you've got to accept the consequences, and I know that's true but it just made me feel really shitty. And today it told me I had my chance and I blew it, and I think it's right.'

'Ah, Zoë! Cop on! You can't let some stupid app dictate how you feel. Good grief! Delete it and move on. What app is it anyway?'

I told her and her mouth opened in astonishment. 'But that's—'

Then we heard a voice above us.

'What are you two doing, coffee-housing behind the weights rack? Don't you know there are pubs for this sort of thing?'

We got to our feet hastily, like school kids caught smoking behind the bike sheds, even though we knew Mike was joking.

'Have you seen this on Twitter, Dani? Your ex is trending all over the place. Load of stuff about some astrology app he started, and how he was paying writers in the Philippines to write content for it, not expert astrologers from NASA like he claimed. And he was using Chinese click farms to inflate the reviews on the app store.' He shook his head in bewilderment. 'It's a whole different world out there.'

I looked from Dani to Mike and back again. Mike was smiling, faintly amused. Dani looked like someone had just chucked a bucket of cold water over her head.

'I think I know the answer to this already,' I said slowly, 'but what's the name of the app he started, again?'

'Stargazer,' Dani and Mike said together.

'And speaking of which,' Mike went on, 'look what the cat dragged in.'

I considered telling him that even if Frazzle had been gifted with superpowers that enabled him to lift a fourteen-stone man as easily as he did a baby blackbird, he wouldn't deign to put his mouth anywhere near Fabian Flatley. But I couldn't, because, as always, Fabian's presence seemed to have robbed me of the power of speech.

He was wearing his usual designer gym kit: a muscle top and skin-tight Lycra shorts. The former had a prominent logo on it that I'd googled once out of curiosity and discovered cost over a hundred quid; the latter showed off far more of Fabian's anatomy than I or anyone else wanted to see. He smelled overpoweringly of the cedar deodorant he always used, which meant that he hadn't started his workout yet, because then he'd have smelled overpoweringly of sweat.

He strolled over to us and gave Mike a slap on the shoulder that looked friendly but would have sent him flying if he hadn't been such an absolute unit, then slipped an arm round Dani's waist.

'Hey, mate. Hey, baby. You over your huff yet? Fancy going out tonight?'

He ignored me, which I felt almost pathetically grateful for. But Dani froze, as if Fabian's arm was made of lead rather than muscle and bone and had rooted her to the spot. I saw her turn her head and look at him, her eyes widening in a mix of fear and desire.

Fabian reached out and pinched her cheek. 'Bit overemotional, were you? Silly girl. It's okay, I'll give you another chance. Just the one, mind.'

Dani reached up and touched the place he'd pinched like it hurt. But she didn't say anything – it was like she physically couldn't.

But Mike could. 'Stop me if I'm wrong. But this woman asked you not to contact her again. I don't know the details and I don't want to. But I won't have my clients being harassed in my gym.'

'Am I harassing her? Does it look like that? Does it feel like that, baby?'

Dani found her voice, although it came out in a thin squeak, as if she could still feel Fabian's hands around her neck, squeezing.

'Yes, it does.'

'Well, then,' Mike said. 'Looks like we're pretty clear on that. This gym is a place where I want everyone to feel safe, and so you won't be welcome here any longer. I'll refund the balance of your membership.'

'But… I pay for daily personal training sessions, and I don't even use half of them!' Fabian spluttered. 'I'm worth almost twenty grand a year to you. These girls pay peanuts. Are you trying to destroy your business?'

Mike folded his arms over his chest. His hands barely reached his elbows because his pecs and biceps were so big. 'Money isn't everything. And I prefer clients who actually follow my advice.

Wherever you go next, Fabian, listen to them when they tell you you need to do cardio as well as lift, and you need to have a healthy lifestyle, too. Maybe slow down on the Colombian marching powder and the little blue pills. No point having the best body in the morgue, right?'

Fabian looked at him like he was getting ready to protest, or even fight. But Mike's face was implacable, and in that moment actually quite scary.

'Fine.' Fabian let go of Dani and spun around on his designer trainers. 'There are plenty of better places than this. See if I care.'

And he flounced off through the gap in the metal shutters. I heard the roar of his car's powerful engine, and then, instead of it fading into the distance, I heard a sickening crunch and a tinkle of glass. Through the open door, I could see the bollard he'd reversed into, his car's crumpled bumper and a group of teenage boys outside the fried chicken shop breaking into ironic cheers.

Dani didn't notice the unfolding drama, though. She was gazing at Mike, wide-eyed, like she'd never seen him before, a huge happy smile spreading over her face.

Chapter Twenty-Nine

There is good fortune in the stars today, Aquarius. Just don't expect any of it to be coming your way, okay?

'Zoë? Earth to Zoë?' Robbie poked me in the ribs with a wooden spoon and I jumped like he'd given me an electric shock.

'What? What do you want?'

'I've asked you four times if you want coffee, twice if you want to use the posh honey we got from Archie in the blondies or the standard stuff, and three times if you wanted to take some of those butternut squash and sage bruschetta out for Maurice and the boys to try, or whether I should do it and get the glory. And you've been completely blanking me. I know you're a bit long in the tooth at almost twenty-eight but it's a bit early to be going deaf, surely?'

'Sorry. I was miles away. Yes to coffee, we may as well go ahead and use the posh honey, and I'll handle the quality control. Thanks, Robbie.'

'No worries.' He switched on the coffee machine, its full-throated roar convincing me that I wasn't in fact going deaf.

I had been lost in my thoughts, and I was still. I picked up the plate of toasted bruschetta topped with rich roast squash, drizzled with sage oil and sprinkled with nduja crumbs and carried them out to the bar, where Maurice, Terry, Sadiq and Ray were beginning their dominoes game. Alice was behind the bar; Kelly was down on her knees with a dustpan and brush cleaning up the crumbs left by the mums and tots group. Fat Don was on his usual stool, sipping his pint. Frazzle was spread out on the chaise longue in a patch of sun.

The Ginger Cat felt the same as it did on any Wednesday morning: bright, cheerful and serenely busy. But I felt different. I felt like I'd been hollowed out inside. It wasn't hunger; Robbie had insisted I ate a bowl of granola when I got in that morning after fussing over me and demanding to know why I was looking like a vampire's cold leftovers, and I'd confessed that I'd had no supper the night before and almost no sleep.

'Are you going to tell us what those are, love?' Ray asked. 'Or are you just going to stand there staring at them?'

'Sorry, sorry!' I'd walked across the room to the dominoes table on autopilot, my mind in another place entirely. 'They're a new snack we're thinking of putting on the autumn bar menu. What do you reckon?'

I put the plate on the table and stood there as I always did, waiting for their verdict.

'What's this brown stuff then?' Terry poked a suspicious finger at the top of one of the bruschetta.

'It's an nduja crumb.'

'And what's that when it's at home?'

'It's a kind of spicy spreadable sausage. Like salami only softer. And we've fried it with some breadcrumbs and sage so it's crunchy. It's got pork in it, sorry, Sadiq.'

'Nduja really want to hurt me,' Terry sang tunelessly. 'Nduja really want to make me cry?'

They all cracked up, and I couldn't help laughing too. Maurice picked up a piece, tucked a paper napkin into his collar and took a crunchy bite.

'Delicious,' he said. 'Really autumnal flavour. I'm going to tell Wesley about this nduja stuff; it would work a treat with rice and peas.'

'Cor, that doesn't half blow your head off,' Ray said. 'Ought to come with a health warning.'

But he finished his piece and immediately took another.

'I'll take that as an approval, then,' I said, leaving them to their game as Alice approached the table with a tray of drinks.

I made my way back to the kitchen, feeling my mind drift back into the tangle of thoughts that seemed to envelop it, tangled and clinging like the fake cobwebs Alice had arranged in the windows for Halloween, which had paper spiders ensnared in them.

For months, I reflected, shaping sourdough into loaves, I'd let myself be governed – or at least steered – by what the Stargazer app had told me to do. I'd followed its guidance on dates and relationships and my own life, not slavishly exactly, but faithfully enough. And now, thanks to Mike, I knew the truth.

I'd read through various threads on Twitter, outlining the story of how Fabian had launched the app, using fake downloads and fake reviews to get it trending. How he'd made all sorts of claims about the authenticity of its predictions being based on genuine astronomical data, when all the time a content mill of writers in Manila had been writing the daily horoscopes based on nothing but a stringent style guide.

I'd read how, when Fabian had unilaterally cut the fee he was paying to the business owner in the Philippines, the writers' already rock-bottom wages had been cut, too. Threatened with losing their jobs if they objected, they'd taken matters into their own hands, writing horoscopes that were darker and more depressing than before, pushing one another to see how far they could take it before the editors noticed.

I imagined them – highly educated graduates working for pennies from their laptops at home, or at shared desks in a café if they had no space or quiet at home – exchanging messages over Slack or glances across the table, taking a bit of glee in getting one over on their exploitative employer. Because the Stargazer brand was all about being edgy, about sending out push notifications that were acid almost to the point of being brutal, it took a long time before anyone noticed. Hell, I'd barely noticed myself. I'd assumed that the app simply knew me well enough, through some mysterious algorithm or through genuine astrology, to reflect my thoughts back to me.

If I hadn't been so invested, I'd have found it funny. But now I couldn't shake the sense of dislocation, of something having changed in my world so significantly that I no longer fully understood it.

The rest of that morning passed in a blur. I worked, I chatted to Robbie, I listened to music on my headphones. But I couldn't remember a word of our conversation afterwards. I could barely taste the food, and had to keep passing the spoon over to Robbie for him to confirm that the seasoning was right. When a new song started on my playlist, I couldn't have told you what the previous one had been.

Robbie seemed distracted too, I noticed. He kept glancing anxiously at his phone, and when it buzzed with an incoming alert he pounced on it like Frazzle on a feathery toy, only to put it down again, disheartened. And then, when the opening bars of 'Half a Man' came through the speaker, I heard the thunk of his wooden spoon falling to the floor and a choking sob.

'Shit, Robbie! What's wrong?'

'It's Rex.' He mopped his eyes on a tea towel.

I put my arm round his shoulder and shushed a bit, my mind whirring. What could have happened? Some sort of horrible accident? Rex turning out to have a wife and kids on the side? Or just Robbie getting ghosted, when things had been going so well?

'Do you want to tell me about it?' I asked.

'I can't believe what he's gone and done,' Robbie gulped. 'The bastard!'

'Ssshh, you poor thing. Whatever it is, you'll be okay.' And, remembering saying almost exactly the same to Dani, I added in my head, *And dump his sorry arse so he can never hurt you again.*

But Robbie went on, 'He says he wants us to be official. Like, boyfriend and boyfriend. The deadass headass.'

For a second, I was too surprised to speak. 'But… but that's good, right? I mean, you're totally into him. You haven't seen anyone else for ages.'

'That,' Robbie said, 'is not. The. Point. We weren't meant to be serious. I was meant to have years of casual shagging ahead of me. And then bloody Rex turns up and not only is he my dream man, but he says I'm his. He told me he loves me, the total melt.'

'But you love him too!'

'So what? I wasn't going to admit I'd fallen for him, was I? So I dumped him. By text.'

I shook my head in bewilderment, then gave Robbie's shoulder a final pat, picked his spoon up off the floor and wagged it at him.

'Now,' I said. 'You've given me your fair share of advice about my love life, and it's my turn to read you the riot act. Are you listening?'

Robbie nodded, his lip trembling.

'Rex is asking you to be his boyfriend. That's all. He's not asking you to marry him, or chaining you up in a dungeon, or making you sign in blood saying you'll never have sex with anyone else again ever. Am I right?'

'I guess.'

'He's saying he wants you two to be exclusive for now – to take your relationship to the next level, and see how that goes. Correct?'

'I suppose so.'

'And that's what you want, really, isn't it? You've just got a massive attack of cold feet.' Like I did when I was twenty and in love with Joe, and ended it because I was too frightened, only to spend years regretting my decision, when I could have just gone with it and let it run its course. I didn't regret that decision any more, not really – but that didn't stop me wanting to prevent Robbie from making the same mistake.

'Maybe you're right,' Robbie admitted.

'Of course I'm right! And another thing. You're allowed to be happy, you know. You're allowed to fall in love, even if it doesn't feel like the right time.'

'So what should I do?'

'Sheesh, you doofus! Pick up your phone right now and text the guy and tell him you made a mistake!'

'I…' Robbie hesitated for a second, then he did the pounce thing again, and seconds later his phone was in his hands and he was bashing away at the screen like a man possessed.

I escaped to the gym after lunch as usual, but I wasn't feeling it and, after a few minutes on the rowing machine, I gave up and did some gentle stretches instead, ignoring Mike's disapproving gaze. And then I went home and got into bed with Frazzle, and had a long afternoon nap, filled with shadowy and confusing dreams.

I thought about sacking off that evening's D&D game, but I couldn't do that – we were at a crucial point in the adventure, with Galena, Annella and Torvid nearing the heart of the castle where we thought Zarah might be imprisoned. Without me, the others would have no fighting power and a real chance of being captured or worse. I'd just have to front it out, and act like nothing had happened between Adam and me. We were friends and that was it.

Of course, I reminded myself, the game wasn't real either. It was an imaginary world, but that didn't make it any less important. If we succeeded in our adventure, we'd have done so as a team, looking out for each other, strategising together, making the best of whatever fate a roll of the dice threw at us.

So, when I woke up feeling no less sleepy than I had two hours before, I told myself I had to get my shit together and make this work, however awkward I felt about seeing Adam again after our last strange and unsatisfying encounter. I showered and washed my hair and put on make-up for the first time in ages, put serum in my hair and pulled on a black jumper dress, tights and boots. I was doing it for me, I insisted to myself. Nothing whatsoever to do with Adam, who clearly wasn't interested in me anyway.

I looked around the tidy, orderly flat. It smelled of my aromatherapy body lotion and coconut water shampoo. The laundry basket was empty and the bed was made. Frazzle was on the sofa, curled up tightly with his paws crossed over his nose. There were worse things than being alone, I supposed. I'd managed it – enjoyed it, even – for years and I could continue to do so.

I locked the door and walked down the stairs, passing the kitchen and entering the bar, a customer again instead of an employee. I bought a bottle of wine and headed over to the Dungeons & Dragons table, where Nat and Archie were already sitting, sipping their drinks and chatting.

'You look amazing, Zoë,' Nat said. 'Heading out somewhere later?'

'Nah. I just felt like making a bit of an effort. I've been dressing like a slob for too long.'

Freddie hurried over and flopped into a chair. 'Looking good, Zoë. Nothing's too much trouble for your fight with the evil lord, right?'

'You've scrubbed up a bit too,' I said. 'Not sure a silk shirt is ideal for crawling through mazes looking for treasure.'

'But think of all the quality gear I'll be able to buy once we find it.'

We all laughed, slightly awkward in the moments before the game began, when we were half our characters and half ourselves; half in the Ginger Cat and half in the dungeons below Castle Drakeford; aware that this was a slightly tragic, dorky game but also caught up in the magic of the story Adam had woven for us.

'And here's the man himself,' Lana said.

Adam approached our table, half-smiling, his heavy bag slung over his shoulder. The shirt he was wearing looked new too – it was a dark bottle-green that seemed to have turned his eyes exactly the same colour. I said hi to him and he replied, but his was more of a general greeting to the whole table. It was like he'd barely noticed me there at all. The others followed shortly after him, and soon the usual rituals of drinks-pouring and food-ordering were complete, and we began.

As soon as Adam started speaking, the real world receded. I stopped being Zoë, stopped thinking about my future as a crazy cat lady who lived above a pub, and became Galena. I wasn't wearing my jumper dress and faux suede boots any more, but leather armour and boots, because Galena had other things on her mind than animal rights, like not getting her head chopped off with a broadsword.

'We return to the upper levels of the castle, where Galena and the others are continuing their quest to find young Zarah. Last week, we left you in an antechamber near to the rooms where you believe the evil Lord Brandrel is holding the girl prisoner. The walls are hung with slightly faded tapestries and lit by oil lamps. There is woven rush matting on the floor and a wooden chest in one corner. On the wall, you notice a large mirror in a heavy wrought-iron frame.'

'Oh God, I'd better not look,' Nat said. 'My root growth will be horrendous after all this time on an adventure.'

I said, 'We should examine the looking glass; it may be somehow enchanted.'

'I sense the power of magic here,' Annella agreed.

'Let's bolt the door we came in through,' I said. 'Then we can examine this place in relative safety.'

'You push the door closed and slide the iron bolt home with a rasp and a click. Strangely, you do not now feel safer in this place but less so – as if you have walked into a trap.'

'Oh shit,' I said. 'Well, there's nothing for it but to take a look around.'

'I will keep watch on the far door,' said Torvid.

'You approach the mirror. In its surface, slightly foxed by time, your frightened faces stare back at you, with the chamber in the background.'

'What if we try and take the mirror off the wall? Could there be something behind it?'

Adam rolled the dice. 'You carefully lift the mirror away from the wall, its iron frame chilly in your hands.'

'Fucking hell, don't drop it, whatever you do, you two.'

'Without letting the glass fall, you lower the mirror carefully to the ground. It was suspended from a fine steel chain, which looped over a hooked spike driven deep into the stone.'

'Is there anything on the back of the mirror? A note, maybe?'

'You turn the looking glass and examine its reverse side. Faintly, on the wooden surface, you can see runes, which appear to have been scratched or etched into the wood.'

'I can read runes!' Annella exclaimed. 'I learned in magic college. Can I understand these ones?'

Again, the dice clicked on the table. Adam smiled, and for a second he was just Adam again, not the all-powerful Dungeon Master. 'You are able to decipher them. The inscription reads, "All is not what it seems."'

'Cryptic, much? I don't see that that's much help, to be honest.'

'Maybe we should hang the mirror back on the wall,' I suggested, 'and check that the reflection of the room is accurate. Maybe there's some weird spell going on.'

'Oooh, good shout!'

'Carefully, you replace the mirror and step back. Again, you see your puzzled faces, the tapestries on the opposite wall, the flickering oil lamps.'

'What about the chest?' I said. 'Didn't we see a chest, when we came into the room? Is it there in the reflection?'

Again, Adam's smile flashed out. 'In the reflection, the chest is positioned centrally, but in the room itself it is in the corner, near the door through which you entered.'

'Let's move it and see what happens!'

'Torvid and I will do it,' Annella said hastily. 'Galena, you stay looking in the mirror and tell us when we've got it in the right place.'

'You tug and heave the heavy chest, but once it begins to move, it slides freely over the rush matting. Galena watches your stooped backs and straining arms, until at last she says—'

'Stop! You've got it!'

'All at once, the mirror moves, opening away from the wall with a creak. Beyond, you see brilliant light, and you are powerless to resists its enchanted pull. You step forward, through the gap in the wall, and you hear a sound like a thunderclap as the magic portal slams closed behind you. Galena, you are alone – at least that is what you think at first. Then you see before you a figure, wrapped in a rich dark velvet cloak, a jewelled circlet on his dark hair.'

'Lord Brandrel!' exclaimed Tim.

'Of course, we wouldn't be there to see what happened next,' Lana said.

'Maybe we should step outside while Adam and Zoë – I mean, while Lord Brandrel and Galena – fight it out?' suggested Freddie.

'But I want to know what happens,' Archie protested.

'Ssshh,' Nat hissed.

'But you guys are in the party,' I said. 'I can't just... How would it work normally, Adam? You're in charge.'

'Well,' Adam said slowly, 'we wouldn't normally have split the party, but all of you have seen what's been going on with the other group, so... Ouch!'

'Sorry,' Freddie said. 'Was that your ankle? My foot must have slipped.'

Kelly came over with a tray laden with a bottle of prosecco and seven glasses. 'Alice sent this over. She mentioned that her office happens to be free right now.'

'We'll step in there, shall we, Zoë?' Adam said. 'Unless you'd rather...'

But Freddie had already poured the wine, and he handed a glass to me and one to Adam. 'Off you go then. Come back soon and tell us what happened.'

'But…' I began, but it was too late. Adam had picked up his glass and headed purposefully off in the direction of the tiny cubicle that held Alice's desk, a filing cabinet that no one ever filed anything in, because all our admin was online now, and often other random crap as well. Today there was a hoover in there, a stack of samples of hard seltzer that a supplier had sent to see how it went down with the punters, and a crate of orange pumpkins we'd ordered in for the family Halloween event.

There was barely room for Adam and me to squeeze in, but we did, pulling the door closed behind us.

Suddenly, he seemed very close to me and very tall. I looked up at him, and he looked down at me, and then we both looked away again and took great gulps of our drinks. Adam hadn't brought any of his notes, I noticed, although I could see his hand tightly clenched around a few of the translucent multi-sided dice.

He cleared his throat. 'Lord Brandrel is alone in this strange room with you. You don't know what form of sorcery has brought you here, or what your fate will be. You feel your gaze irresistibly drawn to his, and you wonder if this is part of the same magic that created the mirror illusion.'

My gaze was irresistibly drawn to Adam's, just like he said. His eyes were the deepest green and his brows were two black arches above them. He had the most ridiculously long eyelashes, I noticed, and they were black too, like his beard, standing out against his pale skin.

'Why have you brought me here?' Galena demanded.

'I think you might wish to ask yourself why you came,' countered Lord Brandrel.

'I – and my companions, who wait without – are here to rescue the maiden Zarah, who was captured by your troops from the village.'

'I think you'll find,' said Lord Brandrel, 'that Zarah merely wished to escape her overbearing mother and is not in any kind of captivity. Rather, she is gainfully employed here at the castle as a kitchen maid.'

'But – but you captured her. You intended to force her to become your bride!'

'I did no such thing. She came here of her own free will, escorted by my soldiers. However, I cannot deny that stewardship of this castle is a lonely life, and should I find someone to share it with me, my heart would be lighter.'

'But I am a fighter!' Galena said. 'I will not set aside my freedom for any man.'

'And I shall make no serf of any woman!' blazed Lord Brandrel. 'I seek an equal in all ways, to fight alongside me, share my board and my bed and my riches, even as she shares my heart.'

I felt a tightness in my throat, and swallowed to try and make it go away.

'So long as she's willing to share her cat with me,' said Adam.

I tried to find Galena inside me, but I couldn't. It seemed like she had… not vanished, exactly, but melted, back into the part of me that had imagined her in the first place.

'There's just one thing,' I said. 'What star sign are you – I mean, is Lord Brandrel?'

'Truly it astounds me,' Lord Brandrel said, stroking his beard, 'that a woman so fierce and learned should put her faith in superstition.'

'Even so. How should I be expected to plight my troth to one who will not indulge an innocent fancy?'

Adam laughed. His whole face seemed to come alive, the stillness and wariness all gone. 'I'm Aquarius, you numpty. Same as you.'

'Well,' I said, 'I guess that has potential. Aquarius man and Aquarius woman is one of the better matches. Our shared fascination with the spiritual world means we'll never tire of exploring wider issues together, and we'll have a rich, fulfilling and inventive sex life.'

I was making it up, just like Fabian's paid writers had been, but it was totally worth it to see Adam blush.

'Come on,' he said, putting his glass down on a corner of Alice's desk. 'I want to show you something.'

Before I could ask what, he'd set my glass down next to his, put his arm round my shoulders and guided me out of Alice's office. And then the closeness and warmth of his body and the juniper scent of his skin was so strange and new and wonderful I don't think I would have been able to say anything if I'd tried. Adam led me into the lobby with the four doors opening off it – one to the kitchen, one to the bar, one to the stairs that led to my flat and one to the garden.

'It's like being back in the D&D game,' I said, regaining the power of speech. 'Four doors lead out from the chamber. Which one will you pick?'

Adam laughed. 'Don't take the piss. We're going outside.'

The beer garden was empty – no smokers had ventured out that night, which wasn't surprising, as it was bitterly cold. The night air bit through the thin fabric of my dress, and I was glad of Adam's warm body next to me. The cold didn't seem to bother him at all, even though he was dressed no more warmly than I was.

We stood there for a moment, our breath forming clouds of vapour that drifted away like ghosts. The garden smelled of damp earth, fallen leaves, the last of the cooking smells being pumped out by the kitchen extractor fan and a distant bonfire. The bird table was deserted and the parasols folded. I could hear a hum of voices from inside the pub, and the faint popping of firecrackers somewhere out in the night.

'Well, this is romantic,' I teased.

'Zoë! Look up.'

I tilted my head, and everything changed. Above us, the clear autumn sky was pitch black but spangled with stars. A thin crescent moon like one of Frazzle's claws hung over the rooftops. On the horizon, the lights of an aeroplane beginning its descent blinked steadily.

'See that bright star just there.' Adam pointed up into the darkness.

'I can see loads of stars.'

'There. In the middle of that dark bit of sky.'

I followed the long line of his arm, pressing my head against his shoulder to keep warm and also so I could look the same way he was looking.

'I think so.'

'That's Beta Aquarii, the brightest star in the constellation of Aquarius. It's about six hundred light years away. The dimmer one close to it, Alpha Aquarii, is a hundred times as big as our sun. It's the right time of the year to see them, and we're lucky it's such a clear night. The third one is called Gamma Aquarii.'

'It's… I never knew you could actually see it,' I said. 'I mean, I knew Aquarius was a constellation and everything, but I thought you needed to work for NASA or at least have a telescope.'

'When I was a kid I used to dream of working for NASA. I thought I'd fly to the moon or be an astrophysicist or something. But I do have a telescope.'

'Is that a telescope in your pocket or are you just pleased to see me?'

Adam pressed me closer, and I could feel the laughter shaking his body. Making this man laugh could get quite addictive, I realised.

'Tell me more about the stars,' I said.

'Their Arabic names are all to do with luck. The luck of kings, the lucky star of hidden things. So if you want to wish on a star, you should pick one of those.'

'Isn't wishing on stars a load of bollocks, like astrology?'

'I couldn't possibly say. Maybe we should try it, then we'd have scientific proof.'

'Okay. You first.'

'We should do it together.'

I nodded, knowing that Adam would be able to feel the movement of my head where it pressed against him. His arm squeezed me closer and we stood in silence for a couple of seconds.

'What did you wish?' he asked.

'I can't tell you! If I do it stops the magic working.'

'But what about our scientific proof?'

I turned around within the circle of Adam's arm and looked up at him, and he looked down at me. He was smiling, and in the darkness it looked like his eyes were sparkling. I felt something shift inside of me, like I was melting, even though it was so cold.

'Okay,' I said. 'I wished you'd kiss me.'

'Funny, that. So did I.'

And suddenly his other arm was around me, too, and both my hands were reaching up to pull him close, so I could press the whole warm, strong length of him against me. My fingers touched his hair, surprisingly soft and silky. The clean man-smell of him joined all the other smells of the night, and as his lips touched mine it was like Aquarius and all the other constellations started spinning round and round at once – although I knew I'd never be able to tell Adam that was how it felt, because he'd say they were stars and planets in orbit and spinning was exactly what they did all the time.

Chapter Thirty

'So what happened after that?' Dani gasped. We were in the gym and taking it in turns on the rowing machine, and she was a couple of hundred metres into her go, and really giving it some.

'Shall I wait until you've finished?'

'No, distract me!'

I laughed. 'Keep going – you've got this. Okay, so we went back indoors and finished the D&D game.'

'No way!'

'Well, we couldn't not. We'd left the others all on tenterhooks waiting to know what happened with Galena and Lord Brandrel.'

Dani half-laughed, half-panted.

'Except it turned out they weren't, really. They were waiting to find out what had happened with me and Adam. Turns out they'd all been in on it, since the party for Tansy and Josh when nothing happened. Basically it feels like everyone who's ever been in the Ginger Cat has been trying to set us up for ages. A hundred metres to go.'

'Oh God, I'm dying.'

'Just a few more strokes. So we went back into the bar and everyone went all quiet, you know how that happens? But Adam had his arm round me still and it was fine. No one said anything, they just looked at us like we were their late-developing babies who were finally taking their first steps or something.'

Dani finished her row and collapsed, laughing, on the floor.

'Right, you're up,' she said, when she'd got her breath back a bit.

'But don't you want to hear what happened next?'

'You can tell me in a thousand metres' time.'

'You're so harsh!' I grumbled, climbing onto the rower and gripping the handle, before taking a deep breath and starting.

'I'm going to need to be,' Dani said. 'I've signed up to do a fitness instructor course and once I'm qualified I can jack in my shitty job at the dental surgery and actually do something I love. So you're going to have to let me practise on you.'

'That's amazing,' I panted. 'You'll be brilliant.'

'Nice long strokes,' Dani said. 'Try and control your breathing. Yeah, to be honest I just don't know why I didn't think of it sooner. It was only when Mike said he was looking to take on someone to help him, because the gym's getting so busy, that I had this light-bulb moment and I was like, "That could be me." Not right away, obviously; I'll have to qualify first and it's really hard.'

'So are you and Mike…?'

'Push with your legs, Zoë. Come on, nearly there. Oh my God, isn't he just the most amazing person in the world? I couldn't believe it when he said yes when I asked him out. I was so nervous I was literally shaking. And we went on this proper old-fashioned date to the movies and then out for pizza. And he didn't nag me when I had extra cheese on mine like Fabian would've done. And he actually listens when I talk to him.'

She glanced over her shoulder to the rack of barbells, where Mike was patiently talking a new client through correct squat form, and I noticed that she had that look on her face again, all wide-eyed and happy, like she was looking at the promised land or something.

'One thousand metres.' I folded down over my legs, which appeared to have turned into two strands of wet spaghetti, and waited until I could breathe a bit more normally. 'That's so cool, Dani. Honestly, you guys are perfect for each other.'

'Right.' Dani hopped back onto the rower and tightened the straps on the footrests. 'Now carry on telling me about Adam.'

I downed some water and towelled my sweating face. I could see in the full-length mirror that my hair had frizzed wildly and my cheeks looked like a pair of tomatoes, but I didn't care.

'Yeah, so like I said, we finished the D&D game and we had another couple of drinks, and everyone was totally itching to ask if we'd snogged, but they didn't. I guess they didn't need to, really.'

It had been pretty obvious, I reckoned, because every time I looked at Adam his face broke into the most enormous, cheesy grin, and I know mine must've done the same. And his hand kept reaching for mine under the table, and his touch sent such amazing shocks of pleasure right the way through me I probably looked like I was radioactive.

'Stop mooning and keep talking!'

'Sorry. It's just... I can't stop thinking about him. Robbie gave me such a telling-off this morning because I was singing along to "Now That I Found You" on my phone and he said I sounded like a constipated cat.'

Dani gasped out a laugh. 'So did you shag?'

'We… It feels so weird talking about it!'

I let myself return to the memory of that night, as I'd done over and over again for the past five days. It was like taking a precious new thing I'd saved up for ages to buy out of its box and gazing at it, turning it over and over, unable to believe it was mine at last. Or like when Frazzle first came to live with me, and I'd wake up in the morning and for a second I would have forgotten I had a cat, and then I opened my eyes and there he was, and I felt like I might burst with happiness.

We stayed in the pub until everyone had left, and Adam helped with the clearing up like it was something he'd always done. And when we'd switched off the lights and Alice and Freddie had said goodnight, we were left alone in the bar. We'd walked through into the vestibule, and this time there was no need to ask which of the four doors we'd choose. We turned left and climbed the stairs to my flat, my heart hammering and my knees feeling all trembly, and Adam filled Frazzle's water bowl while I scooped out his litter tray, and although it shouldn't have been the most romantic thing ever, somehow it was. It was like there was an electric current running between Adam and me that intensified whenever we passed each other, and sent sparks flying between us when our eyes met and we smiled. He'd probably say it was just static from the cheap nylon carpet, but I knew better.

'Two hundred metres to go,' I said. 'You're doing brilliantly, keep pushing. Yeah, we did. And it was off. The Scale. Like we'd had years of practice. Or maybe he's just a natural at it, I don't know. But it wasn't awkward or cringe or anything, just lovely. Even when my cat jumped on the bed in the middle of it. Honestly, he and Adam have this total bromance going. Frazzle thinks he's the best thing ever.'

'He's not the only one,' Dani said, giving me side-eye from her position on the rower.

'Oy! Who was it who just referred to her new boyfriend as "the most amazing person in the world"?'

Dani opened her mouth to argue – possibly to make the point that clearly, from her objective point of view, Mike was the most perfect man ever to have drawn breath, in which case I'd have had to argue the toss and tell her that clearly, going purely on the evidence, Adam was a superior human being, and it would all have got a bit silly – but fortunately she didn't have the breath to say anything at all.

'One more pull,' I encouraged her, feeling like someone on *Call the Midwife*, 'and you're there.'

'Right.' Dani lay on her back on the floor, her chest heaving. 'Your turn next, and then we're done, right?'

'Then can we go to that place down the road that does the incredible cupcakes?'

'For sure.'

I got back on the machine, telling myself that I'd be finished in just another couple of minutes. But my legs were still feeling trembly with fatigue, and I knew I'd need all the help I could get to last the final kilometre.

'So I take it you haven't heard from Fabian again?'

'Oh. My. God. I was saving this up to tell you over cake, but do you want to hear it now?'

'Go on then.'

'I didn't hear anything from him for ages. Like, over a week. I was so relieved the calls and the bloody flowers had stopped, because

I was starting to feel like I was living in a flaming funeral parlour and I kept having to go round to the old people's home with these ridiculous bouquets, and I was worried they'd start thinking I was crushing on one of the residents. So I reckoned Mike warning him off had worked, and I was right. Kind of.'

'What happened then?' I panted.

'Then, last Friday, I was at work, and he walked in through the door. Only he wasn't alone.'

'Oh shit.'

'My mum was with him.'

'What?' Literally thrown off my stroke, I slowed down and almost stopped.

'Keep going, Zoë. Think of the cupcakes. Yeah, he turned up with my mum, at my work. I almost died.'

'But how…?'

'Obviously I had no idea what had happened, but Mum explained it all to me afterwards. I'd told him a bit about her, how we didn't have the best relationship and stuff, and how sad it made me, and how I hoped one day we'd be able to make things right again. I thought at the time he wasn't listening, because he never really did, but he must've been. Because he found out her address and wrote to her.'

I kept rowing and didn't say anything, but my mind was whirling. Fabian Flatley? Getting in touch with Dani's mother to try and arrange a reconciliation between them? It seemed about as likely as Frazzle setting up a shelter for homeless mice.

'He sent her photos of me,' Dani almost whispered. 'Of me… you know.'

'Revenge porn?' I gasped. 'The bastard!'

'Bastard is right. God knows what he thought was going to happen. I mean, it couldn't have made things that much worse between her and me than they already were, right? But he picked a fight with the wrong person when he did that. Twenty metres to go… ten… and you're done.'

'Never mind done, I'm broken. So what did your mum do?'

'She went full mama bear. She looked him up on LinkedIn – I didn't know she even knew what LinkedIn was, but she did – and she found his work address and she got a train from Liverpool and marched right into the office and demanded to see him.'

'What?'

'I know, right. And when the receptionist told her he was in a meeting, she was like, "That man is trying to blackmail my daughter" – although he wasn't really; he knows I don't have two quid to rub together – "So you fetch him out of his meeting or I'll walk in there myself and tell everyone what kind of person he is."'

'No way!'

'Yep. So the receptionist went and got him and they sat in his office and Mum gave him the bollocking of his life and told him he ought to be ashamed of himself and she was going to go the police, and that must've put the fear of God into him because you know he doesn't pay anything like the tax he ought to and he's really paranoid about scrutiny of any kind. So he literally begged her not to, and she said she might reconsider if he deleted every last pixel – I didn't know she knew what those were either – of every image he had anywhere of me, and got in an Uber with her right that second and went round to my work to apologise to me.'

'Shut the front door!'

'Yep. So the first I knew of it was them turning up and Mum saying, "Mr Flatley would like a word with you in private, Danielle," and I was like, what the fuck? But what could I say? So we went outside and he said he'd treated me appallingly and he was deeply sorry, and he accepted my decision to end the relationship and wished me every happiness. And then he got in another Uber and went away, and I took the afternoon off and had tea with Mum.'

'That's amazing!'

'Isn't it? And she said she felt awful about having been cold to me all this time, and she should have supported me wanting to make a life for myself away from home, but she'd never known how to say sorry, and now she was. And I said I was sorry too, for not making more of an effort, and we agreed that Mike and I will go there for Christmas.'

I stood up and finished my water. 'Well, that calls for a celebration.'

'Prosecco with our cupcakes?'

'Word.'

And we swished out of the gym together, Dani only pausing to blow Mike a kiss over her shoulder.

Chapter Thirty-One

Christmas Day

The sound of church bells woke me just before seven. It was still dark outside and I could feel cold seeping in through the window, which was open just a crack because Adam got too hot otherwise. But under the covers I was perfectly warm. I turned over, pulling the duvet up to my chin, and opened my eyes.

There was Adam's dark head on the pillow next to mine, the black eyelashes sweeping down over his cheeks. And there, lying on his chest, gazing adoringly at him and purring like a freight train, was Frazzle. In the corner of the flat, a tiny Christmas tree twinkled with gold and silver lights, and under it was a small pile of carefully wrapped presents.

For a minute, I let myself luxuriate, still half asleep, looking at my two boys.

Then I sat bolt upright and said, 'Shit, fuck, bollocks! The turkey stock!'

'What?' Adam pushed himself up on his elbows, careful not to disturb the cat who was already half his. 'It's Christmas Day, Zoë. The pub's closed. You're not going near a kitchen today.'

'Oh. Oh my God, of course it is. Merry Christmas.'

'Merry Christmas. And happy day off. You've been working too hard.'

I smiled. 'I've been working just right.'

He did have a point, though, I thought. The last couple of weeks had passed in a blur of mince pies, Brussels sprouts and chestnut wellingtons, Robbie and I both rushed off our feet. The Ginger Cat had been buzzing from the moment we opened the doors until late in the evening – or, as it seemed to me, from spiced pumpkin muffins to roast dinners, via turkey sandwiches, Christmas cake at teatime and sausage rolls on the bar at six o'clock.

Robbie had complained that he'd almost forgotten what Rex looked like, and Maurice had told me I looked like I needed a nice sit-down in front of the telly. The only night off I'd managed had been to go with Adam to his work Christmas party, at a five-star hotel. I'd been terrified of having nothing to wear and not knowing what to say, but he'd assured me that they'd all loved me and, amazingly, they seemed to, even though my dress was from eBay and my hair had frizzed.

But now it was all over, and I had two blissful days off in which I could do anything I wanted, or nothing at all if I wanted that.

I snuggled closer to Adam in bed, and felt the comforting warmth of his body and the weight of Frazzle's. It was strange, I reflected, how the flat, which had always felt too small when Jude was there, seemed to have expanded, Tardis-like, to accommodate Adam. He spent most nights there, and I teased him that it was because when he went back to his place, he missed Frazzle too much.

'Of course I do,' he'd said. 'But he's not the only one I miss.'

'So what do you want to do with your Christmas morning?' he asked now.

In answer, I ran my hand up the hard length of his thigh, and Frazzle grumpily got up and moved to the end of the bed, where he spent the next half an hour looking pointedly away from us while we celebrated Christmas in the best way ever.

'You know,' I said afterwards, 'I never thought this would happen. I thought I'd completely blown my chances with you. I was sure you weren't interested, and if you were, I'd managed to put you off.'

'Ha! I was interested from the moment I first saw you, when you came over to ask me about D&D.'

'But you didn't even want to do it! I practically had to beg.'

'That was just because I was too worried about showing myself up in front of you and the entire pub, and blowing my chances. And then whatsisname came on the scene…'

'Jude. You know a weird thing? I saw him a couple of weeks back, when I went into town for a drink with Dani. He was with a girl. His friend, Indigo. But they didn't look like they were just friends.'

'You didn't mind, did you?'

'Mind? God no. Why would I? She's welcome to him. I've got you, now.'

Adam pulled me closer. 'You do. For as long as this lasts.'

'What's that supposed to mean?'

'It's just… I can only truly thrive when I find someone who shares my world view and my long-term vision of the future.'

'I…' I began, and then I stopped. I wasn't sure what to say and, more importantly, I wasn't sure what Adam was saying. Was he telling me he wasn't as confident in our relationship as I was and trying to put that on me? Was he going to dump me on Christmas morning, right after we'd had sex?

If he was, it would surely be a new low in my dating life – possibly in everyone's dating life, ever. I'd be the world's most disastrous dater, officially. In years to come, there'd be a blue plaque outside the Ginger Cat, saying that Zoë Meredith, the unluckiest woman in love, had lived there.

I swallowed and waited for him to carry on, still in the warm embrace of his arm. If this was the end, I was going to enjoy every second of happiness with him while I could.

'I find it hard to conform to society's norms and expectations,' Adam went on. 'Many people who think they know me, don't really. And of course, because I've been single for so long, I'm often thought of as the eternal bachelor. My friends all say I'll never settle down until I find a woman who's one hundred per cent perfect for me.'

'But…' Then I stopped again. I might as well hear him out.

'My attitude to sexuality can appear somewhat transactional,' he said. 'Casual friends-with-benefits arrangements appeal to me while I flit through life, relishing my independence, wary of putting down emotional or practical roots. And because I have the image of the perfect woman in my head, it's often hard for a real-life relationship to live up to that.'

I turned my head against his shoulder and looked up at him. His eyes were solemn, but there was the beginnings of a smile turning up the corners of the lips I loved to kiss so much.

Suddenly, I realised what he was up to.

'Adam! You've been reading stuff about Aquarius men, haven't you?'

He burst out laughing. 'I wondered how long it would take you to realise.'

'If your work ever sack you, you could get a job working for Fabian Flatley. And I'll have you know that Aquarian women can be prone to bouts of fierce temper, so you'd better watch out.'

'What does your app thing say about today then? Because if it says there's a picnic hamper hidden behind the bar downstairs, containing what Fortnum & Mason describe as a luxury plant-based feast for two, I'll be seriously impressed.'

'What's in the feast, though? Because you might want to bear in mind that Aquarian women, while unencumbered by the expectations of society, have exacting standards that are entirely their own.'

'Let me check.' Adam reached sideways for his phone, careful not to disturb Frazzle or me. 'Organic Perugian olives. Fair trade dairy-free chocolate ganache selection made from single-sourced Ecuadorian cacao beans. Sourdough bread made with wild Cotswolds yeast. Sustainably produced mushroom pâté. Smoked Catalan almonds from bee-friendly orchards. Half a case of champagne. And three packets of truffle crisps, only I got those from Archie, not Fortnum's.'

'Hmm. It's not sounding too bad so far.'

Frazzle got up from his perch at the end of the bed, stretched all his four legs in turn, then strolled up and nestled in between Adam and me. I thought about the parcels under the Christmas tree that I'd wrapped for Adam, which were from both me and my cat, and hoped he'd like the signed edition of the Dune books I'd got off eBay, the bottle of his favourite shampoo I'd found out the brand of from Tansy, and the framed picture of Freezer I'd asked his last shared cat's owners to send. I was just as proud of them as he was of what he'd bought me, but there was no way I was hinting at any of it.

'Anything else?' I asked.

'Four packs of Oreos, a box of cat treats and two bottles of extra-hot chilli sauce,' Adam finished smugly. 'They were from the corner shop. So what does your Stargazer app make of that?'

'I haven't a clue,' I told him. 'I deleted it round about when you kissed me out in the garden.'

'How about Tinder?' He looked at me again, now definitely smiling.

'I deleted that, too,' I said.

A Letter from Sophie

Dear reader,

I want to say a huge thank you for choosing to read *Thank You, Next*. If you did enjoy it and want to keep up to date with all my latest releases, just sign up at the following link. Your email address will never be shared and you can unsubscribe at any time.

www.bookouture.com/sophie-ranald

On the day this book is released into the world, I should have been waking up with the mother of all hangovers, dragging myself into the shower, eating cold pastry with leftover roast pork for breakfast, then carrying my share of at least forty empty prosecco bottles out to the recycling.

It should have been the final morning of my eighth annual Book Club Retreat, which sounds ever so intellectual but actually involves me and sixteen of my best mates spending a weekend cooking, eating, drinking, reading, gossiping and singing show tunes badly. Generally, someone starts on the cocktails at about ten in the morning. Usually, someone has a good old cry, knowing they'll get all the hugs. Heroically, at least three of us make it out for a run on at least one morning.

But this year it's cancelled, like so many of the Lovely Times. It's not a big deal in the grand scheme of things, I know. My wonderful partner is fond of pointing out that he and I have done the Covid crisis on easy mode: we have no children, no caring responsibilities, we're both set up to work from home anyway, we get on with our neighbours, we have a fabulous community of people at our local fitness studio to keep the lockdown lard at bay and the cats love joining us for afternoon naps.

I've never been so conscious of my own privilege.

And I'm also conscious that this year has been terribly hard for many, many people. I'm genuinely touched and honoured by how many of you have got in contact to tell me that my books have helped you through this time – made you laugh, distracted you for a few hours, or kept you up all night (sorry about that).

One of the things I love most about being a writer is hearing from my readers, so please do keep reaching out on social media or just by leaving a review on Amazon to let me know what you thought of *Thank You, Next*.

A huge thank you for choosing this book among all the other books out there clamouring for your attention. I hope you enjoyed it, and I wish you all the very best until next time.

Love, Sophie

🐦 @SophieRanald

📘 SophieRanald

📷 @SophieRanald

Acknowledgements

When I was writing *Thank You, Next*, it sometimes felt as if Zoë spent her days ricocheting from her upstairs bedroom to her downstairs workplace to the gym and back again in a never-ending loop. There's a reason for this – it's pretty much what my life consisted of while I was working on this novel. Only when I was about halfway through did pubs and restaurants reopen in the UK and some semblance of normality return.

This meant that the usual face-to-face research that I so enjoy doing when I'm working on a book wasn't able to happen. Nonetheless, there are many people who have helped me enormously during the process, and they all deserve a massive thank you.

Over socially distanced outdoor drinks, my lovely friend Nathan answered my questions about Grindr hook-up culture with breathtaking honesty, and I am so grateful for his insights. I know he will be disappointed that I gave Robbie a happy ending, but I have my fingers crossed that his own is just around the corner.

It's been more years now than I care to count, but the Dungeons & Dragons games played with my sister Jassy as DM are as fresh in my mind as if they were yesterday. I could have written a whole book just about the adventures in Castle Drakeford, but – quite rightly – my wonderful editor would have taken a scalpel to it. But thank you, my darling sister, for all the happy hours we spent on those imaginary journeys.

Which brings me on to the team at Bookouture. I am so fortunate to have such an amazing publisher and work with such a professional, supportive, all-round bloody lovely team. Christina Demosthenous, my editor, holds my hand throughout the horrible solitary process of producing a first draft and the lovely, collaborative editing stages that follow, and makes my books the best they can possibly be. She also has endless patience when I whine that I can't do this. Thank you, you are a star. Noelle Holten, Kim Nash, Peta Nightingale, Lauren Finger and Alex Crowe have also provided invaluable support behind the scenes on publicity, production and promotion, Lisa Horton came up with a totally gorgeous cover design, and Rhian McKay smashed it with a brilliant copy edit as always.

I also owe huge thanks to the team at the Soho Agency, who have looked after me since I started writing eight years ago. I couldn't be more grateful for the expertise, wisdom and support of Alice Saunders, Araminta Whitley and Niamh O'Grady.

To Amanda, Becky, Carla, Catherine, Eleanor, Hazel, Helen, Jen, Jess, Katie, Kez, Lisa, Lou, Lucy, Lynda, Nikki, Rache, Sarah and Sian – love you all. Thank you for being my best friends and for the daily Covid chats that have kept us all sane over the past few months.

And finally, thanks to my darling Hopi and Purrs and Hither the cats. I couldn't be cooped up with a nicer crew.